To Jeanne,
Class of

GUIDING
MISSAL

FIFTY YEARS.
THREE GENERATIONS OF MILITARY MEN.
ONE SPIRITED PRAYER BOOK.

Believe!

NANCY PANKO

Nancy Panko

Torchflame Books
An imprint of Light Messages

Guiding Missal
   Fifty Years. Three Generations of Military Men.
   One Spirited Prayer Book.
Nancy Panko
gnnpanko@yahoo.com
www.nancypanko.com

Published 2017, by Torchflame Books
   an Imprint of Light Messages
www.lightmessages.com
Durham, NC 27713 USA
SAN: 920-9298

Paperback ISBN: 978-1-61153-240-1
E-book ISBN: 978-1-61153-239-5
Library of Congress Control Number: 2017931795

PRAISE FOR GUIDING MISSAL

"An inspirational story told from an original viewpoint. Nancy Panko's clever tale is as comforting as a guiding missal in one's shirt pocket, tucked close to the heart."

Scott Mason, author of *Faith and Air: The Miracle List* and host of the emmy-award-winning *Tar Heel Traveler* series

∽

"A heartfelt tale of a family's service to our country and devotion to God."

Jim DeFelice,
co-author of *Fighting Blind* and *American Sniper*

∽

"...a unique, intense and reverent tribute to our troops through three modern eras. Part fantasy, part history, the experiences of three different military men are recounted by the spunky little book that was their constant companion."

E.E. Kennedy,
author of the *Miss Prentice Mysteries*

∽

"A tiny, prayer book narrates a story about the divine protection experienced by three generations of military men who carry it. ...an inspiring story with both whimsy and grim reality. This 'Guiding Missal' definitely hits its mark!"

Ann Ault,
author of *Hi From the Sky: On the Road to Happily Ever After*

"Read the touching journey and inspiration provided to the Panko family by the Guiding Missal. Discover how a small paper book provided strength and hope in the face of tragic adversity. Read the true miracle, *Guiding Missal*."

Tim Forrest, IslandSunrises.com

❦

"A masterful storyteller, Panko weaves a soul-stirring tale of history, faith, and grace from the foxholes to the gates of heaven … absolutely stunning."

Barbara Parentini,
author of *Living Letters*®Seminars

❦

"This cleverly woven story is a journey through generations which immediately draws the reader in and holds them there through love and loss, crisis and triumph. Guiding Missal is a must read for all ages."

Debbie Dillon
Publisher *Joyful Kitchen Magazine*

❦

"Guiding Missal weaves an unexpected perspective, detailed research and quiet faith into a compelling, informative and uplifting read. Nancy Panko honors all who serve and speaks to all who appreciate the sacrifices of so many."

Cynthia Wheaton,
author of *Are You Ready to Start Your Own Business?*

To the men and women of the United States Armed Forces
who give all to keep us safe
and to their families who share their sacrifice.
Thank you for your service.

ACKNOWLEDGMENTS

I give honor, praise, and glory to our Almighty Father, without his guidance this book would have been relegated to an outline.

Guiding Missal would not exist if the some of the brave men of the 289th Cannon Company who served with George Panko during the Battle of the Bulge weren't willing to tell their stories. Thanks to Al Roxburgh, Ray Vittucci, and Harold Shadday who shared stories about Dad that we, the family, had never heard. A heartfelt thank you goes to Joe Panko, who wrote a 10-page letter regarding his brother's service and about their reunion in France. The story is priceless.

Many thanks to Ellen and Harold Kennedy for convincing me I had a wonderful story to tell and was capable of writing it. Bless you, Harold for your unique talent to come up with amazing title suggestions. Ellen, you have my eternal gratitude for mentoring my writing, for editing, and for believing, like my mother, that I "had a book in me." You both are priceless friends.

To my husband Butch, thanks for your service to our country, for allowing me to interview you in depth, and for your patience in waiting for dinner many nights when I was engrossed in writing.

Thank you to the men who make up the composite of the third character in the book: my brother, Terry Emmick, my brothers-in-law, William Reinbold, and Sam Owens. They all served bravely and selflessly, each coming home a different man than when they left. My thanks and forever love goes out to my grandson Andrew who, although not in the military, has waged many battles in his short life and was an inspiration to me in writing this third character. To the actual third character, who prefers to remain anonymous, thank you for serving.

Thank you to my dear friends who agreed to be readers, Sally Lagoy, Terry Hans, Linda Loegel, Ellen Kennedy, James Lewis and Tammy Roode Smith who weren't afraid to give me the unvarnished truth and the perspective needed to make valuable revisions.

To The Cary Writers Circle, thank you, Ellen, Janet, Mac, Joanne, Jim, Marilyn, Terry, Barbara, and Linda for listening and giving me great feedback each week. Thank you to the late Harry Zoller and good friend James Lewis veterans of WWII and Vietnam respectively, who gave me their viewpoints of war and life in uniform.

To Barbara Parentini, founder of Light of Carolina Christian Writers' Group, who always told me to believe the words of Jeremiah 29:11. To fellow members, Jan, Pat, the two Ellens, Karen, Cynthia, and Terry for your encouragement, guidance and unflagging faith in me.

To my forever friend, Debbie Dillon, publisher and editor of Hearth and Home magazine, who gave me my first publishing break. I will always be grateful.

To my friends at Chicken Soup for the Soul, publisher Amy Newmark and editor D'ette Corona thank you for your encouragement and friendship. It has been my honor to be a contributor to this fine book, "changing the world, one story at a time."

Acknowledgments would not be complete without mentioning my editors, Ellen Kennedy, Terry Hans, Linda Loegel, and Alice Osborn. Thank you all, Guiding Missal is a better book today because of each of you.

My deepest gratitude goes to my publisher, Wally Turnbull and the staff at Light Messages/Torchflame who shepherded me through this process. It has a been pleasure to work with you.

Contents

PRAYER FOR SOLDIERS

(To St. Sebastian)

O St. Sebastian, brave in battle and strong in faith, who gave a perfect example of courage in fighting for your country and your God alike, through thy intercession help the soldiers who like you fight for the country they love. Help them, that it can be said of them, as it was said of you, "He was a good soldier." Make them strong and brave, ready to give their best for that cause for which their country fights. You were found perfect in the testimony you bore of your faith in Jesus Christ. Grant that the same may be said of those who wear our country's uniform, that they too, strong in battle, may be strong also in the faith for which you died. Preserve them from the wounds and dangers of battle and bring them safely home. Amen.

My Military Missal

PROLOGUE

More than seventy years ago, Private George Panko tucked me into a pocket of his combat jacket. The country was in the second year of World War II. George and I served together until September 1945. Since then, two more generations of military men have carried me. My mission as a Military Missal was to guide and protect each of my charges. One may ask, "How?" My answer would be, "By the power of The Holy Spirit."

During my journey, I bonded with each of the men who carried me in their pockets knowing them better than they knew themselves. This knowledge gave me the insight to narrate our story. From covert operations behind German lines in 1944 to bloody firefights in the streets of Mogadishu, Somalia, in 1993, I've seen, felt and heard it all. Before I can start with the action, I need to go back to the beginning of this odyssey.

1

1941
THE AWAKENING

Visiting the book distribution hub, Author Monsignor Joseph F. Stedman was in the process of blessing cases of his book, "My Military Missal." The priest had arrived earlier than expected and, instead of being neatly stacked, some of the boxes scheduled for shipping to military bases all over the country had not yet been closed and sealed. Assuring the warehouse manager the blessing could still take place, Father Stedman proceeded to walk the length of the concrete floor sprinkling holy water on each of the cartons.

> I was one of those prayer books distributed from 1941 to 1945. The priest had no idea what the holy water did to me as it hit my cover.
>
> That one drop spread a warmth throughout my pages and down my spine. The heat awakened me, infiltrating every precious word printed between my covers. I became aware of my surroundings. I could think. I knew this event made me uniquely different from the rest of the missals, but how?
>
> Suddenly, I knew I had become infused with the Holy Spirit. I had total clarity that my omnipotent God could bend time and events to suit His needs when and where He saw fit. I was only a part of His plan, but that was the extent of my knowledge. I trusted Him.

2
MARCH 1942
MAKING MYSELF COMFORTABLE

As the soldiers moved through the assembly line of haircuts, showers, and immunizations, and after receiving their government-issued clothing and toiletries, they entered another area where Army chaplains were handing out Bibles and prayer books for all denominations. As a recruit stepped up, I felt an odd, unfamiliar tingling.

I heard the chaplain ask, "Would you like one of these books?"

The sensation became more intense. What was happening to me?

I heard the man reply, "Yes, I'm a Catholic, I'll take the black prayer book on the end of the third row." He pointed directly at me.

The chaplain turned to the array of religious books on the table and reached for the specified missal. He asked the man, "This one?"

"Yes, sir. That's the one."

Suddenly, I was plucked from the pile of military missals and placed on the stack of clothing nestled in the man's arms. I can't explain what happened because every recruit before him received the same offer. None of them wanted a specific book. I surmise it was part of the plan that this man and I were supposed to be together.

The tingling was replaced by a soulful connection with the soldier now carrying me. I had no sooner wondered how far my sphere of influence and intuition would extend into his world when I began to have flickering flashes of visions. My soldier is dangling precariously on the side of a troopship about to be crushed. Blinding, drifting snow is covering the mine fields. Supply lines can't reach the soldiers. There is much danger. The invasion begins. The forest, teems with enemy forces and becomes a place of slaughter. Great red flashes set the trees on fire. I see frozen bodies stacked like firewood. My soldier is stranded behind enemy lines. There is danger all around. I see two lines of weary, unshaven men trudging along with bandoliers of ammunition strung across their chests. Another flash reveals my soldier wading in cold, black water while big guns are firing artillery shells dangerously close. Lord, have mercy! I hear laughter while at the same time sensing feelings of unrelenting fear, sadness, and longing. I feel weighed down by sights and sounds.

I never expected these premonitions. Although my metamorphosis is happening at an astonishing rate, through the grace of God, I find myself totally in sync with my soldier. That connection tells me everything about him and much of the strife to come. Heavenly Father, I implore you to guide and protect this man.

He knew he had been drawn to me, but he knew nothing about my gifts.

Twenty-six-year-old George Panko was drafted in March 1942 and reported for basic training at Fort Benning, Georgia.

He carried me in his pocket whether in or out of uniform and referred to me as his "soldier's Bible." He'd been an altar boy in the Russian Orthodox

Church, and I gave him a feeling of comfort and familiarity which was a good start to our relationship. I went where he went while making myself comfortable.

After Basic, he was assigned to Camp Stewart in Georgia, as a baker. He made friends easily with all the men in the kitchen. It was common knowledge that George was always looking for a ride to Dickson City, Pennsylvania, whenever he could get one. Married only two years to his wife Gladys, George was sure his being drafted would put their lives on hold.

Little did he know what was soon to come.

One day a fellow cook, Buddy, approached him. "Panko, I met a guy from Scranton yesterday, and he's got a car on base. Are you interested in talkin' to him?"

"Heck, yeah! Thanks!"

While replenishing a tray of hash, Buddy spotted the soldier from Pennsylvania coming down the chow line with his tray. He nudged George, and they waited for the man to get closer. Buddy made a short, inconspicuous introduction so he didn't hold up the line.

"George is from Scranton, too," Buddy announced, as he grabbed an empty pan and strode off toward the kitchen to refill it.

With a mug of coffee in one hand and a hunk of bread in the other, George took a short break and sat with Vince at a crowded table.

"I have a car and drive back and forth to Scranton, as often as this place will let me, Vince stated. He sipped his steaming coffee.

George tore off a hunk of bread and dunked it in his cup. "I don't mind sharin' expenses and gas rationing coupons. If you want, I can help with the driving too. My wife and I are still newlyweds, and I can't stand being away from her."

"I think that would work out. I can let you know when I'm planning to go home and you can make arrangements on your end."

"I'd like that. I'd like it a lot, Vince. Thanks."

"It's settled, then. Glad to have you travel with me, George." They clinked coffee cups.

Apparently, the arrangement between Vince and George worked out because, in July of 1942, twenty-two-year-old Gladys told her husband he was going to be a father.

George had no idea what was in store for him and his family, but I did.

3

1942
SWEET GLADYS

O n his last trip home George and Gladys cuddled on the sofa talking. I heard and felt everything.

"I've been having awful dreams about you in combat. They're so life-like, these nightmares that wake me up. I can't get back to sleep. I get out of bed and pace ..." Her voice trailed off as she twirled and un-twirled a lock of dark hair around her index finger.

"Glady, you have to remember what I do in the Army. I'm a baker, which means I bake. The biggest danger to me is burning myself on those dang big ovens when I'm baking bread. If and when I deploy, I'll be in the rear in some kitchen." He reached out to the end table and stuck his hand in a bowl of salted peanuts, grabbing a handful. He turned to her, winked, and popped one in his mouth.

"But, the dreams, they seem so real." She shuddered. "I'm thankful you're a baker, but I'm still gonna pray that the war ends before you have to deploy." Her hand dropped to her expanding waistline. "You know what else I pray for?"

George popped another peanut into his mouth. "What? That Marilyn Monroe will drop by to help you clean the house?" He laughed, and that made her giggle.

"No silly, I pray that we have a little boy who looks just like you." She was deeply in love with this kind, handsome man.

I knew The Lord had heard her prayer and her prayer would come to pass.

"Remember when we first met?" Gladys leaned her head on his broad shoulder. "'Tall, dark and handsome' is how I described you to my girlfriends. I never expected to fall in love with the man behind the counter at the Dickson City Bakery. You know it was meant to be. Mom sent me to pick up the bread that day because she didn't feel well and I happened to be home from work. You had me hooked with those warm, brown eyes and knock-out smile. And you didn't even know it."

"Well, I never told you this before, Glady, but you were all I could think of from the first day you walked into that bakery. I'd never seen you before, but I sure hoped I'd see you again. And when you started comin' in regular, I finally got up the nerve to ask you out."

She remembered quite clearly. "You were a little jumpy and awkward. I thought it was cute." She reached over to take a peanut out of his hand and pop it in her mouth. "Do you remember what you said to me?"

"Sure do. 'Wanna go on a picnic in the park at Weston Field? I'll bring fresh bread.'" He had it right down to the cadence. He chuckled, rather pleased with his recall ability.

"I noticed your accent then. I thought you were an Italian from New York City. I remember telling you I'd bring kielbasa, thinking you'd never had it before. Then I handed you my address and phone number on a piece of paper."

"Yeah, and you smiled that smile that melted me into a puddle, Glady. Oh, boy, after that I stammered and looked at my feet shufflin' around on the floor and before I could tell you that the park was the ball park and I'd be playing on the home team, I heard the door bell jingle, and you were gone."

She laughed at the picture in her mind.

"You know my knees were weak after you left. I couldn't figger out why you made me so nervous. You had me muttering to myself for the rest of the afternoon!"

They passed the peanut dish back and forth. "As I recall, George, the picnic and the ball game were lots of fun. I love baseball."

"I remember the kielbasa was real good and I ate too much!"

"I didn't realize you were four years older than me until that afternoon. Me being eighteen didn't matter one single bit. I loved you from the start." Turning toward him, she looked into his warm brown eyes. "I enjoyed watching you play ball, and the way you moved on the field and I remember how my heart pounded when you were near me. I couldn't take my eyes off you, George. You were, and are still, beautiful to watch."

He enveloped her in a bear hug, covering her face and neck with peanut breath kisses. She giggled and squirmed in his arms.

George released his grip. "Yup, when I walked you home and kissed you on the cheek at your door, I knew this was the beginning of sumthin' big."

Gladys closed her eyes and released a sigh, "I only wish your parents had given us their blessing. They just couldn't get over the fact that I wasn't Russian Orthodox like you."

"Mom and Dad are from the old country. They couldn't stand for my converting to Roman Catholic." He looked down at his feet with a somber expression and quietly remarked, "Glady, it was the first time in my life I ever defied their wishes."

"I was hoping they'd come around when we were married. I was so sad for you, George, when they didn't come to our wedding."

"You know, Glady, I hope and pray that when they see their grandchild, they'll change their minds."

On February 25, 1943, their son, George Jr., was born. The proud father came home on leave the following weekend.

As he held his newborn son, he pulled Gladys to his side. "This deployment is gonna be harder than I ever thought, Glady. I love you both so much." There was an indescribable pain in his heart as he thought about having to leave them. Their tears mingled as they kissed.

The couple heard a car horn honking outside. Gladys slipped out of his arms and went to the window. She parted the curtains seeing the familiar dark green Packard sitting in the driveway. She was about to confirm that it was Vince when George spoke up from behind her.

"That must be my ride. Vince knows we have a new baby. You'd think he'd have enough sense to come to the door. He always has to honk that dang horn."

I felt George's spirit sinking and surmised Gladys felt the same. It was always difficult when George had to head back to the base hundreds of miles away.

What was this? Resentment, too? Yes. And from both of them, loud and clear.

4

SEPTEMBER 1944
CHANGING ARMY OCCUPATIONS

F eeling his contribution as a baker was insufficient to assist in the war effort, George volunteered as a scout/ forward observer (FO) with the 75th Division, 289th Cannon Company. His impulsive action came after learning that two of his three brothers, Andy and Joe, had been sent to the European Theater of Operations (ETO), one as a medic and the other in the infantry. George was determined to do more than just bake bread.

His new occupation required a few more months of training. George rationalized that this might give him more time in the States and hoped that the war would end before he had to deploy.

It was a dangerous job because it involved gathering information from behind enemy lines and assisting the Fire Direction Center (FDC) by giving coordinates to guide the aim of the big guns. A forward observer often had a shorter lifespan than most infantrymen. He wasn't sure he would tell Gladys the whole truth about his new job since she took such comfort in knowing he was just a baker.

> *Ooooh, Gladys isn't going to like that one bit. George still had no idea of the scope of my God-given gifts. I didn't want him to think that he could behave recklessly while in battle. Soon, through me, he'll communicate with The Holy Spirit.*

George will have a sign which will encircle him in golden rays of light. I hope he'll recognize it. His relationship with Our Heavenly Father is surely going to mature. I feel it in my spine.

After he completed his scout training and before his deployment to Europe, George came home to Scranton on leave. Their son slept that first evening as Gladys bustled around their small rented duplex preparing a meal for her husband and herself.

George stepped up to his wife at the sink and took the knife out of her hands. "I'll peel the potatoes." Working side by side in the kitchen with his wife, he knew he was completely at home. He loved watching her move gracefully around the room. It certainly stimulated all his appetites.

"After you're done there, would you please set the table, honey?" She gave him an encouraging smile.

"Sure Glady, anything for My Lady of Perpetual Motion." He grabbed for her apron ties and missed.

Scooting away from his grasp, she giggled and looked over her shoulder at him. Her shiny dark hair framed a flawless olive complexion and full lips. Her deep brown eyes sparkled with love and mischief.

With impeccable timing, the baby awoke. The couple had just set their forks down. Gladys got up from the table and prepared his bottle. Eager to spend as much time with his son as possible, George gave his boy the bottle while his wife cleaned up from dinner. He watched his ravenous son gulp down the milk. After several loud burps, Junior was full and content to play with his toys while spread-eagled on a soft blanket placed on the living room floor.

George got up and walked outside onto the porch. He stared at the brightly lit sky. Looking up at the blanket of stars surrounding a large half moon reminded him not to waste a single moment. He came back into the house and said, "Let's go for a walk, Glady."

The couple bundled Junior, donned their coats, hats, scarves and gloves, put the baby in the carriage and walked out into the crisp, clear night. As they strolled around the neighborhood, George placed his strong hand over hers to help steer the baby buggy.

Gladys tipped her head to the side to look at her handsome husband. "What'll we do after the war?"

"Whaddya mean?"

"I have such a hard time dealing with uncertainty. I keep wondering how things will change in the world and for us. I wonder where we'll live and what work you'll find and I worry about Junior having playmates nearby." They skirted the uneven sections of sidewalk to avoid bouncing the carriage, but needn't have worried about the bumps, because the baby was already sound asleep.

"Wow, that's a lot of wondering, Glady. Well, first, I know your parents want us to live with them, and it'll give us a chance to save money for a house someday. It's okay with me, as long as we're together. I think we'll figure it out. Second, maybe it's better not to worry about things so far in the future." Neither of them spoke of the war consuming the world.

She pondered her husband's wise words, wishing with all her heart for stability in their lives. She wanted to share in that deep, abiding faith her husband possessed.

A slight gust of cold wind made George hunch his shoulders and fasten the top button of his coat. He was relieved that Gladys wore a thick wool hat and scarf. The baby was snug under a warm blanket. The blast of cold air reminded George he had something important to tell his wife: that he had changed occupations from the safety of the kitchen to the battlefield, but he couldn't find his voice.

He must have sensed her anxiety. "You know Glady, we're a family now, you, me and Junior here. That's not gonna change. As for the rest, with the help of God, we'll figger everything out as we go."

She smiled up at him, and he gave her a big hug as they watched a shooting star streak across the starlit indigo sky.

"The Lord is our Shepherd, Glady," George proclaimed quietly as they made their way home.

> *The shooting star was just for them, a sign of reassurance from God. George seems to get that message. I pray for God's blessing on this beautiful little family.*

At bedtime, they clung to each other, making love tenderly as if they had all the time in the world. They fell asleep in each other's arms, dreaming of the life they wanted to live in a peaceful world without war.

George left the next day to continue training, uncertain of a deployment date.

> *I waited for the circle of light.*

5

OCTOBER 1944
PREPARING FOR DEPLOYMENT

During this last furlough before his deployment to Europe, George had a deep need to help Gladys care for his son. Diaper changes, however, confounded the competent soldier. Fumbling with the unruly length of cotton cloth, he'd ask Gladys repeatedly, "How do you fold this diaper?" Over and over his wife showed him how do it. He'd watch studiously while leaning over his wife's shoulder, then become distracted by the scent of her perfume. He never did learn to do it without her help, and he was no dummy.

The natural part of caring for Junior was feeding him. He loved bottle time with his son, gazing into his little blue eyes until heavy lids closed in blissful contentment. George felt his heart swell with incredible love. Continuing to hold and rock his son until Gladys signaled it was crib time, George reluctantly placed the baby on his belly and covered him with a blanket. Immediately, he felt the child's warmth leave his arms and chest.

Bath time each night was full of squeals and laughter with everyone getting wet. No one laughed harder at his son's antics than George. He was like a kid, and the scene never failed to warm Gladys' heart.

Stealing lots of kisses throughout the day, the couple cuddled on the sofa in the evening listening to their favorite comedy shows on the radio trying to ignore the news broadcasts from the war front. Listening to the correspondent only reminded them of the dark cloud of deployment hanging over their heads. As the time drew near, their lovemaking became more urgent. They couldn't get enough of each other.

Snuggling one morning as the baby slept, George and Gladys both realized the day of his departure had arrived, yet neither wanted to throw back the covers and get out of bed.

As he spooned Gladys and nuzzled behind her ear, he whispered, "We have a big trip today, honey." He planted a gentle kiss on the nape of her neck. He loved the way she smelled and the softness of her skin.

"I know." She sleepily rolled over and laid her head on his chest. "I've been tryin' not to think about it. I can't bear the thought of you being so far away from us."

"I'll always be right here, Glady." George placed his hand on his wife's beating heart.

She covered his hand with her own. A tear escaped her right eye and slid down her cheek.

"I'll never let our son forget you. I'll read him your letters and remind him how much you love giving him baths and rocking him to sleep. Whenever I take him for a ride in the carriage, I'll make it a point to go by the church and light a candle for you." Her rambling was interspersed with small shaking sobs before her chin quivered and she could no longer talk, then the tears flowed freely. She wiped her eyes on the bed sheet.

Hearing the sad desperation in her voice, George pleaded, "Glady, I love you. Please don't cry." He stroked her back and shoulders. "It's wartime, babe. I need you to be strong for Junior and me. I'll be countin' on you lightin' those candles. We're a team, hon. We know your parents will help whenever you need them. In fact, they told me that they want you and Junior to move in with them as soon as I leave. It'll help you, they'll feel better, and it would be a comfort to me. We'll write letters every day and, hopefully, this war will be over soon."

I heard him offer up a silent prayer for that to be true. He was going to miss his family more than he could ever articulate. I knew what was in his heart. I would do my best to return him home safely.

They made love one more time before finally getting out of bed. Taking a little longer to savor the time alone, this moment was theirs to treasure. It was cut short when they heard Junior calling, "Da Da Da Da."

"See that, he's calling for you. Go get him, and we'll change and dress him."

After taking care of the baby, the three of them stood in a loving embrace. A ray of sunshine streamed through the bedroom window encircling them.

"Look, George! Look at how this light is shining on us. It feels like a warm God hug."

"I'm sure it is, Glady. I'm sure it is."

My goodness! It was a circle of light. What a blessing! Through months of never-ending battle and in each night of fitful rest, George and Gladys were sustained by the memory of their "God hug." I'm happy that they were aware of God's love light. When I'm around them, I can't help but think of the words of Jeremiah 29:11, For surely I know the plans I have for you, says the Lord, plans for your welfare and not for harm, to give you a future with hope.

A short time later, the couple bustled around the kitchen, preparing food for the train trip. George had put his baking talents to good use and made homemade bread the day before, and Gladys now assembled ham sandwiches, wrapping them tightly in waxed paper.

Gladys carefully packed a picnic basket. "We have a couple of surprises in here."

"What? Surprises? Is it you?" He smiled with a twinkle in his eye, not thinking of the food.

She lowered her head looking sideways at him with mischief in her eyes, remembering the *kielbasa* and the *kolache*, sweetened walnut pastry, wrapped tightly in waxed paper, nestled next to jars of baby food. Gladys usually made Junior's baby food, but this new jarred food was convenient for today's adventure to New York City. It was going to be a long day, and she'd never allow there to be a shortage of food for the baby or any adult. She'd also make sure George stashed some goodies in his duffle bag for the ocean crossing.

Gladys, an integral part of George's life, was loud and clear in my sphere of knowledge and intuition. She certainly softened all his rough edges.

"I just love watching you, Glady." He adored his woman not only for her sexy body and lovely features, but she was a darn good cook, too. He walked up behind her and wrapped his arms around her waist. He nuzzled her neck and smothered her with kisses murmuring, "I love you, I love you, I love you, and if I keep doing this, I'm gonna hafta drag you upstairs for a special good-bye."

"I love you too." She turned to face her handsome husband and wrapped her arms around his neck. She swallowed hard. She loved his warmth and affection. Denying the lump in her throat she thought, "If I start crying now, I'll never get through this day. There'll be plenty of time to cry later."

This deployment would be a journey of faith for both of them, according to my premonitions.

6
NOVEMBER 1944
I'LL BE SEEING YOU

George cherished those last hours together on the train ride to New York City. His in-laws accompanied them on this difficult day, in order to help Gladys and the baby.

The aroma from the hamper of food between the four seats caused the other passengers to salivate. "Glady, this kielbasa is the best we've ever had." George reached for another piece of sausage to feed his wife. They enjoyed every bite of the delectable feast Gladys had packed so carefully.

George held his son and in between bites of food, sniffed his little head, enjoying that unmistakable baby smell. "What do you put on him that smells so good, Glad?"

"Baby powder, baby lotion and baby oil."

"At the same time? Wouldn't that make a gooey mess?" His face contorted in feigned disgust in an attempt to make her laugh.

It worked. Her smile turned into laughter. "No, silly."

It was music to his ears.

She knew what he was trying to do. She'd miss these verbal exchanges. She'd also miss watching him interact with his son when he fed him and at bath time. Good Lord, she was going to be lost without him!

Much too soon, the train arrived at the station and the family all bunched together in a taxi for the ride to the port. The

RMS Franconia, now a hired military transport (HMT), had already started the boarding process of its uniformed human cargo.

After a tearful, heart-wrenching good-bye, George and Gladys pulled themselves apart.

"Stay right here where I can see you." He gave her and the baby one last kiss and held them tightly before abruptly letting go. Laden with his gear, he turned and briskly strode away to board the ship.

> *God bless you, Gladys and Baby George. Stay strong. God made him my charge and the Holy Spirit will do his job.*

Sobbing uncontrollably, Gladys watched him walk away. "I'll love you forever!" She called out with a catch in her throat.

Minutes later, George appeared at the railing. Gladys hugged the baby as she and her parents stood on the pier, looking up at her departing husband. They waved and blew kisses to each other. The scene repeated itself up and down the pier as other families bid their soldier goodbye.

George made the letter J with his finger and thumb and signed the numbers two, nine, and eleven. He put his hand over the left breast pocket of his combat jacket where he carried the military missal. He hoped those gestures would remind Gladys to read the words of Jeremiah 29:11. He knew it would give her comfort.

> *The Lord did know His plans for them and I was happy to have given him the thought of that particular Bible verse.*

Gladys nodded her head in acknowledgment as the dockhands completed their work. The ship moved away from the pier and out into the harbor. She watched the vessel until the wind picked up, making it very uncomfortable to stand there any longer. Clutching at the collar of her favorite deep purple coat, she held her baby tightly and tucked his blanket around him. She shivered from the cold and pulled the baby's hat down over his little ears.

Her parents protectively gathered their daughter and grandson in their arms as they left the dock to catch a taxi to the train station for the ride home. Gladys robotically followed. Both in the cab and on the train, she prayed for her husband as the baby slept peacefully in her lap.

After arriving home in Dickson City, Pennsylvania, Gladys stood at the front window, holding the curtains aside, watching a cold rain run down the glass in rivulets. She picked up the skirt of her gingham apron to wipe the tears from her face. Just then the baby started to cry. She turned from the window, realizing she alone was now responsible for their child. She vowed she'd do her best to help him remember his daddy. Sobbing several times, she took a deep breath to pull herself together before trotting up the stairs to comfort her son.

Several days later, George disembarked from the *Franconia* in rainy Liverpool, England. His tears ran together with the rain drops on his face as he remembered who he left behind. He was about to board a troop transport truck for a month of artillery training in Wales before leaving for the fighting in Europe.

To my surprise, my intuitive sphere was expanding halfway around the world, proving to me our Heavenly Father has no boundaries or limits.

Over and over, George had turned my pages to read Scripture on the journey across the Atlantic. Distraught at leaving his family, he simply couldn't find the words for prayer. Instead he settled for reading what someone else had written. I knew he'd want to pray for his own safety as well as that of his wife, son, and his brothers. He relied on the words within my pages to guide and sustain him.

He repeatedly read Psalm 85:4: Gladden the soul of your servant, for to you O Lord, I lift up my soul.

7

DECEMBER 9, 1944
TRUCKS, TRAIN AND THE
SS LEOPOLDVILLE

*T*he men of the 289th were itching to get into the fight. They were leaving the hills and rain of Wales after a month of intense training in the latest field artillery methods. Hundreds of infantrymen sat in the back of troop transport trucks, some laughing and joking, others somber and pensive; all uncomfortable on hard wooden benches during the long bumpy ride. The snaking convoy carrying these souls made its way over narrow country roads to the train station. One by one the canopied trucks unloaded the young soldiers onto the platform.

Boarding the train in an orderly fashion, the men found seats like cattle instinctively finding their stanchions in a barn. They stowed their packs and settled down for the ride to the port of Southampton, England. This leg of their journey was a little more comfortable and certainly warmer than the last one. The conductor rang his bell and called out in a distinctive accent, "All aboard who's goin' aboard!"

As the countryside fell away, the monotonous click of the rails lulled the men of the 289th Cannon Company, 75th Division of the United States Army.

Nancy Panko

Those who couldn't sleep stared blankly out of the windows of the train, wondering about the dangers their troop ship would face in the English Channel from German subs lurking below. It was the third year of World War II, and none of these men had seen battle before. They had gone through grueling months of training and now were afraid the fighting would end before they even got there.

Through the power of my God-given senses, I was flooded with their thoughts. I knew they were going to be in the thick of some of the most intense fighting of the European war. I also knew who would not return home alive. It grieved me to have that knowledge, but I was sustained by knowing that our Heavenly Father held most of them in His hands.

I was continually intrigued by George, the man who carried me in his combat jacket pocket. I could feel his body heat and had a good sense of him as a soldier prepared for battle. He'd always been rather quiet and also somewhat resentful for being taken away from his family. That resentment had been gradually replaced by an intense feeling of patriotism, partially fostered by being part of a military brotherhood. God-fearing and faithful to a fault, George was a good man. I knew he would probably be overwhelmed to discover the extent of divine help he had at his fingertips, within my pages. My task was to act as a conduit for the Holy Spirit to keep him alive, strengthen his faith and bring him home safely.

We had been together since 1942. My pages were now dog-eared, my cover becoming worn. The Word of The Lord was a source of guidance and encouragement for George even before the war. Now, I was very grateful the two of us were in this together.

Cannon Company disembarked the crowded train to board yet another mode of cramped transportation

*to Europe, the SS Leopoldville. The eager warriors
had trained to become a tightly-knit, group totally
in sync with each other. They were ready for
battle. The sooner the war was over, the sooner
they could go home.*

When the converted luxury ship left Southampton, England,
to cross the English Channel bound for Le Havre, France,
she was at capacity with fresh American soldiers ready to fill
the thinning ranks of the 289th Cannon Company created
by the men killed or wounded in action.

Due to rough seas, the ship was unable to dock at the pier at
Le Havre. Consequently, a decision was made to unload the
troops onto landing craft (LC) and take them ashore, one
boatload at a time. Large swells tossed the two ships about
as the men began to descend a rope network hanging on the
side of the *Leopoldville*. A few made it onto the LC before
some of the lines lashing the two craft together broke loose.
In increasingly heavy seas, the flailing LC rose up on the
waves repeatedly crashing into the side of the larger ship.

*George was the only man left hanging on the
swinging ropes. He had been unable to scramble
back up to safety. I was in his jacket pocket.
Instinctively, we both sensed danger. The partly
untethered LC pulled away as we dangled there.*

Troops on the upper deck who were waiting to descend
watched as the LC rose on a swell, poised to crash into the
side of the *Leopoldville*.

They yelled in unison, "Look out!"

Desperately needing a miracle, George spotted an open deck
and positioned himself on the edge of the ropes parallel
to it. Watching the LC rise and move toward him in slow
motion, he knew he had to act. There was no question he'd be
crushed to death unless he could get himself onto the deck.
Gathering all his strength, George swung himself free of the
ropes. With 70 pounds of equipment on his back, he hurled

himself into the opening as the LC smashed into the side of the ship. A loud cheer erupted from the soldiers watching from the deck above.

> *My God is an awesome God! Thank you, Lord, for this burst of agility.*

Because of George's narrow escape, Command curtailed further disembarkation until the seas were calm enough to dock at the pier. The Army was already short of combat-ready troops, and the senior officers were not about to unnecessarily lose a single man.

Sprawled on the deck, George crossed himself. Oddly, he quoted his Irish mother-in-law as he prayed aloud, "Thank you, Lord, for 'savin' me sorry arse.'"

> *His gratitude and humility pleased me. A thankful attitude opens windows of Heaven through which spiritual blessings flow freely. He's brave, this one. The Lord says, "I am your refuge and strength, an ever-present and well-proved help in trouble."*

George looked up to get his bearings and saw his buddy Harold gripping the railing to steady himself. Harold offered him a hand.

"Jeez, George, that was somethin'! You must've had some divine help." Harold shook his head in amazement. "I ran down here when I saw the LC break loose. Got here in time to see what happened."

Slipping out of his pack, George stretched his legs out then reached for Harold's hand to pull himself up. Using the railing to steady himself, he nodded. "Harold, you're right about divine help. I swear I felt the hand of God on me. I'm in good shape, but couldn't have made that jump on my own."

A massive wave thoroughly doused the two men at the railing.

"Let's get inside!" George hollered to Harold. He grabbed his pack, and the two of them lurched the short distance for the door leading to an interior hallway.

Sheltered inside the ship, Harold wiped the salt water out of his eyes and attempted to dry his hands on the front of his combat jacket. "Nothin' gets a guy in shape like the Army."

"This is true. But, playin' ball got me in shape even before I was drafted." George also ran his hands over his wet face. The sea spray burned his eyes.

Harold led the way to the stairwell. "Let's sit and catch our breath. What kind of ball did you play, George?" The men braced themselves as the ship pitched and rolled.

"Baseball. Ten years in American Legion ball 'til I was seventeen." He looked sideways at Harold before delivering the grand slam. "Then I had a chance to try out for the Boston Red Sox farm team."

Harold eyebrows lifted in surprise. "What position?"

"Shortstop or third base."

"Did you make it?"

"Yes, I ..."

Harold interrupted. "Holy mackerel, George. How long did you play on the farm team?"

"I was with the Sox for three years. I was in great shape, my batting was consistent, and I was a fast runner. They wanted me to move up."

"What? Move up? As in: 'up to the majors'? For the Sox? Did you go?"

"Nah, my mom wouldn't let me." George wiped his wet face again.

"Whaddya mean; she wouldn't let you?" Harold was beside himself. The ship rolled again, and so did his stomach.

"When your Russian mother says, 'Nyet!' you listen. Mom thought all baseball players in the majors were beer drinking,' woman-chasin' bums. I was twenty years old, but I didn't want to cross my ma, so I stayed in the minors for another year and a half before I went to work in a bakery." Another wave hit the ship and knocked them both against the bulkhead. "We gotta get to the upper deck soon, Harold. While we're here, I've got some great *kolache* I smuggled in my pack."

"What the heck is *kolache*?"

"It's good; that's what it is." George fished the sweet flakey contraband wrapped in waxed paper out of a hiding place in his pack. Sweet Gladys had even sliced it into portion sizes.

They continued talking baseball and munching on the pastry. Now unfazed by the rocking of the craft, the two men continued talking about America's favorite pastime. It certainly took their minds off the frightening disembarkation attempt and the war they'd be fighting in the months ahead.

The men of the 289th didn't know who among them would return home and who wouldn't make it out of Europe alive.

But I did.

Twelve days after the Cannon Company disembarked from the *SS Leopoldville*, she was sunk in the English Channel by a German torpedo, with a loss of over eight hundred men from the 66th Infantry Division.

8

DECEMBER 1944
CANNON COMPANY

With God, there are no coincidences. The Cannon Company, 289th Infantry was activated at Fort Leonard Wood, Missouri, on Friday, the 13th of August 1943. There was a total of thirteen dollars in the company treasury. They were thirteen men short of being tactically operational, and the commanding officer was assigned to room thirteen in the officers' barracks. The old superstition of the number thirteen made the men work harder, pulling together, becoming more cohesive, efficient and effective. They became the best at what they did. These work habits later saved many lives.

Having been commissioned by God, I was tuned in to all the numerology. I was pleased that George was going to have a place in this stellar group of men.

The Company achieved first place for accuracy in the entire division and continued proving themselves many times over as excellence prevailed.

From December 1943 to March 1944, the 289th zig-zagged through Europe across France into Belgium, Germany, and Holland. There were fierce battles and intense fighting, tens of thousands of brave troops on both sides were killed and many more wounded. George was one of the new American replacements sent into battle in December 1944.

He was just an ordinary man carrying a uniquely endowed military missal with the Word of the Lord to guide and shield him from harm.

The winter weather of 1944 took a terrible toll on men and machines. Blinding snowstorms and massive drifts made it almost impossible to detect deadly minefields, hampering the movement of the troops. Supplies, warm clothing, boots, and mail were often not able to catch up with the erratically moving army, but the most crucial item in short supply was ammunition.

Oh Lord, protect us in these harsh conditions and help us endure the challenges.

The 289th encountered the Germans in the Ardennes Forest for the first time on Christmas Eve 1944. From his slit trench, George gazed at the serene scene of enormous pine trees laden with snow. It was breathtakingly beautiful, reminding him of the Currier and Ives Christmas cards his wife sent out last year. The heavy snow muffled all sound and, considering the battle about to take place, created an eery silence. The hairs on the back of his neck stood on end. He was glad he hadn't told Gladys about his change of occupation to forward observer. He thought, "She'd be out of her mind worrying about me. It was bad enough when I was a baker. I made the right decision. I'll tell her in the next letter home." He felt better about that decision as he prepared his weapon for battle.

Knowing they were short on ammo, the commanding officers came up with a strategy. The CO spoke with his First Sergeant about getting a count on all of their grenades.

"Jackson, I wanna see what we've got."

"Yes, sir."

Jackson crawled from trench to trench counting grenades and reassuring the shivering men. Some were down to a dozen rounds of ammo.

"Sarge, I gotta take a leak," groaned one young private, obviously in pain.

"Kid, when the shooting starts you'll forget all about it. When it's all over, I guarantee that most of you guys will have taken a leak. Now keep yer head down and follow orders. Do not leave yer cover!" He patted the youngster's helmet and moved on.

George hunkered down. While checking his ammo, fixing his bayonet, and adjusting his helmet, he prayed he'd live to see his wife and baby again. He was scared like everyone else.

> *Good grief, why not? After all, it was the first time someone would be trying to kill him. Stay calm, George, you'll be shielded by the Holy Spirit.*

When First Sergeant Jackson returned with the grenade count, the CO issued new orders. "Let the Krauts get on this side of the tree line and lob your first grenade. Wait till the smoke clears and look for any Krauts standing and any pushing through the tree lines and throw the next grenades. Repeat until none of them are advancing or until we are out of grenades, whichever comes first. Fix your bayonets and be prepared for hand-to-hand combat. Try to save at least six rounds of ammo for close combat. Remember, men, you trained for this."

They hunkered down, steeling themselves for the battle to come.

Suddenly, the silence of the thick forest was shattered by enormous explosions as the Allied cannons began their barrage. Along an 80-mile front, every big gun seemed to be firing non-stop. The bright sky illuminated the ghoulish silhouette of giant pine trees. Thunder filled the air, and the earth shook from the impact of the cones of fire.

A frightened George crouched in his trench, waiting until the Germans broke through the tree line and got close enough to be targets for the grenade assault. He hoped and prayed he and the men in his company could avoid slaughter.

As the enemy penetrated the fiery tree line, the American troops reacted by pulling their grenade pins.

> *My consciousness was filled with a chorus of countdowns before the grenades were lobbed at the advancing Germans.*

Men ducked into the trenches to avoid being blasted with debris. Weapons fired on both sides made the once peaceful forest a shooting gallery. Occasionally, a German fell into one of the American slit trenches and suffered the consequences. For the newest replacements of the 289th, it was an intro to war.

> *It was biblical fire and brimstone deep in the Ardennes. I felt souls writhing in protest at their deaths throughout the haze of battle. They rose into the darkened sky, many accompanied by angels.*

When it quieted, the 289th was out of both ammo and grenades. Keeping their heads down, each soldier remained on alert. At this point their bayonets were their only means of defense. They waited for daylight to come. Groans and pleas for help were heard, but no one moved. Now and then a shot rang out, and they heard another grunt.

> *I saw two more wispy forms move upward.*

Dawn's early light filtering through the skeletal remains of the giant fir trees revealed the success of the grenade offensive, confirmed in the German body count. Strewn along the line of American foxholes and slit trenches lay the German corpses, frozen stiff into ghoulish poses.

Emerging from their covered positions, the men slowly assessed their situation. Miraculously, the company had only lost two men. Their bodies were wrapped in tarps and prepared to be loaded onto one of the supply trucks after they had delivered their load of ammo and supplies.

The desperation strategy worked, but they were defenseless now.

The CO barked orders. "Gather up all the enemy weapons and ammo you can carry. Make sure we get it all; it's less for them to use against us later." The men took stock of their commandeered weapon and ammo supply and reported to their commander.

Praise the Lord, at least now they could defend themselves with German weapons until they connected with their supply lines.

The CO barked, "Let's move out, men."

The young private walked next to George. "I notice I'm not the only one with cold, wet pants."

An equally embarrassed George growled, "Just keep moving, kid."

I hummed Psalm 135:1: Give thanks to the Lord, for he is good, for his mercy endures forever.

Dawn not only illuminated signs of a successful offensive, it also allowed the supply trucks to move faster. As the brave men of the 289th moved on, the supply lines caught up with them.

At last able to get the necessities of ammo, food and some much needed dry clothing, the men rallied; their morale lifted. It was a good day.

It was a good day; but for the 289th, the war had only just started.

9
DEC. 27, 1944—JAN. 1, 1945
LIKE A GHOST

Harsh weather didn't take sides; it affected the Allies and Axis, equally pounding the men and machines. The 289th and 290th Companies encountered the 12th Panzer Division the week after Christmas. The fierce German tanks split the Allied lines, forcing them to regroup in order to mount a strong counter attack that required covert intelligence.

The CO called his men together. "I need one man to scout the Panzer positions over that hill. The bastards have stopped our forward progress and split our lines. We're pinned down and they're gonna wipe us out unless we can get the coordinates on their tanks for our cannons to take 'em out. I want one of my forward observers to volunteer to get over that hill and give the Fire Direction Center (FDC) some guidance to hit those German guns."

George stepped forward. "I'll go, sir. I can move fast and they'll never see me."

"Thank you Private. God go with you."

> I understood the CO knew George was good at what he did. I heard the CO think to himself, "Hell, that man's like a ghost, slipping in and out of German lines undetected." I read the relief flooding the

officer's mind knowing Panko would deliver the exact information the FDC needed.

Of course, I went too. I'm wasn't at all happy with my soldier volunteering for the mission, because it was going to be dangerous, but there was no denying his bravery.

He moved low and fast. He had a radio, compass, handgun (for all the good it would do him against tanks) and his map for the coordinates. George infiltrated the German lines by crawling from tree to bush to tree. He found cover in the bombed-out shell of a building. Hunkering down, he charted the German tank positions.

I heard his clear, soft voice calling coordinates into the FDC. His radio crackled; they'd received his transmission.

The barrage began. The first rounds hit their marks. The tanks not incapacitated by American artillery shells began to move defensively. In spite of the enemy's attempts at evasive action, the strikes repeatedly found their marks. The Germans realized someone had to be directing the Allied fire. Through their field glasses, they began to look for a place where a scout could take cover.

George saw the turrets of the tanks turn toward the bombed-out ruin where he was hiding. He knew the Panzers were intent on leveling his cover. "Oh, Sweet Jesus!" he muttered.

Lord, we have our work cut out for us now. He needs speed, agility and protective holy armor. Give me strength, Father.

George dove through an opening on the opposite side of the stone wall and high-stepped through the snow. Both of us heard the sound of the tanks blasting away the remaining ruins.

Sprinting through the trees in the direction of his cannon company, George prayed all the way, "Lord, don't let my legs fail me." His high-stepping zig zag pattern got him through the snow-covered trees, making it difficult for any of the cumbersome tanks to set their gun sites on him. Every blast missed by yards, but George just kept on moving like he was protected inside an impenetrable bubble.

I could hear the pounding of his very brave heart. He ran as if he was carried on the wings of angels. Thank you, Lord, for the gifts you've bestowed on this man and thank You for taking care of my soldier. I knew the power of the Lord and I was still in awe of His visible assistance. God is good.

Having made it safely over the hill, George dropped to his knees gasping for breath in the thick blanket of snow. He gave thanks. He knew it was the grace and protection of The Holy Spirit. There was no doubt in his mind that he was spared for a reason.

The shelling continued for days, but the Allies prevailed, moving deeper into the enemy stronghold.

10
WINTER 1945
A VISITOR IN THE FOXHOLE

I n the bitter cold, the company strengthened its defensive positions at the Salm River, preparing for another bloody battle. George was assigned a difficult scouting mission.

> *Not all soldiers had protective tarps or supplies of warm, dry clothing; some froze to death in their foxholes, as France and Germany experienced one of the most severe winters on record. I genuinely felt this tragedy and the unnecessary loss of life.*

George was one of the lucky ones to have a tarp in his gear. It kept him from freezing more than once. Now, deep in enemy territory, having gathered and transmitted enemy coordinates to the Fire Direction Center, he sought shelter as the barrage on the gun emplacements ramped up. As he radioed his FDC on the success of the mission, dusk deepened the shadows of the heavily-wooded mountain. George knew he wouldn't make it back to his company that night.

The temperatures plummeted, and George did what he had been trained to do. Clearing a spot in the moisture laden snow, he dug a trench to serve as his shelter for the night. As he dug, he prayed, "Our Father who art in heaven hallowed be thy name. Thy Kingdom come, Thy will be done," he paused at "Thy will be done" to reflect. It truly was all about God's will. He resumed his prayer.

I can offer no explanation for the strength and perseverance he exhibited, creating a safe spot in the frozen ground. He simply amazed me with his survival instincts. Burrowing down, he covered himself with the tarp.

Unable to risk a radio transmission to tell his company he'd be taking cover for the night, George dozed off and on, curled up in a ball. Heavy snow fell for hours. He aroused himself as the fingers of dawn reached gently through the dense trees. Desperately wanting to stretch his stiff limbs, he quietly and slowly lifted the snow-covered tarp, remembering he was behind enemy lines. His movement ceased. He froze in place. Another man was in his trench.

Letting his eyes adjust to the dim light, he saw the outline of the soldier's helmet and realized his visitor was a German soldier, only an arm's length away. The German wasn't moving. Neither was George. Staring at the man so close to him, George noticed stark white facial features, covered with snow. The man wasn't breathing.

"Holy Mother of God!" He did a double take. The kid, who looked to be in his mid to late teens, was dead. Frozen stiff. George made the sign of the cross, as he'd been taught as a child, head, heart, left shoulder, right shoulder. "Rest in peace," he whispered.

I noticed a halo around the young German's head. His weapon had never been fired. He was young, very young. Probably a new replacement unwillingly conscripted off the street and sent into battle. Perhaps his parents had no idea that he'd been taken.

After folding and stowing his tarp, George grimly removed the boy's weapon and ammo to take with him. He slipped silently out of the foxhole and disappeared into the trees. Concerned that he might cross paths with a German patrol, he checked his compass and map and headed in the last known direction of his company. Within the hour, he was back with his company, who were overjoyed to see him. They told him they thought he might have been killed or captured, but instead, he had a story to tell.

> I know the young German was an enemy, but he was also a child of God. I pray that he is with the Lord and that his soul may rest in peace. Praise be to God that George survived the night and wasn't discovered by the enemy.

With the information George provided, the regiment aided in the clearing of several towns and villages and, after nine grueling days of battle, was pulled out of line for a short rest.

> Praise God, for these totally exhausted, battle-weary men.

On that day, Sergeant Bill Corner, a fellow scout, received a battlefield commission to Lieutenant. All the scouts of the 289th were extremely proud of him and grateful to be serving with one of the bravest soldiers they had ever met. In this capacity, Lieutenant Bill Corner was going to save George from certain death.

11

WINTER 1945
FINDING FOOD AND
BESTOWING NICKNAMES

As the 289th moved into Odeigne, Belgium, they discovered an abandoned farm house which hadn't been bombed to bits. After clearing each room and determining the place was safe from booby traps and snipers, the men began to relax; they had found a house which offered badly-needed shelter from the unrelenting cold and snow. The CO felt it was safe enough to build a small fire in the fireplace of a back room. Some of the men stripped off their wet clothing and hung their pants and shirts to dry. All of them jockeyed for positions near the fire to warm their cold, stiff limbs.

The house was explored for hidden panels and hiding places. Suddenly, someone hollered out, "Holy smoke, what a find!"

Men came running, weapons ready. "Whaddya got?" hollered Jenks.

"A cold cellar with potatoes in it!" Smitty bellowed. "I'll go down and throw some up to you. Wipe 'em off and start roasting 'em over the fire."

Some of the guys from the FDC were so hungry they ate them raw, like apples. Others stuck them on the ends of their bayonets, turning the spuds slowly above the flames.

The door to the potato cellar was nothing more than a loose section of four wide floorboards slid to one side to gain entry. In the haste and joy of finding edible food, none of the men had bothered to put the boards back into place.

George and I were returning from patrol with three other scouts, the newly commissioned Lt. Bill Corner, Ray Vittucci, and Harry Sachs. Having slogged through the heavy, wet snow, they needed warmth from the fire and something to eat. Relieved to have a roof over their heads, these men were looking forward to some rest.

I was frozen stiff.

George strode purposefully into the back room. He never saw the uneven opening in the floor. Stepping on the edge of the loose floorboards, he suddenly and silently disappeared into the cellar below. The pressure of his foot flipped the boards around and snapped them perfectly into place, covering the hole.

"Ta-da!" Smitty waved his arms with a flourish as if performing a magic trick. "One minute George is there, and the next he isn't. What a feat, ladies and gents."

Shocked at first, the men broke the silence with bursts of laughter.

As quickly as the floorboards had flipped over and snapped shut, they flipped open and a red-faced soldier pushed the trap door to the side, pulling himself up from the dusty cellar, loudly cussing in an unrecognizable language.

"Presto, changeo, he reappears!" Smitty removed his helmet and took a bow as if he were a ringmaster in the circus.

Jumpin' Jehoshaphat, I must say the disappearing act was unexpected. My spine is still reverberating from being jostled. Oh, boy, George is upset. If Smitty knows what's good for him, he'll zip his lip.

Smitty held out a roasted gem. "Want a potato, George?"

"Hey Panko, yer bleedin' a little, maybe you can put in for a purple heart. They'll make it a purple potato instead," Vittucci cracked.

Someone else asked, "What language was that, Panko?"

"Russian." George snapped, brushing spider webs off his sleeves and out of his hair.

"Do you speak Russian or just swear in Russian?" Lt. Corner rubbed the stubble on his face while waiting for the answer.

"I speak it, read it, write it and swear in it, Lieutenant."

Lt. Corner seemed genuinely interested. "Seriously, Panko, how is it that you're fluent in Russian?"

"My parents are from Russia. Came to the States when they were kids. They spoke both Russian and English at home. My brothers and I were brought up speaking both. We lived in an all immigrant neighborhood outside of Scranton. It was like a small Russian village, and the men were all coal miners like my dad." His facial features softened, and he smiled. "In fact, if I didn't speak Russian, I'd never get anything to eat." He bit into the potato with a loud crunch.

"Whaddya mean, you'd never get anything to eat?"

Chewing with his mouth open, George explained, "In that little community we got together all the time, any excuse for a meal. The women would be in the kitchen fixin' food, men in the back yard settin' up croquet and figurin' out teams. Everyone spoke Russian." A wave of homesickness hit him.

Vittucci scratched his scruffy head. "Okay, Panko, I get the neighborhood gatherin' thing, but why did you have to speak Russian to eat?"

"When you walked through the food line, you had to tell the Russian *babushkas* what you wanted in their language, Russian. Only the little kids could get away with pointin' at the food. That neighborhood was a great place to live."

Vittucci stepped a little closer. "What the heck is a *babushka*?"

"That's what we call an older Russian lady or a grandmother, *babushka.*"

Lt. Corner reiterated, "So you're fluent in Russian, Panko?"

"Yep." George emphatically nodded his head.

> *Within the year, Lt. Corner would pass this information up the chain of command and George would have an unexpected assignment.*
>
> *Everyone was too cold and hungry to make a big deal of George's bilingual skills. The guys were concentrating on keeping the small fire going to warm themselves and cook their potatoes on the end of their bayonets without someone losing an eye. George had provided the entertainment for the day when he disappeared through the floor. The laughter was good for all of these men. The cussing, well that's another story.*

He'd softened up after talking about home and family. It had been a long time since they'd had anything about which to laugh.

That day, Lt. Corner dubbed George Panko, "The Mad Russian."

Not one to be outdone, Vittucci chimed in, "From now on, you guys call me 'V2.' I'm the American version of the German rocket wreakin' havoc here in Europe. I plan to wreak havoc on the lousy Krauts!"

"The Mad Russian" and "V2" both looked at Lt. Corner and Sachs quizzically. "Well?" V2 challenged.

The Lieutenant answered, knowing what they wanted. "I'm just Corner."

Sachs shrugged his shoulders and shook his head. "I got nuthin.'"

> *That night, George wrote his sweet Gladys a long letter explaining that he was no longer a baker, but an infantryman. He couldn't bring himself to*

explain the forward observer duties. He knew she would be out of her mind with worry. Before falling asleep, he turned my pages and read this prayer: "St. Michael, the Archangel, defend us in battle; be our protection against the malice and snares of the devil. We humbly beseech God to command him, and do thou, O prince of the heavenly host, by the Divine power thrust into hell Satan and the other evil spirits who roam through the world seeking the ruin of souls. Amen."

12

FEBRUARY 1945
CROSSING THE RHINE

George was known as the "Mad Russian" in his company, but to the artillerymen in the Fire Direction Center (FDC) who heard his smooth voice repeating accurate coordinates, George was "the sweetest voice in the ETO."

Guided by a map and his compass, and armed with a .45 caliber handgun, he crawled deep into enemy territory, remaining calm and speaking clearly into his radio. On covert missions behind enemy lines, he studied his battlefield map, plotted the coordinates, and called them into the FDC. Accurate artillery strikes subsequently rained down on tanks, German bunkers, and gun emplacements to give the advancing troops a clear field ahead. George credited his training and field experience for fine tuning his English.

> He also had me as his guide and protector and was beginning to believe the Word of the Lord was protecting him at all times. I was always in the breast pocket of George's combat jacket, my cover and pages worn and dog-eared. I was able to give him guidance, strength, and comfort through the words on my pages. His dependence on reading them was the beginning of an epiphany regarding his "soldiers' Bible," as he called me.
>
> George refused a battlefield commission to Sergeant. I was flabbergasted at that decision, but

hands down he wanted no part of being responsible for the lives of the men he had trained and worked with for so long. His focus was surviving this horrible war and getting back to Gladys and his little boy at home. His focus was also mine.

Lt. Bill Corner fostered a strong sense of brotherhood among the forward observers (FOs). This bond was not entirely understood by the others in the company, but it was highly respected. The FOs could argue with, fight and tease one another, but let someone else mess with one scout and the perpetrator would have the other scouts jumping all over them. It was the same situation at home for George and his three brothers. They fought amongst themselves but became a united front when an outsider picked on one of them. For the wartime brothers, each day was the definition of bravery; they were scared to death most of the time, but conscientiously doing the job they were trained to do.

The first week of February, the strategists made preparations to cross the Rhine. With steep rocky banks and rapid, debris-filled polluted waters, the undertaking posed a challenge. Ideally, the commanding officer would wait until their big guns were in place, but the heavy artillery had been slowed by the deep snow.

Lt. Corner was promoted to the position of Executive Officer and a fresh from the states, Lt. Snyder took his place.

In spite of not having the cannons in place, the new guy insisted his forward observers cross the Rhine River. He demanded his scouts give him the coordinates of German cannon emplacements and machine gun bunkers at any cost. None of the men could figure out what he was going to do with the information they gathered when the guns of the 289th weren't ready to fire.

The young, inexperienced officer was calculating that if his unorthodox strategy was successful, he'd make a name for himself and gain stature with his command.

Crossing the Rhine was extremely dangerous for the scout patrol under ideal conditions, but without the cannons set up and ready to take out the targets, the bizarre mission was going to be suicidal.

Lieutenant Snyder had joined the regiment fresh out of officers training. Everything he knew came from three months of officer training school, not combat experience. Snyder was a little know-it-all who managed to irritate every soldier with whom he came in contact. Behind his back, the men referred to Snyder as a "ninety-day wonder."

Following Snyder's orders, three scouts including George attempted the crossing and encountered withering enemy fire from the east bank. Their rubber raft was soon riddled with bullets and sank. The men managed to swim back in the frigid water, crawling up the river bank on their bellies and over the snow-covered ground until out of machine gun range. They lay exhausted, wet and cold.

"Where's my scout patrol?" Snyder barked, storming into a circle of men gathered around a fire.

The freezing scouts came forward. "Here, sir." George chattered and shivered while pulling a wool blanket tighter around his shoulders. His lips were blue. Someone was trying to find dry clothing for him and the other two scouts who survived the unsuccessful mission.

"Here, sir." Sachs and V2 echoed, chattering with cold.

"I want you men back in a boat for another try as soon as you get dried off."

"Yes, sir." George looked at the other two scouts with a nod. They nodded back acknowledging what George was thinking.

It was stupid to participate in another doomed mission led by an incompetent man. I heard their thoughts clearly. I felt helpless other than to pray for their protection.

"Dontcha just love takin' orders from this ignorant ninety-day wonder?" George muttered to the others as they picked up another raft and headed toward the frozen river bank.

Sweet Mother of God, this young man is a square peg in a round hole! The 289th had run like a finely-tuned machine without his irritating presence. His lack of combat experience was sure to get his men killed or wounded. My print raised in alarm. We call upon you, Lord. Please save these men from an unnecessary demise. Frustrated, I heard mental chatter from dozens in the company, and I was not able to console them.

At the Lieutenant's order, the scout patrol made another valiant attempt to cross the Rhine. Again, they were driven back. Again, another rubber raft was riddled with bullets. For a second time, the men managed to swim through the freezing water and low-crawl over the snow covered bank to safety. Miraculously, the scouts were unharmed.

Lt. Snyder met the three men once they were out of range of the German machine guns. He screamed, swore, and berated the men for not carrying out the mission assigned to them. Everyone within earshot was appalled at this treatment. Word got out.

"Saddle up, you're going again," the red-faced junior officer barked.

Lt. Corner had been alerted by some of the others in the regiment about the impossible mission his scouts were being ordered to carry out. He was also aware of the inappropriate tongue-lashing his forward observers were taking from the new lieutenant. The senior officer approached the group and overheard Lt. Snyder demanding they make a third attempt to cross the Rhine. Observing his men and their miserable condition, Lt. Corner shook his head.

Duty-bound to intervene on their behalf, the Lieutenant calmly approached the new officer. "It would make better sense to wait for some of our machine guns and cannons to get in place to soften the German lines and give these men some cover, Lieutenant Snyder. Additionally, they'll be risking their lives to obtain coordinates for our cannons to hit the German machine guns and their cannons, but we don't even have our firepower in place. That part puzzles me. They've tried your innovative plan twice unsuccessfully. Fortunately, no one got hurt."

"I don't want to wait until our cannons are in place, sir! I want them gathering coordinates now!" the little man screamed.

Corner exercised every bit of his patience in trying to stay calm. Through gritted teeth he issued his next statement, "Lieutenant Snyder, I have been on FO missions with each one of these men. They are the best I've ever worked with. This exercise is a suicide mission, as proven by two bullet riddled-rafts. Fortunately, we haven't lost any of these valuable men. It's downright dangerous to continue the same tactic. The Germans are waiting for us to try again and they know we don't have the heavy armaments in place."

"I don't care, I want them to complete their assigned mission," Snyder snorted, while stamping his feet and kicking at the snow covered frozen ground in emphasis. He then launched into another tirade of obscenities.

Lt. Corner had had enough of this pompous, ignorant man. He pulled out his .45 caliber sidearm and was on Lt. Snyder's flank in less than a second. Holding the gun to the smaller man's head he said calmly, "Okay, the mission is on, but Lieutenant Snyder, you're going with them. What's more, you're going to ride point in the raft."

Snyder's eyes bulged and his face blanched when he felt the cold metal on his head. He swallowed hard.

Corner snarled into the smaller man's ear. "Would you like to reconsider your order, Lieutenant Snyder?"

"I-I think waiting for the cannons to be in place is a good idea, Lieutenant Corner. Now, p-p-please put your weapon away, sir."

> *Thank God for Lt. Corner. He'd been with the 289th from the beginning and, if you'll pardon the pun, was the cornerstone of the forward observer teams.*

The Allied cannons arrived and started battering the German resistance, allowing the scouts to cross the Rhine. The "sweetest voice in the ETO" recited enemy coordinates to the Fire Direction Center (FDC) as the scout platoon completed their intelligence-gathering, finding every well-hidden German gun emplacement and machine gun nest. Not one scout was lost in the effort. The information they gathered aided the rest of the allied ground troops who followed to cross the Rhine and drive the Germans out of France.

13

MY THREE SONS IN COMBAT

My sphere of knowledge and understanding extended home to George's entire family.

Large headlines in The *Scranton Times* heralded the Allied advances. It was sometimes hard to determine specifics about troops involved and their location. Newspapers held back details to protect wartime strategy and the troops, but still boasted about successful operations. Headlines made bold proclamations of the daring bulge offensive through German lines and praised the American troops for pushing through German lines and driving the aggressors out of France.

However, in truth, either side still had the potential to win this war.

I knew the outcome, but it all had to be played out.

George's parents, Tom and Mary, had the news reports read to them because their comprehension of the written word in English was sometimes difficult. With three sons in the European Theater of Operations (ETO), even thinking of the danger their boys were in was almost too much to bear.

Their neighbor, Ruth Hritzko, had planned to come to their Dickson City home for a visit that day. After they had poured their visitor a cup of coffee, Ruth sank into Tom's deeply cushioned chair in the corner of the warm kitchen. Tom eagerly relinquished his favorite spot today, since Ruth planned to read the newspaper to them. Tom and Mary sipped their strong, black coffee while seated across from each other at the red and gray Formica-topped kitchen table. If they didn't understand a word or a phrase, they would ask in Russian, and Ruth answered them in their language. There was not a lot in today's paper, but the couple hung on every word while holding rosaries wound around their fingers.

"'The Battle for the Ruhr Valley is pivotal because it produces eighty percent of Germany's coal, iron, steel, chemicals and synthetic rubber.'" She looked up to see if Tom and Mary understood. They nodded their heads for her to continue.

"'The 75th Division had the task of taking the Ruhr Valley in a battle beginning March 31st.'"

Mary gripped her apron, rocked back and forth and moaned, "My son, my son! Tom, our George is in the 75th Division."

Ruth tried to comfort the couple. "You know the papers can't always report which companies are fighting in that battle. Maybe it's not the 289th."

"Read more, Ruth," Tom insisted

"'To take control of the Ruhr Valley will certainly shut down the German Army and win the war in Europe.'" Ruth looked up to see Tom reach over the table to grasp Mary's hand. It was hopeful news, but it was all they had on the European front for today.

Mary rose and walked to the opposite end of the big kitchen. She reached for a plate in the cupboard and put it on the counter. Carefully retrieving a cookie sheet from the oven, she scooped a dozen warm, nut-filled cookies, called kiffles, on the decorative plate and carried them to the table. Beckoning to Ruth to help herself, Mary bowed her head to pray for all her sons.

I could smell freshly baked kiffles. Too bad my endowed gifts didn't allow me to pass this on to George. He'd never believe it, anyway.

14

MARCH 1945
THE DORTMUND-EMS CANAL
CROSSING

"Men, the 289th Cannon Company, first battalion, has been tasked with the Dortmund-Ems Canal crossing. As you know from your maps, the Ruhr Valley is interlaced with a series of canals, averaging ten feet deep and as much as a hundred feet wide, with very steep, slick concrete banks. Certain areas are more narrow and shallow. Our mission is to infiltrate German lines and take the town of Ickern. But, we got a problem. The German artillery covers the entire canal because it's their last line of defense." The commanding officer of the Cannon Company looked around at all the faces with which he had become so familiar during these months of combat. He knew this was going to be fierce fighting. He continued, "The Germans are desperate to hold the line and fend off the American invasion. We have to be more desperate than they are to take Ickern and defeat these bastards. We'll be sending our scout patrols out to gather intel and to guide our FDC to soften the line with artillery fire. Be safe, men. God go with each of you!"

At 0100, George and two other forward observers, V2 and Lt. Corner, stealthily made their way along a rutted dirt road next to the canal. The water-filled ditches on both sides offered some protection from the German artillery which came whistling in, one after the other.

"Hey, Lieutenant, aren't you glad you volunteered to go on this mission with us?"

"I never wanna lose the feeling we have as scouts. But I'll tell you one thing, Panko, I hate the sound of those 88's coming in," griped Lt. Corner. "Only good thing is, it gives us some warning to dive in the ditches for cover."

George was glad Corner was part of the group. Highly respected by every soldier in the company, he was the bravest man with whom George had ever served. The lieutenant could spot a camouflaged gun emplacement when no one else could. He was simply the best at the job.

The repeated shelling and diving for cover impeded the scouts' progress, but they finally reached their predetermined crossing point.

> I heard George say to V2, "I'm gonna start praying now. We gotta get the coordinates for these gun emplacements before they kill us all."

"Hail Mary, full of grace, the Lord is with you." George took me out of his pocket and put me in his helmet because I had a better chance of staying dry there than in his pocket. "Blessed art thou among women and blessed is the fruit of thy womb, Jesus. Holy Mary, Mother of God, pray for us sinners now and at the hour of our death. Amen."

Over and over, he prayed in a hoarse whisper. Corner and V2 listened to George as they moved. His prayers helped to calm their nerves.

Securing their rope ladder over the edge of the concrete bank, they descended. Once in the canal, they were careful to get their footing before wading a little faster to keep ahead of the relentless shelling.

Suddenly, V2 lost his footing and disappeared beneath the surface of the cold, black water, managing to hold the radio above his head.

Grabbing it out of Vittucci's hand while George pulled V2 out of the water by the back of his combat jacket, Corner said, "I got the radio."

"I got the V2." George mimicked Corner as the man struggled to stand. V2 coughed, gagged, and spit snot and water.

George pounded Vittucci on the back. "V2, you're not s'posed to drink this putrid stuff."

Bill could no long contain his laughter as they watched V2 continue to gag and cough.

"Jumpin' Judas, V2, we have a job to do here," implored Bill, "Pull yourself together." They all flinched as they heard the whistle of another 88 shell.

"Man, I just pissed my pants," Vittucci whined.

Bill looked V2 up and down. "We can't tell. You're soaking wet from head to toe. You shoulda just kept yer trap shut."

Looking at each other, both Bill and George looked back at V2 and burst out laughing once more. In spite of the 88s, they found themselves giddy. It seemed reasonable, like a group of guys fooling around in the swimming hole at home. It brought a moment of sanity and calmed their frazzled nerves.

"Come on guys, gimme a break!" V2 sputtered. He looked like a slimy drowned rat. "Considerin' how you guys are laughin' at me, I must really look funny."

"You not only look funny V2, you smell funny," Corner replied, holding his nose.

Corner and George burst into laughter again.

"Glad you dogfaces enjoyed it." V2 snorted.

The German artillery had not stopped the laughter. Although inappropriate, the levity broke the tension. The men pulled themselves together, crossed the canal and dispersed within enemy lines, each calling in coordinates to the Fire Direction Center. The scouts' calls were always said to be "right on the money." Accuracy was their trademark. They completed the mission assigned to them that night, signaling the beginning of a difficult, but successful two-week battle to defeat the Germans and take the city of Ickern.

> I was proud of the job George was doing. He hated the war, but was superb at what he did. He had learned from the best, Lt. Bill Corner. At this point, they wanted to accomplish their missions, win the war and go home to family and friends. Who could argue with that?

15

GOOD NEWS
FOR THE FOLKS AT HOME

R uth Hritzko sat in the upholstered chair, once again reading from The *Scranton Times*. Tom and Mary had settled on the vinyl padded chrome chairs and were holding hands across the Formica tabletop. The coffee was hot and a plate of freshly baked walnut *kolache* sat in the center of the table. The aroma from the second batch of *kolache*, still in the oven, enticed the three of them.

Ruth looked forward to reading the news to this couple because Mary's baking skills were incredible, and there was always something fresh from the oven on the table.

"'Allied artillery pounded the German machines and emplacements to soften enemy lines for the infantry to cross to Dortmund-Ems canal and take the city of Ickern,'" she read aloud. "'The two-week battle broke down German defenses and the Nazis were driven back toward Berlin.'"

"Two-week battle? It lasted two weeks?"

Ruth looked up. "Yes, Tom, but they did it. They took control of the city." She couldn't have been happier for this couple. Returning to the newspaper, she read: "'War correspondent Ernie Pyle reports that the 289th was relieved on the river line April 13 by other elements of the Army.'"

"Dat was our George!" Mary cried out. She turned to Tom, "Dat was our son. He's in da 289th! He was one of da soldiers in dat battle!"

Ruth showed Tom and Mary a cartoon which showed haggard soldiers, who had apparently not bathed in weeks, wondering when they would get their first hot meal for all their hard work. She read the caption to them, "Infantry soldiers to get $10.00 a month extra in 'fight pay' thanks to the 'Ernie Pyle Bill' passed by Congress in 1944."

Ruth condensed the next bit of news. "'Although there's a decline in fighting, the 'mop-up' operations are still dangerous. Hundreds of German soldiers are surrendering to any Allied soldier they meet. However, pockets of enemy troops who refuse to accept that they are on the losing end are continuing to attack.'"

Tom and Mary pulled out a chair at the table for Ruth. They were very grateful for her kindness in reading to them. Mary wiped the tears from her eyes and offered her a piece of nut and poppyseed *kolache*. Tom invited Ruth to stay for a lunch of *halupki*, the stuffed cabbage still simmering in the pot, and freshly made *pierogies*. Ruth graciously accepted. After they finished their sweet treat and coffee, they compared notes about their respective families. An hour later over lunch, the three of them speculated how soon each son would return home.

"Wit' da grace of God, all of my sons will be home soon," Mary announced with finality.

16

APRIL 1945
LIBERATING THE CAMPS

G eorge's service was not over. He had no idea of the inhumanity of man he was about to witness. The Lord God Himself held him upright as he experienced unimaginable horrors.

The Allied troops, energized by victory after victory, now advanced even further into Germany. As they did, "camps" were discovered which challenged all human understanding. The evidence of Nazi brutality was overwhelming.

The Germans had imprisoned vast numbers of displaced persons of all nationalities. At a camp near Ickern, Americans liberated hundreds of Catholic captives, as well as other prisoners of war, long thought dead. These people were unspeakably grateful to the Allies for setting them free. "Thank you!" "*Danke!*" "*Heil Americans!*" Over and over, gratitude poured out for the liberating army.

As the troops liberated the camps, General Eisenhower gave orders to take as many pictures as possible of the survivors of the Nazi concentration camps. "These were death camps for Jews and others the Nazis deemed undesirable in their utopian society. Much of the world will not believe what we say without pictures," the wise general directed.

The Germans had disguised these torturous places as displaced persons camps. Thousands and thousands of Jews had been imprisoned, gassed and cremated; thousands of other bodies piled up in mass graves awaiting cremation to destroy the evidence. Many, near death from malnutrition and disease, were freed, only to die within hours. For them, freedom came too late.

Eisenhower wanted definitive proof of the crematoriums, the gas chambers, and all other evidence. "Let there be no doubt as to the atrocities which occurred here."

The liberating forces were stunned at the sights of the emaciated surviving prisoners and the piles of human remains in various stages of decomposition throughout the camps.

"Get pictures of the bodies and the survivors. Give them whatever food and water we have."

George stopped to pass his canteen to a small group of emaciated men clad in filthy wide-striped uniforms. Sitting on his haunches and looking at the ground to keep from breaking down, he waited as they drank every last drop. Glancing to his left, George saw large buckets of blood-spattered dental work containing gold fillings and crowns lined up along a fence line. He got up and walked along the enclosure taking in, but not believing, the images his eyes were sending to his brain. Beyond the teeth buckets were piles of discarded children's shoes and box after box of eyeglasses. The evil Nazis had robbed each prisoner of every shred of human dignity they had before killing whole families. George held on to the wire fence and vomited repeatedly. When his stomach was empty, he continued to retch at the smell of death.

> Oh, the cruelty and hatred of men! I pray for the souls of these people; men, women, and children who were tortured and killed. This treatment of fellow human beings is unfathomable. How will the survivors live with what they have lost and

experienced? Heavenly Father, let us never forget what we see here lest it happens again!

The American troops were now an occupying force.

Signs of Allied advancement were evident on buildings, bridges and other flat structures with graffiti stating, "Kilroy was here." The bald character with the big nose peeking out over a wall became a symbol of Allied troop occupation and brought a smile to all Americans who passed by. The Kilroy cartoon was a sign of hope and a sign that, in time, many men would start rotating back home.

17
LAST DAY OF COMBAT FOR THE 289TH

Gladys turned on the radio in the kitchen as she prepared her son's breakfast. The child had lost his baby face, had experienced his first haircut, and now looked like a little boy. Gladys' sister Dorothy had given her nephew the nickname Butch, and it stuck. When she wrote to her husband, Gladys softened his nickname to Butchie. It fit the active toddler. Sitting in his hand-painted, wooden high chair, the youngster watched his mother fix his meal. While munching on finger foods Gladys had placed on his highchair tray, Butchie bobbed his little head to the music coming from the radio sitting on the kitchen counter.

When she heard the war report would be up next, Gladys turned up the volume. The announcer seemed almost jubilant to read his morning news. "For some forces in Germany, April 13, 1945, was the last day of combat; this includes the 289th, 290th, and the 291st Companies. They fought an amazing campaign, traversing Europe more than once, and fighting wherever they were needed. Exhibiting extraordinary bravery, these soldiers, the best of the best, prevailed against the German war machine."

She knew that was her husband. "The last day of combat? Praise the Lord!" Gladys crossed herself and, with tears streaming down her face, sat at the table to pray as the radio announcer droned on in the background.

I knew that history would call the men and women of World War II "The Greatest Generation" because they saved the rest of the world from the unbelievable horrors and cruelty of Adolph Hitler and his Nazi killing machine.

"Mama, Mama," Butchie's little hands started slapping up and down on his tray sending cracker crumbs and little round cereal O's to litter the floor under his chair.

Gladys pushed herself back from the table and crossed herself again, "Okay, sweet boy, it's coming." Her thoughts were somewhere in Europe with her husband. When would he be coming home?

She was comforted by one of her favorite verses in Psalm 17:2-4, I love you, O Lord, my strength, O Lord, my rock, my fortress, my deliverer. My God, my rock of refuge, my shield, the horn of my salvation, my stronghold! Praised be the Lord, I exclaim, and I am safe from my enemies.

18

CAMP LUCKY STRIKE, RHEIMS, FRANCE

"Panko, you're wanted in the CO's tent."

What? What's happening? Now that no one was shooting at us, I had dozed off. Did I hear correctly? Is he wanted in the CO's tent? Oh, yes, now I remember what's going to happen; I think George will be surprised.

George wondered if they'd tell him he was shipping out soon. It seemed to him all he was doing in France was marking time. Impatient to get home, he dreamed about holding his wife in his arms every night and wondered how his son had changed. George was surprised to learn through his wife's letters that his boy was nicknamed Butchie. It didn't quite fit the baby he remembered, but he was two years old now. He hoped his son would live up to the name and be a tough, independent kid. He was also anxious to see his parents and prayed his brothers had survived and would be there when he got home. He headed for the CO's tent in eager anticipation.

George was ushered in by an aide

His commander was seated behind a desk with pen in hand. "I heard from Lieutenant Bill Corner that you understand and speak Russian fluently. Is this right?"

"Yes, sir, it is."

"Do you read and write it?"

"Yes, sir, I do."

"We need an American interpreter in Berlin for signing the peace agreements the day after tomorrow. Lieutenant Corner says you're my man. You're gonna leave right now by truck. They'll bring you back as soon as it's over." They discussed the details and logistics, and within ten minutes, George left the CO's office with a new assignment.

"Holy smoke! Is this the reason I haven't gotten orders to go home?" George wondered aloud as he made his way back to his tent. Throwing his cleanest uniforms into a duffle bag, he prepared to leave for Berlin.

The guys in the company had dubbed him "The Mad Russian" several months earlier. Interpreting between the Russians and Americans would add fuel to the fire. He was just grateful that he'd be in the background for this new assignment. Here he'd be an active participant, no longer a forward observer.

> I knew this opportunity was coming. I also knew George would be humbled and astounded by his new responsibility when he'd have time to digest it.

George thought about the last three years: starting out as a baker, volunteering as a forward observer, participating in the Bulge Offensive and the liberation of the concentration camps and now, being present as an interpreter at the official surrender of the Germans to the Russians. Regardless of the delay in shipping out for home, he was sure this was all God's doing.

> I was acutely aware of God's plan. I want him to be proud of this legacy he's leaving to his son. I pray the words he hears and the words he repeats are correctly interpreted for all to understand.

19
MAY 10, 1945
NEWS OF SURRENDER

An episode of Fibber McGee and Molly was interrupted by a news bulletin by Edward R. Murrow. Gladys and her parents were gathered around the radio in the small living room to enjoy the favorite comedy.

Morrow began his broadcast, "The newly-appointed German President sent General Alfred Jodl to negotiate a peace agreement with Allied Commander Dwight Eisenhower. On May 7th, General Jodl signed the instrument of surrender in Reims, France. A very unhappy Joseph Stalin demanded, and got, a separate German surrender ceremony in Berlin. Stalin could not abide with the agreement signed at a place outside of the area conquered by the Soviet forces. Stalin's signing event with German leaders occurred on May 9, 1945. Ladies and gentlemen, a peace agreement has now been penned by all parties."

There were whoops of joy when the announcer finished the broadcast. Gladys turned to her parents and outstretched her hands, "Does this mean George will be coming home soon?"

"I sure as hell hope so," growled her father. "Wish I knew why they're keepin' him."

20
WHAT'S OPULENT MEAN, ANYWAY?

The Scranton Times newspaper reported on developments in the peace treaty signings and meetings of leaders. To the average reader, the details were boring. Every once in a while, a correspondent threw in a little humor to try to liven up the report.

In July, Gladys' father began reading aloud at the dinner table. It was always amusing to hear his interpretation of the printed word. "Sez here, President Harry Truman, Joseph Stalin and another high mucky-muck got together in Potsdam, Germany. They called it The Meeting of the Big Three. Sez they had an opulent marble bathroom just for them." He slurped noisily from his coffee cup.

"What's opulent mean, anyway? And why do they need a marble crapper?"

"Dad, it means fancy and these men are prominent heads of state." She sipped her tea and broke a cookie in two for dunking.

"Marble crapper," he muttered. "I just don't get that. They put their pants on just like I do." He picked up the paper again to read. "Okay, Glad, here's the best part. Sez here, on the second day, Stalin come flyin' outta the fancy bathroom yellin' in Russian. One of the translators heard him ask,

'Who's Kilroy?' And, are you ready, Glad? Looks like Kilroy made it to the summit meeting!" He tipped his head back and had a hearty laugh.

Gladys giggled at her father's antics.

"Don't that beat all?" He asked as he slapped his knee. His giddiness was infectious. Neither of them could help the laughter bubbling up inside them, the war in Europe was over. They knew George wasn't fighting anymore, that he was relatively safe, and they hoped he was awaiting transport back to the States.

As they finished dinner, they both pondered just how long it would take for George to return home.

George wondered why he wasn't shipping out as well. He didn't know a big surprise awaited him.

21
Camp Lucky Strike
a Surprise Visit

After his translation duties, George returned to his base camp in Rheims, France. Unknown to him, his younger brother Joe, also in France, had heard from a supply truck driver that George was stationed at Camp Lucky Strike. Joe's unit had a replacement parts depot for their heavy equipment in Poix, about ninety miles outside of Rheims. He was so close, and yet so far. All he needed was a ride.

Approaching his supply sergeant, Joe humbled himself. "Sarge, I haven't seen my brother since March of '42. The next time you fill a request for replacement parts at Lucky Strike, can I ride along to see my brother?" It would cost him a couple of cartons of cigarettes, but it was going be worth it!

The sympathetic and bribable sergeant filled out the necessary paperwork and gave them to Joe. "Go find your brother, but be back tomorrow morning."

> This reunion was a special surprise that the Lord arranged for these two brothers. They needed the uplifting presence of family and to enjoy some time off with each other.

After ninety miles of bumpy, bomb-cratered road, Joe arrived in Rheims. Once at Lucky Strike, he was given directions to his brother's tent, only to find it empty.

Joe stood there scratching his head. "Where would I be?" Looking up, he saw a crudely made sign for the PX (Post Exchange). "Best bet, he's in there, 'cause that's where I'd be." As Joe burst through the door, he came face-to-face with his brother.

George couldn't believe his eyes. He shook his head, gasped, and reached out to touch Joe. "Holy Mary, Mother of God! Whaddya doin' here?" The brothers hugged, cried, laughed and hugged some more.

"I bumped my backside off just to come see you. I wanna spend some time with my big brother."

George was a good three inches shorter and twenty pounds lighter than Joe, who was a good bit over six feet tall. George certainly didn't look like the older brother.

With their arms around each other, they walked out of the PX toward the mess tent.

"I can't offer you a beer, but how 'bout a cup of coffee?" George suggested.

"Great, let's go."

Joe reached into his jacket pocket and pulled out two cigars. "Here, I brought you somethin' and one for me too." He clipped the ends of both cigars and pulled out his matches.

They had so little time and so much catching up to do. Both men carried letters in their helmets. Taking them out, they shared the latest news of home and brother Andy, an army medic somewhere in the ETO. The cigars and conversation lasted most of the night.

Under orders to return to Poix the next morning, Joe asked, "George, can you get a pass to go back with me for a few days? They won't turn you down. You're Mr. Big Shot after translating at the surrender."

Prepared to beg, George went to see his first sergeant, who accommodated the request, with no begging necessary. The two brothers boarded the supply truck for another bumpy ride, but neither seemed to notice. They enjoyed ninety miles of talking, laughing and catching up.

In Poix, the club for enlisted men was open and, because everyone was preparing to leave for the States, all drinks were free. The brothers had a few beers, played cards and talked some more.

> George learned that by the time he had disembarked from the *Leopoldville* in Le Havre, his brother Joe had already been a combat casualty. Wounded by machine gun fire while in northern France, Joe spent three months recovering in England before returning to duty.

Leaning forward, Joe eagerly explained. "I was assigned to a C-47 airplane group responsible for droppin' gliders over the Rhine. They were so short on manpower from battle casualties they all but kissed my mug when when I joined them. It's been a good fit, George."

The brothers swapped stories of combat, travels and the terrible homesickness so common to a soldier.

George pulled me out of his pocket and held me in front of his face,"Joe, I got so much comfort from this little missal. Sometimes I was so homesick and down in the dumps that I would never have made it through without this here book. Somethin' else, Joe, I swear this prayer book kept me alive the whole time I was bein' shot at. When I think of the number of times I coulda been killed or captured ..." His voice faded away as his eyes welled up. He picked up his beer, took a swig and wiped his mouth with the back of his hand.

Seeing his older brother get so choked up, Joe confessed, "I got one too, George. The prayer book gave me strength when I didn't have any. It gave me the courage to get through the hard times and trust in the Lord when I got shot up."

> I was pleased to hear that both George and his brother were aware of the power within the pages

of his soldier's Bible. George was beginning to understand some of the power with which I was commissioned by Our Lord.

Joe lifted his beer in the air. "Here's to us and survivin' this blasted war."

George touched his beer to his brother's. "Here's to gettin' home soon so I can beat the pants off you bowlin'!"

They burst out laughing, knowing that no one ever beat Joe at bowling. They had never been so happy to see each other.

The next day Joe posed a question to George. "Have y'ever flown in an airplane?"

George hesitated, "Nope."

"Wanna fly with one of our pilots on a run to Paris? Come on, George, it'll be swell."

"I guess if I survived the Battle of the Bulge, I can survive a ride in an airplane."

Joe saw a pilot he recognized and walked over to inquire if any flights were scheduled and asked if they could ride along. The two huddled in conversation for a few minutes before Joe walked back toward George. "It's all set; we're hitchin' a ride with Mac on a run to Paris, it'll be a gas." The brothers jogged to the runway and boarded the plane.

Mac, a friendly guy, was happy to have company and an audience. He bellowed, "Welcome aboard. Strap yourselves in and enjoy the ride."

It was a short flight to Paris, and on the way back to Poix, the pilot decided to have some fun with George. Mac, being an ace fighter pilot, decided to show off some of his maneuvers to both men flying with him. As fate would have it, there were a few unsuspecting French soldiers on the runway. He banked the plane and swooped low, flying in a strafing maneuver. The Frenchmen turned, stared in disbelief and scattered in many directions.

George was horrified and started hollering, "Pull up, pull up, you crazy fool!" Repeatedly he screamed at the pilot and wondered why Joe was not doing the same. He looked over at his brother and saw him hanging onto an arm strap, laughing uncontrollably, tears streaming down his face.

"You planned this? You set me up, Joe! What the hell?"

Joe laughed heartily. "You shoulda seen the look on your face! Remember how you teased me growin' up? I gotcha back, brother! This takes the cake for being the best practical joke ever, George."

They could both see Mac laughing in the cockpit. Mac skillfully landed the aircraft and taxied to the hanger. His passengers were still laughing and punching each other on the shoulder as they deplaned.

George approached Mac. "I hafta admit, you had me. You're quite a pilot, Mac. I enjoyed the flight right up to the *kamikaze* dive." He laughed.

George gazed at his younger brother. "Seeing you has been great, Joe. I've enjoyed every minute of it, even though you and Mac almost made me crap my pants. I gotta get back to Lucky Strike. Sad to say, my leave is over."

"Hey, George, maybe I'll ride back with you. Nuthin' like another bumpy ride back to Rheims in a supply truck. We'll have another hour and a half to talk."

After arriving at Camp Lucky Strike, the brothers bid each other an emotional farewell as the supply truck had to return to the depot.

"I'm not sure when we'll see each other again." Joe examined his shoes and sniffed.

"Just keep thinking of home and the family gatherin' we're gonna have when all three of us get back from this bloody war. It makes my mouth water just thinking about Mom's homemade *halupki* and *pierogies*." George pinched the bridge of his nose with two fingers in an attempt to keep tears from flowing.

The brothers hugged, and the dam broke. Both men cried unashamedly. Joe got in the passenger seat of the supply truck, gave his brother a salute and a wave. George returned the salute and waved until the truck was out of sight. He turned and walked slowly to his tent, grateful that he'd had time with his younger brother.

> *I enjoyed the reunion of these two. The time the brothers had together was a balm for both their souls. This respite from a terrible war is quite a tale they'll have to tell their children and grandchildren. George was able to share with his brother some of the incidents that gave him frequent nightmares. Thanks be to God.*

22

September 1945
It's a Long Way Home

George left Europe on a crowded troop ship sailing for the United States. He'd told Gladys he'd be shipping out soon, but he couldn't tell her when. He'd probably get home before that very letter reached his wife's hands. Needless to say, his arrival would be a surprise.

On board the troop ship leaving from Le Havre, France, soldiers read and swapped their letters and pictures from home. The deck teemed with men as soon as they left their cramped bunks, stacked five-high below deck. Sharing both government-issued matches and cigarettes, the warriors gathered to smoke and talk. Although no longer targets for snipers, each man was superstitious about being "the third on a match." They believed if three soldiers lit their cigarettes from the same match, the enemy would note the first light, take aim at the second light and shoot his weapon with the third. One of the three smokers would be killed. Many had seen it happen to fellow soldiers, so being "only two on a match" seemed to banish any perceived danger and made it hard to break a life-saving habit.

With timed showers only every other day, they found the air was fresher on deck. These homeward-bound warriors often exchanged funny anecdotes of where they'd been, who they'd been with and memorable battles they had fought. Many of these stories would never be told at home. If one hadn't been in battle, there would be little understanding of it. After sharing some of the most intense experiences of a lifetime, the wartime band of brothers would all go their separate ways, some only to meet again at yearly company reunions.

When the ship docked in New York eight days later, the men streamed down the gangways onto the docks in a rapid, but organized disembarkation.

George had rehearsed his exit plan time and again in his mind. Making his way to the train station, he boarded the express to Scranton, Pennsylvania. Grateful fellow passengers bought him drinks and food, which he modestly accepted. The ride seemed painfully long, but when the train pulled into the station, George got butterflies in his stomach. He grabbed his duffle bag and walked out to street level, raising his arm to hail a taxi. Before a cab could pull up to the curb, a passenger car pulled in front of him with the window rolled down.

An older white-haired gentleman with a kind face peered through the window at George. "Need a lift, soldier? I'll take you anywhere in Scranton you want to go."

George said, "Thanks! I live in North Scranton just off North Main Street on Commercial." After the man confirmed he knew the way, George put his heavy duffle bag in the back seat and got in the front passenger side of the late model Packard. He mentally planned to pay this kind man what he'd pay in cab fare. The fellow probably needed the money to put food on his table.

The older man smiled, "I'm happy to do it for any serviceman. You're not the first and won't be the last."

"How's that?"

"I had a son in the Army. He went in right after Pearl Harbor. We lost him in North Africa."

"I'm so sorry." George went quiet thinking that could've been him. They rode in silence for a few minutes as George remembered another time, arriving home from tech school in Georgia in a beat-up Packard driven by his pal, Vince. That seemed so long ago.

"Every time I pick up another soldier to take him home, I feel I'm doing something right in delivering a man to his family, something that my wife and I didn't get to experience."

"Well, I really appreciate the ride. I'm so excited and nervous to see my wife and little boy."

"You have a son?" The white-haired man asked as he pulled out of the train station parking lot.

"Yeah, he's two and a half now and out of diapers. It's been quite a while since I've seen him. My wife wrote in her last letter that I'll hardly recognize him." George's eyes were bright with tears.

The two men talked non-stop for the rest of the ride.

George pointed, "Turn right here, the house will be on the left about half-way down the block. Would you like to come in and meet my wife, have somethin' to eat?"

"No, no, I don't intrude on emotional reunions. I just enjoy delivering soldiers to their families so the reunions can take place. You go and make up for lost time. God bless you and your family. I wish you many years of happiness now that you're home."

As the car pulled up to the curb and George got out, he reached into his pocket for money to pay the white-haired man.

"Oh no, I don't take money. Giving rides to brave service members is my payment."

"Thanks, sir. Thanks so much. I've enjoyed talkin' to you." He reached across the length of the front seat to shake the kind man's hand, thanking him once again.

Opening the back door of the new Packard, George retrieved his duffle bag.

The car pulled away, and the returning soldier waved before lifting the heavy duffle bag over his shoulder and racing up the slate walkway to the front porch.

He thought to himself, "I better knock on the door before I just barge in and scare 'em half to death."

He knocked, waited a minute and knocked again. He heard someone come, saw the door curtain pulled aside, and heard a scream, "It's George! George is home! He's back!"

The door flew open and Gladys burst out of the doorway as if shot out of a cannon. She jumped into his arms, smothering him with kisses. He dropped the duffle bag and as he enveloped his wife with both his arms, his hat fell off.

"How did you get here? When did you get in? When did they let you go? Oh my gosh, I have missed you so much." So many questions to ask and have answered.

"Let's go inside. I wanna see Butchie and everyone, where is he?" No sooner had the words come out of his mouth when his mother-in-law appeared, holding his toddler son.

"Oh my gosh, he's gotten so big. He looks like a little boy. He looks like a Butchie! His nickname fits him." George stared at his son in utter amazement.

Junior eyed his father suspiciously and clung even more tightly to his grandmother.

George didn't quite know how to act at this apparent rejection.

"It's gonna take some time," Gladys assured him. "I think all the excitement has him a little startled." She grabbed George's hand and pulled him into the parlor.

George sat next to his wife on the sofa. He draped his arm around her shoulders. Gradually, Butchie crawled onto his mother's lap. As the conversation progressed, the little boy moved from one parent's lap to the other as he played with a stuffed animal. George's eyes welled up with tears of thanks when he was able to hold his son.

Butchie looked up at his father with a big toothy smile, "Daddy home." Both George and Gladys' eyes misted.

That about summed it up. Daddy was home, and all is well. I was thankful for all God's blessings as I know George was.

Dinnertime consisted of a wonderful array of the homemade food that George had dreamed about for the last year. Gladys modestly insisted it was just leftovers thrown together. "Nothing special, certainly not fancy enough for your homecoming."

"Not to me, honey. This is a feast and I'm gonna enjoy every bite."

George found himself fatigued after dinner, both because he'd overdosed on the mashed potatoes and because he hadn't had a good night's rest in weeks. He couldn't wait to sleep in a real bed next to his precious wife. His homecoming was everything he'd hoped it would be.

23

A REUNION OF BROTHERS

Final separation from the military came at Indiantown Gap, Pennsylvania, on November 28, 1945. George had earned numerous citations and medals from the United States, France, Belgium, and Germany, including a silver star and a bronze star embellished with an oak leaf cluster.

Two weeks later, George sat on the edge of his bed, holding me in his hands. He trembled as he felt the power of God. Tears coursed down his face as he recalled the hell of combat and the guidance the power within my pages gave him time after time. God had seen fit to answer his battlefield prayers to come home safely. He bowed his head in prayer once again. I heard his sincere words entreating Heaven that none of his children would experience what he had experienced. Then, holding me up, he spoke directly to me. "I hope you will only be a special memento of this war for my kids and grandkids. History will tell them why we went to war to protect our homeland and our families."

With that, he placed me inside the cedar chest at the end of the bed. I was due for a rest along with his citations, medals, badges and souvenirs from Europe.

A few weeks later, George reunited with his brothers Joe and Andy when they returned from Europe. Their youngest brother, Tommy, who was living in New York City, came home to Dickson

City for the weekend. It was a boisterous, tearful family gathering with all four of Tom and Mary's sons, their wives and children. Tom and Mary could not have been happier. The boys were like puppies playing with each other, and the reunion wouldn't have been complete without a huge, celebratory, neighborhood feast. Tables were laden with platters of meats, studzienina, pots of halupke, pans of pierogi, red beet horseradish, and plates of kolache for dessert. Kegs of beer were tapped and big fat cigars were passed around as bursts of laughter punctuated funny war stories.

Gladys sat talking with her three sisters-in-law while watching their children play. The frost had not thawed between Gladys and her mother-in-law, Mary, and was only emphasized at these gatherings because Gladys was the only non-Eastern European family member.

For months, George recalled stories of the war whenever he had a questioning audience. He readily related the humorous times of camaraderie with other ordinary men who became war heroes. Often stopping in mid-sentence, he'd fall silent, his expression somber and his eyes filling with tears. Uncomfortable painful flashbacks became the subject of occasional nightmares.

George went to work in the coal mine for a few years before he got a job on the railroad. In 1947, Gladys had another son, Ronald. The couple looked forward to living the American Dream, raising their family and going to Little League ball games.

I lay dormant in the bottom of the cedar chest.

24

1948
A CHILL DESCENDS

After the war, the Allies divided the city of Berlin into sectors. The French, British and American sectors comprised West Berlin; Russia's sector became known as East Berlin. Located 110 miles inside the Communist border, the city of West Berlin was accessible by air, land and water routes only through East Germany.

One lazy Saturday morning in early 1948, George was sitting at the breakfast table, drinking his coffee and reading sections of the folded newspaper out loud to Gladys as she scurried around the kitchen, making fresh cinnamon buns. Five-year-old Butchie and infant Ronnie were still sleeping, and they had some quiet time to themselves.

"Sez here Glad, that Russia is pushing the western governments for more influence in the economic future of Germany. Ain't that somethin? America and Britain both said no. Glad, do you hear this?"

She nodded, smiling at her husband. Now that he worked two hours away on the Erie Lackawanna Railroad out of Hoboken, New Jersey, all week long, it was good to have him home for the weekend.

I was still very much in tune with everything to do with this family. They were always in my thoughts and prayers. George was still my charge until he, himself, passed me to someone else. Until such time, I am totally invested in George, Gladys, and their boys.

On June 24, 1948, George started to worry about being called up by the Army to serve once again. Gladys steeled herself for the worse and doubled down on her prayers.

Newspaper headlines screamed, "Soviet Union Blocking All Travel To and From West Berlin." The Soviets had stopped all supplies from entering the city. The people were suffering from lack of food, heating coal, oil and other vital goods.

George and Gladys listened carefully to each radio broadcast for reports on the tense conditions, hoping and praying the conflict wouldn't lead to a showdown. One day, George heard encouraging news while Gladys was hanging wash on the clothesline strung across the back porch. She heard a whoop of joy from inside the house and ran into the kitchen. George was moving toward her with a huge smile on his face.

George grabbed his wife in a bear hug, "Honey, listen, President Truman ordered an airlift of supplies into West Berlin. They're sending in food, clothes, water, medicine, fuel and other stuff! I just heard it on the radio. Thank God!"

Gladys hugged him back in joyous relief.

American planes flew round-the-clock missions for almost a year, supplying two million citizens of the city. It was a massive endeavor, known as the Berlin Air Lift.

George had strong opinions before and during the crisis. One day, as Ronnie was napping and Butchie was playing quietly in the living room with his army men, he confided in his wife, "You know Glad, I saw those Russians up close. They were bullies during the signing of the peace agreements with the Germans. I'm glad they were on our side during the war, but they sure were downright mean '*blatnoi*.'"

"What in the world is that?"

"It's Russian slang for hoodlums, really mean hoodlums."

"This stupid blockade, threatening people with starvation and death, ended up being a big fat embarrassment for them and it serves 'em right!"

Gladys trusted her husband's spot-on judgment of people.

On June 25, 1950, the Korean War began. By July, American troops deployed to South Korea. It seemed when one war ended, another began.

In 1951, George and Gladys prematurely welcomed a third son, Joey. He was a tiny four-pounder, and his mother now had three boys to raise. George still worked out of town all week, and she had to depend on her parents to help with four-year-old Ronnie and eight-year-old Butchie.

With each year that passed, she prayed for her sons to thrive and grow up in a stable world. Gladys was by nature a worrier.

Depending more and more on Butchie's help with his younger brothers, she didn't allow him to get involved in after-school sports or other activities. Gladys needed Butch, and he had to learn, "it was family first." The two younger boys, however, were able to play Little League baseball and Pop Warner football. Butch dutifully obeyed his mother's instructions in taking care of his brothers and completing his many household chores, but he couldn't help the growing resentment every time he watched one of his brother's games.

Gladys readily gave him the credit he deserved to family and friends when they praised her for doing such a fine job in raising her boys. When George was able to change his base of operations on the railroad from Hoboken to Port Jervis, he got home more often and had time to take the boys to their games and watch them play. But, by that time, Butch was in high school and had missed out playing the sports he loved.

As it does when one is raising a family, the years passed quickly giving Gladys pause to think ahead to the future, always with the fear that the military might draft each of her sons. Daily she bowed her head in prayer for her boys. "Oh Lord, spare them! I couldn't bear it,"

The conflict between Communist and democratic nations became increasingly tense. Each side strengthened its armed forces. Settling disputes through compromise was next to impossible. This new situation, termed the "Cold War" by presidential advisor Bernard Baruch, created fear that one spark might touch off World War III.

> I knew I was going to be called to action in the coming years. The knowledge I had was going to worry both Gladys and George. For now, I was helpless. What could I do, stuck in the cedar chest? Hey, someone, let me out of here!

> Well, that didn't do much good, did it?

25

1960
A RESTLESS YOUTH

The Cold War continued to cast a dark cloud over Eastern and Western relations into the Sixties. George began to worry.

A chill traveled up his spine and fear crept into his consciousness when he thought about it. He couldn't share this with Gladys, at least, not yet. Their seventeen-year-old son Butch, newly graduated from high school, occasionally talked of following in his dad's footsteps by joining the military.

"Dad, I'm not happy doin' this trade school thing. I've been listening to some of the things John Kennedy is saying on his campaign about each of us giving some time in service to our country." He pushed himself away from the breakfast table and took his dishes to the sink.

"Well, Butch, trade school is gonna offer you a skill and then, a job. There's certainly not much else to do in Scranton. You know your mom and I don't want you to work in the coal mines like both your grandfathers and I did and there's no work on the railroad with me right now." George sipped on his hot coffee while his eyes never left Butch's face.

"Dad, my part-time job on the construction crew is never going to pay me enough money to ever move out on my own. I'm running out of options." Butch shoved his hands in his pockets and paced around the kitchen table.

I knew this young man wanted more out of life and he was going to have to leave Scranton to find it. His parents had no idea how far away he would go. I knew I'd be with him. My powers were being renewed by The Lord to prepare for the task. I was getting out of the cedar chest soon. I could feel it in my spine.

26
DECEMBER 1960
BUTCH'S PROPOSAL

While running errands one day, Butch happened to pass an Air Force recruiting office. He did a double take, backtracked, parked the family car and went in to meet the recruiters. What they had to say interested him. Offering college classes while in the service, they'd continue to pay for his education after an honorable discharge. For the first time since high school graduation, he was excited. There was only one catch; his parents were required to sign for him because he was only seventeen.

Butch knew that his enlistment might bring back unpleasant memories for both his parents. He hoped they'd listen objectively. He hoped they'd understand his justification for wanting to join the Air Force. Butch prepared his argument as he drove home.

Butch strolled into the kitchen as his parents were preparing dinner. He carefully closed the door behind him since his mother was a stickler for keeping out the winter drafts.

Gladys turned her head to look at her son. "You didn't work today. Were you job hunting?"

"Kind of." Leaning back against the door, he calmly said, "Mom, Dad I'd like to talk to you."

The determined look on her son's face sent a feeling of alarm through Gladys.

"Shoot," his father said.

"I just came from talking to the Air Force recruiter at the square." He cleared his throat and before continuing, "I ..."

"What?" His mother turned from the sink where she was peeling vegetables. "What did you just say?" That feeling of alarm became a reality for her.

"I went to talk to the Air Force recruiter," Butch repeated.

The potato peeler clattered to the floor as his mother's face blanched.

George had taken the train home the night before and was breading chicken breasts at the counter. He stopped what he was doing, wiped his hands on the dishtowel draped over his shoulder and turned to face his eldest son. Leaning against the counter with his arms crossed over his chest, he asked his son, "What did they say, Butch?"

"For one thing, they'll pay for my college education."

"What college? We didn't know you had any interest in college." Gladys had finished high school, but her husband had only completed the tenth grade. College hadn't held much importance for their generation.

"Mom, I was college prep all through high school." Butch countered. "I guess I just never pushed the issue. Maybe I assumed I'd be able to go, or maybe I really didn't think seriously enough about it to make a plan. Now that I've thought about it, I'd like to go to college and major in business."

"You could go into business here in Scranton. The factory down at the square, they're hiring."

Butch winced. "Mom, I don't want to work in a factory on the assembly line. That's not what I had in mind. I'd like to go to school and major in business so I could manage or someday own the factory. I need a career where I can make enough money to support a family."

"Well, you don't have to go into the Air Force to go to college," his mother protested.

"Mom, we can't afford four years of college. Through the Air Force, it's free! I can start taking classes as soon as I complete tech school and get assigned to a base."

Gladys moved to the table, pulled out a chair and sat down. She lifted her eyes and looked expectantly at her handsome son.

"You know what else, Mom? It's not wartime. I won't be fighting anyone, anywhere."

> George, dropped his arms, turned to resume breading the chicken breasts, reached to turn down the sautéing onions for the drained *pierogies* on the stove, and pondered a Bible verse from Luke 11:11, *You fathers: if your children ask for a fish, do you give them a snake instead? Or if they ask for an egg, do you give them a scorpion? Of course not!*

Both Gladys and George were quiet and contemplated their son's proposal. They could see the excitement on his face and knew that there'd be no stopping him; he had made up his mind. They agreed to sign for him.

> Almost twenty years old, I was up for any assignment God wanted to give me. Yes, I was older, I showed some wear and tear, but the Word of God within my pages is infinite, timeless and everlasting. My days in the cedar chest were growing shorter. I was now certain of what was going to happen.

27

1961

FREE AT LAST

*I*t had been sixteen years since I'd seen the light of day. Placed gently in the bottom of the cedar chest in December 1945, I was hopeful each time I heard the lid open. Instead, I felt quilts and blankets on top of me, and I heard silver dollars dropped into a box beside me. I needed to stretch my spine, and I yearned to offer guidance and hope. Maybe this was the day.

Searching through the contents in the cedar chest, George moved heavy blankets and quilts aside, finding the treasure for which he was looking. He sat on the edge of the bed, gently turning the thin, fragile pages, and reminisced. With old memories flooding his mind, he barely heard the call from downstairs. Dinner was ready. Jumping up, he tucked the treasure into his shirt pocket, ran downstairs to the kitchen and found his place at the table.

"Joey, would you say grace, please?" Gladys watched as her nine-year-old bowed his head and offered the blessing he'd learned in Catholic school.

"Amen." He looked up and smiled, waiting for his mom's approval.

Gladys nodded her head and smiled back at Joey. She looked around at her three beautiful sons. Butch was slight in build, 5' 10" tall and still growing. He had his mother's

89

olive complexion and thick, dark hair. Blue-green eyes, like those of his maternal grandmother, made him a strikingly handsome young man. Olive-complexioned, thirteen-year-old Ron was a big boy, weighing almost 200 pounds at six feet tall. He had put on a lot of weight having been bedridden with a seriously fractured leg that year. He also had dark hair, almost black, and deep brown eyes like his mother and father. Nine-year-old Joey was the fairest of them all. He had light brown hair with a light complexion and his brown eyes sparkled with mischief.

Butch started teasing his younger brother Ron, "I saw you flirt with that cute girl across the street."

"Flirt? Whaddya mean flirt?" Ron assumed a defensive posture.

"Well, do you like her? She's blonde! You always go for blondes. Does she like you back?"

"I wouldn't tell you if she did." Ron blushed and concentrated on shoving food into his mouth.

While waving a carrot stick as if conducting an orchestra, little Joey sang out, "Ronnie has a girlfriend!"

Ron glared at him and with his mouth full of mashed potatoes muttered, "Do not!"

"Do too."

"Do not."

"Do too."

George looked at Gladys and held up his hands to silence the boys. He had to admit they were a brilliant combination of genes. He struggled to keep a straight face. "Okay, okay that's enough, you three."

The table talk turned to school, sports and weekend plans.

When dinner was over, George cleared his throat. "Your brother has an announcement to make." He nodded to Butch.

Butch looked around at his family and said calmly, "I've enlisted in the Air Force, and I'll be leaving for basic training next month."

"What?" Ron cocked his head and laughed, "You're pullin' my leg. How long will you be gone?"

"No, I'm not pullin' your leg. I'll be home after basic training and again after tech school and then probably overseas for a few years."

"Cool! Can I have your room?" Ron was downright gleeful.

"Well, I ..." Butch didn't get to finish his thought.

"Ronald Panko, enough! We'll talk about the room situation later." Gladys admonished.

"Now it's my turn. I have somethin' important to say, so listen up!" George reached carefully into his shirt pocket to retrieve the military missal, which he referred to as his soldier's Bible. He chose his words carefully. "When I was fightin' in the war, this here Bible gave me comfort and hope when times were tough."

Four pairs of questioning eyes stared at him. Talking about the war and his time in Europe was not his style.

George turned to Butch, "This soldier's Bible is special, Butch. By the grace of God and by the guidance of the prayers in this book, I was spared during combat. I can't begin to tell you how many times I thought I'd be killed or captured, but I wasn't. I know it was the grace of God and I want that same protection and guidance for you as long as you're in the military, son."

> As the words spilled out, I realized this was a momentous occasion and I knew what was going to happen. I felt a tingle of spiritual energy course through my pages. The Lord was preparing me for another charge of spiritual power and the responsibility of guiding another man in uniform. George was handing me over to Butch.

George rose from his chair and slowly walked around the table. He put his hand on Butch's shoulder and passed him the military missal, his precious soldier's Bible. With a quivering chin, George spoke to his seventeen-year-old son as from one military man to another. "I want this soldier's Bible back."

> The time-honored tradition of one military man passing on a missal or a Bible to another military man is significant. The message is from man to man, factual and unemotional. It's supposed to save face and keep men from crying. That part doesn't always work.

Butch held the missal in his hands, only partly realizing the significance of the gift.

> I now belonged to Butch.

He swallowed hard, "Thanks, Dad, I promise to keep it safe." Butch turned the little book over in his hands. As an afterthought he added, "I'll bring this back to you, I promise."

> The kid didn't get it, at least not yet. It was not about him keeping me safe; it was about me keeping him safe. His maturing faith would bring understanding.

Gladys had tears rolling down her cheeks as she watched this tender moment unfold between her husband and their first born.

> I felt a jolt as a memory struck her.

> She had a flashback to that day at the pier in New York as she held her baby boy, blowing kisses to her departing husband on the deck of the RMS Franconia. It took her breath away.

Ron and Joey's eyes widened as they watched. It sobered them to see their mother cry. Silently, they got up from the table and took their dishes to the sink before putting their coats on and going out into the back yard to toss a ball.

After dinner, George helped Gladys clean up the kitchen and do the dishes. It was their time to talk quietly while the boys were either doing homework or playing catch.

George recalled what it was like when he returned from Europe in 1945. "You know Glad; Butch was a toddler when I got back and didn't remember me except from pictures you showed him. That was hard for me. I thought my heart would pop the first time he crawled into my lap." George's eyes filled with tears, remembering that day.

Gladys remembered as well. "I know, but you worked real hard at developing a relationship with him before you had to leave home to work on the railroad."

"Was it enough? I wish I could have been there for him during the week when he needed a man around. You know, Glad, the weekends are hardly enough time for a teenager. At times, it seems like Butch and I are strangers. We didn't bond and have a connection like I have with Ron and Joey."

"George, we did the best we could at the time. After fifteen years of trying to make up for lost time, you and Butch are going to be separated again. He's gonna grow up in the service, George. When he comes back, he'll be a man. You two will have a different relationship, but you'll be able to build on the common bond of being in the military." Gladys wanted to reassure her husband. She wished she was more confident that her words were true.

Butch was scheduled to leave for basic training at Lackland Air Force Base in Texas. He was looking forward to the adventure, and it was all he could think about these days.

In January 1961, John F. Kennedy was inaugurated President of the United States. His famous quote: "Ask not what your country can do for you, ask what you can do for your country," resonated across the nation creating a wave of national pride and a spirit of volunteerism. The new president came into office at a difficult time in history. Cold War tensions were at an all-time high, and the worst was yet to come.

As of January 1961, I had a new charge to guide and protect. As the Holy Spirit shielded his father in combat, the same Spirit would guide the son in peacetime. I was off on another adventure and glad to be out of the cedar chest.

If only I could shake the odor of moth balls!

28

1961
OFF WE GO
INTO THE WILD BLUE YONDER

Departing from Wilkes Barre/Scranton Airport in January, Butch headed for six weeks of basic training at Lackland Air Force Base. In technical school, he specialized in intelligence and cryptography at Sheppard Air Force Base, Texas. He performed beyond all expectations in this school and, as a result, the Air Force sent him back to Lackland for more intensified training in cryptography.

Upon graduation, he got his overseas assignment. To his delight, it was his first choice, one of the countries his father had fought to liberate, Germany.

> George and I had been through months of combat under tough conditions all through Europe. I wondered if he was struggling with stressful memories as his eldest son prepared to go to Germany. It flipped my pages to think of returning to Europe, but this would be different. It was peacetime, and Europe was undergoing a transformation.

Butch couldn't wait to get home on leave before shipping out to Germany. He missed his family. He missed sitting in the bleachers at his brothers' ball games. He missed his father's homemade bread and breaded chicken. This time spent at home was going to be special.

While at the dinner table, Butch closed his eyes and savored his Mom's excellent cooking. Conversation was at a minimum because everyone had their mouths full. Butch smacked his lips, "Mom, no one makes *halupki* like you and Grandma Panko do, and I'm gonna tell her that at our next Sunday visit."

His mother smiled, "Make sure you give grandma my best when you see her." Gladys swallowed the bitter taste in her mouth from wishing for acceptance that wasn't ever going to happen. She didn't want those feeling to interfere with the happiness she felt when her three boys were around the dinner table enjoying her cooking. "Eat and enjoy" was her stock answer to any compliment about her cooking.

Butch spent a lot of his leave time with his brothers playing ball at Weston Park and fishing in a nearby stream with Joey. Each Sunday, Gladys stayed home while Butch accompanied his father and younger brothers to Dickson City to visit his paternal grandparents.

Before he knew it, the day arrived. It was time for him to pack for his deployment to Germany.

Joey stood next to the bed watching his oldest brother methodically fold his clothes and place them inside the open suitcase. He had a question mark all over his face. "Why do you have to go, Butchie?"

"There's a job waiting for me in Germany, Joey. I want to go. This assignment is a chance for me to travel and get an education."

"Can't you do that here?"

"Not like this, buddy. I'll be back, I promise. I'm not going forever. Besides, you'll be busy in school and sports. Do me a favor, will you? Study hard, get good grades, and do well in baseball. It'll all pay off one day."

"I'll try." The little boy looked down at his shoes and shuffled his feet back and forth.

Butch knew that his little brother was getting upset at his imminent departure. He swallowed hard and reached out to ruffle Joey's hair. "I sure am gonna miss you," he murmured, choking back sudden tears.

The little boy's arms wrapped themselves around his brother's waist for a tight hug, then he quickly turned and scampered away. Butch wiped his eyes with the back of his hand and was grateful he had to finish folding and packing before going downstairs.

His mind drifted to thinking about the next three years. In spite of the excitement of leaving, living in Europe was going to be difficult because there would be no occasional trips home. He'd miss the solitude of fishing with Joey and helping his brothers with their pitching and catching. He'd miss birthdays, holidays, and other family celebrations. Conversely, he knew loads of new experiences awaited him.

The next day, the whole family made the trip to McGuire Air Force Base in New Jersey. There were spurts of conversation and nervous laughter, punctuated by awkward silences. Gladys' sadness permeated the vehicle.

When they arrived at the base, the public address system squawked loudly, "Paging Airman Panko; Airman George Panko, please report to the departure desk."

Hearing the page, George automatically stiffened his spine, put his shoulders back and stood at attention. He relaxed when he realized it was his son being paged. The father's eyes teared up as he glanced sideways at the young man in uniform by his side. His son was going to be stationed in Germany where, less than twenty years ago, he fought a brutal enemy in the very same country.

"Last call for Airman George Panko, please report to the departure desk." They were boarding the aircraft and Butch was uncharacteristically late. It turned out to be a blessing in disguise, as their tardiness didn't allow for prolonged emotional goodbyes. The entire family broke into a run behind Butch as he sprinted down the concourse. When they reached the departure desk, hasty good-byes had to suffice. He was the last passenger to board.

> *What a sight to see! Four people running down a long concourse seemingly chasing a man in uniform tickled me. I could have told them to take their time, he was going to be on that flight. My sphere was widening further to encompass Butch and his future. Lord bless us!*

Gladys and George remembered their train ride to the port of New York when George left for Europe. Butch was a babe in arms then. They were quickly brought back to the present when they realized that this sharply-uniformed United States Air Force airman was walking away from them, ready to make his way in the world. Gladys swallowed hard, stifling the sobs bubbling up inside of her. Although sad to see him go, both parents were exceedingly grateful that their son wasn't going to war.

Butch was flying on a commercial aircraft, but as he boarded, he had a fleeting thought of his father taking a crowded troop ship to Europe. Times were different. The plane was filled with Air Force personnel and dependents, all heading for their assignments in Germany. George found a seat next to Fritz, his friend from both basic training and tech school.

Scattered chatter and laughter filled the aircraft. The uniformed and civilian passengers settled down in their seats as the attendants handed out pillows and blankets for the long flight. Butch was excited, eager to begin his tour of duty. It was quite a difference from the eager but frightened soldiers heading to battle in World War II.

Having had only minutes to say their farewells, George, Gladys, Ron and Joey stood at the floor to ceiling window, looking out at the aircraft. They waved until the plane pulled away from the gate and began to taxi. With hands and faces pressed up against the glass, each of them hoped to get one last glance at Butch. Gladys cried out when she saw her son at a window waving to them. "Butch, my Butch!"

Frantically, they all waved back. The plane taxied onto the runway. After watching the takeoff, the family turned and slowly walked through the airport to the parking lot.

The trip home was quiet, except for the baseball game broadcast on the radio. In the back seat, Joey fell asleep with his head in his mother's lap. Gladys worried about the little boy missing his big brother. The two of them, although eight years apart, were very close.

"Is he asleep?" George asked, looking at Gladys in the rearview mirror.

Gladys nodded. Joey cried whenever he saw his mother cry. She now felt free to shed a tear. She sniffled gently, not wanting to wake him.

"Glady, it'll be okay."

Butch had been her right hand in his father's absence, and she was already missing him in that role. With George working out of town all week, he helped his mother with chores around the house and kept his younger brothers in line. Pondering that thought, Gladys whispered in the dark, back seat of the car to no one in particular, "It was a lot of responsibility on his young shoulders, but the family had to come first. That's the way it was, but why do I feel so guilty?"

George was silent as he drove the car, listening to the game, while at the same time praying for the safety of his departing son.

Ron could only think about how thrilled he was to ride shotgun next to his dad.

I was dismayed Butch didn't put me in his pocket before he left. My prayer for this family was offered up from inside of a duffle bag in the cargo hold of an aircraft. I remembered the words from the Gospel of Luke 11:9-10, *And I say to you, ask, and it shall be given to you; seek and you shall find; knock, and it shall be opened to you. For everyone who asks receives; and he who seeks finds; and to him who knocks it shall be opened.*

29

JUNE 1961
GERMANY: SIXTEEN YEARS
AFTER VICTORY IN EUROPE

B utch arrived at Hahn Air Force Base at the end of June 1961. As members of the 2184th Communications Squadron, he and his seven roommates were billeted according to the common shift they worked. The base was old, built by the German military and relinquished to the Americans after World War II. Nonetheless, Butch found his living quarters acceptable.

Unpacking his gear, he had time to anticipate his first day in Germany. He was looking forward to meeting his co-workers and exploring the base.

> Finding me in his bag, he carefully placed me in his footlocker. What? Now you're putting me away? I don't believe it. I have a job to do. Hey, hey, hey, you're my new charge! I'm not letting you get away with this. It was one thing to put me in your duffle bag for the trip, but another thing entirely to be stored in a trunk again. Your father presented me to you for a reason. How can I do my job from the dark corner of a footlocker? What is this silly boy thinking?

> The footlocker opened, and Butch reached down and picked me up.

He addressed the cover of the military missal. "I could've sworn I heard someone talking to me."

> *He shook his head and turned me over in his hand. Putting me in his shirt pocket, he remembered how much I meant to his father who felt I saved his life through months of combat and hard times behind enemy lines. In honor of his father, Butch decided I would also be part of his uniform.*

For the next five days, the new airmen of the 2184th Squadron registered at payroll, took care of administrative paperwork, went to the base hospital for a physical and saw the base dentist. By the time Butch reported for duty at squadron headquarters, he was acclimated to his new home.

He and his friend, Fritz, also from Pennsylvania, had been adjusting to their specific jobs for approximately five weeks. They often managed to meet up at lunch time in the mess hall.

One day at lunch, Butch told Fritz, "I'm gonna be working swing shifts. Not sure how I feel about that."

"Hey, I guess I'm lucky. I'm on daylight only. That's what you get, Panko, for being in crypto and intel."

"Stop rubbin' it in." Butch bit into a thick Reuben sandwich, chewed and swallowed before he commented, "Even with crypto and intel, I still have to start at the bottom, and that means working the switchboard at squadron headquarters." He made a face.

"What's the face for, the sauerkraut or the switchboard?" Fritz asked sarcastically.

"The switchboard."

"Hey man, that's not so bad, nobody's gonna be shootin' at you!"

"That's true. I can do anything for a week. By the way, for future reference, this sandwich is delicious. Meanwhile, working the switchboard gives me somethin' to do while I wait for my Top Secret clearance. When it comes through, I'll rotate to the Combat Operations Center (COC) for orientation to the communications center (Com Center)."

"It's too much for me to remember," Fritz muttered as he pushed a french fry through the puddle of ketchup on his plate.

"Get a grip, man. It's just one communication function after the other."

After a gooey, made-from-scratch dessert, the two men finished lunch and left the mess hall.

It didn't take long for Butch to become friends with the other enlisted men. He also developed respect for the Intelligence and Flight Control officers in the COC; they all had immensely important responsibilities. A professional interdependence within that operating area would prove to be vitally important in the coming months.

The Combat Operations Center itself was unimpressive. Butch's orientation guide described the two-story structure as they headed in that direction. "It's entirely underground. As you can see, the décor is 'European gray cement.'" He added, "The COC is only accessible by one stairway, this one. It's heavily guarded at all times by Air Police both inside and out and they don't tolerate any nonsense. There aren't any windows; no daylight at all, but it's well-lit. Every bit of work done here is sensitive and top secret."

Showing the new airman around, he proudly pointed out, "We have the latest communication and crypto technology."

Butch was impressed.

> I knew that after working the Com Center for approximately one year, Butch was going to be shift supervisor. He'll have obtained yet another Top Secret security clearance, and his superior officers were going to recommend him to work in the Victor Alert area. His future looked bright.

I was proud of my boy! He had been trained well, carried a tremendous amount of responsibility on his young shoulders and thrived in it. At nineteen years of age, the kid had done an impressive job. God had blessed him with a quick, calculating mind. My job had been easy so far, but I knew personal challenges awaited young Butch.

30

1961
WORLD LEADERS DISAGREE

B utch and Fritz weren't the only Americans in Europe becoming acclimated to a new job in June of 1961. The young American president also had his challenges.

The two friends were in the mess hall eating lunch. Butch was reading a newspaper while finishing up a bottle of root beer. "Hey Fritz, President Kennedy is meeting Nikita Khrushchev in Vienna, Austria. Khrushchev is demanding a free Berlin and an end to military occupation. Kennedy's not on board with that and, 'Nikki' is threatening to sign a separate peace treaty with East Germany." He looked over the top of the paper. "Where do you think this is going to go, Fritz?"

Fritz had just bitten into a bratwurst sandwich. He chewed and swallowed. "It can't end well, Butch. We could end up being in the soup where we are. Whaddya think?"

"Me? I honestly don't know. I'm new at guessing what makes world leaders tick. Guess we'll just have to wait and see."

In July, personnel at Hahn Air Force Base became aware that the USSR canceled scheduled cuts in its armed forces and instead, increased its military spending. Tensions were rising.

Nancy Panko

Suspecting the Soviets were going to seal off East Berlin from West Berlin and perhaps begin hostilities, East Germans fled in droves to the freedom of West Germany.

> Uh oh, Butch, this is going to get dicey. Could this cold war be heating up? Heavenly Father, guide us now as the diplomats negotiate a minefield. It's not tanks and cannons these days; it's nuclear armed warheads. I remember the words of Psalm 138:7, *Though I walk amid distress, you preserve me; against the anger of my enemies you raise your hand; your right hand saves me.*

31
1961
LET THE GAMES BEGIN

Hahn Air Force Base took great pride in their football team. Practice started in August. Butch tried out and made the practice team the first year. He had grown taller but was not fast enough or strong enough for the travel team. Regardless of what he lacked in size, speed and strength, he made up for in determination.

Butch played with enlisted men and officers alike. They all noticed his focus, enthusiasm, and love for the game. One of those officers, Lt. Ray Perkins, was impressed with what he saw. One day he and two other football players, also officers, approached Butch.

"Airman, what kind of workout are you doing?"

Butch proceeded to iterate his regimen.

"All of that's a good start, but can we make some suggestions on how to beef it up?"

"Yes, sir. Anything to improve. I'd like to make the travel team."

The next day Butch was handed a workout sheet for the week, and the training began. Over time, he became bigger, stronger and more confident. It was one of the best things to happen to him.

Lt. Perkins and other officers on the football team became his mentors, both on and off the field. They recognized his intelligence and eagerness to learn, something neither of his parents had ever understood about him.

After a strenuous practice one day, Lt. Perkins and Butch were doing cool down stretches on the grassy football field.

Perkins mused, "I never get tired of seeing the beautiful snow-capped mountains of Germany. We are so lucky to be stationed here, don't you think?"

"Without a doubt. I love it!" Butch returned to stretching his tired, tight quad muscles.

"What are your plans for the future, Butch? Have you thought about a career in the Air Force or do you want to go after a civilian job?"

"I'm not sure I'm cut out to be career military as an enlisted man. I've been doing a lot of reading, and I think I'd like a business career. I know this is going to sound funny, but I enjoy looking through the financial news. I want to be a part of that. I've always been a math whiz, and economics have always fascinated me. I must take after my mom; she won every card game we played because she could remember who played what card."

"Wow, remind me never to play cards with your mother! Do you have any college under your belt?"

"No, sir, but I thought about enrolling while I'm here. I can at least get in some general education courses."

"That's exactly what I was thinking. I'd encourage you to take advantage of every opportunity you have here on base. You've got a quick mind, and I see you being a great success at whatever you go after. In fact, you could probably pass some of the challenge exams and get full credit for the semester. You'd sure save time that way and be able to move on to core courses sooner than you thought."

It was just the push Butch needed. Lt. Perkins had faith in his abilities both academically and athletically. He thought, "Man, that's a good feeling."

During the football season, he could only take one course a semester; however, he took several challenge exams and passed. After football season was over, he signed up for two classes a semester. Butch soaked up knowledge like a sponge, he was the ideal student.

> My feelings were summed up in Psalm 118:24, *This is the day the Lord has made; let us be glad and rejoice in it!"*

> I was so proud of the man he was becoming. Thank you, Lord, for these mentors who saw the promise in this young man.

32
1961
BUILDING THE BERLIN WALL

George was watching television in the living room while Gladys was in the kitchen putting the finishing touches on dinner. The evening national news began with an ominous report.

Newsman Walter Cronkite was at the microphone. "On August 13, 1961, the East German Communists began building a twenty-six-mile wall of cement and barbed wire between East and West Berlin. Some lucky East Germans have been able to escape to West Berlin. This is not a good development in the Cold War."

Gladys walked into the room holding a dishtowel. In her anxiety, she had twisted it into a knot. "What does this mean, George?"

"Now, Glady, you know the diplomats are gonna try to get this all smoothed over before anybody gets hurt." He walked over to the television set and shut it off. Putting his arm around Gladys, he turned and led his wife back into the kitchen. "Say, what smells so good?"

In the coming months, disturbing newspaper reports revealed that the wall split Berlin in two, not only physically but also ideologically, politically and economically. East

German guards patrolling the wall were excellent shots and quite cruel, often leaving bullet-riddled bodies of East Germans to hang from the barbed wire as a grim reminder for all those who dared to think of escaping to the Western part of the city.

Additional headlines screamed, "United States Sends Troops to West Berlin" and "American Tanks Enforce Western Rights To Enter East Berlin." Storm clouds gathered, and the winds of war blew with increasing speed.

> Gladys hated seeing The *Scranton Times* headlines. Each day she had one of the boys bring the paper in from the front porch and deposit it in a basket for their father to read.

The evening television news reports repeated over and over. "Tanks representing the USSR are lined up, fifty yards apart, all turrets and guns pointed toward West Berlin and the American troops. Up and down the borders of all the Soviet Bloc countries, Eastern tanks and troops on one side, Western tanks and troops on the other, the men and weapons of war menace each other. The dangerous standoff threatens world peace." Although not solely confined to the city of Berlin, historically, it was called "The Berlin Crisis."

After each newscast and every newspaper article or headline, Gladys bowed her head in prayer for the safety of her son. "Thank God, they're not shooting at him. Lord, please don't let it come to that."

George had faced tanks in World War II. By the grace of God, he'd been able to outrun them. Now his oldest son was in the midst of this crisis. "If I could change places with Butch, I would in a second. God be with him."

Only two hours away from Berlin by car, the commanders and airmen of Hahn Air Force Base watched, prepared and prayed. The base was on alert, anticipating hostile action by the Soviets.

Although no one was shooting at him, Butch was worried. His dad had relied on the Military Missal to keep him grounded, and Butch now carried that same small prayer book with him. He began to read it, turning the delicate pages slowly, digesting the word of God.

> When at work, he only had to place his hand on the book in his pocket to be reminded of God's promises. Comforted, Butch thought of his parents and younger brothers and hoped that he'd see them again. He came upon Luke 11:2-4, *And He said to them, When you pray, say: "Father, hallowed be thy name. Thy kingdom come! Give us this day our daily bread, and forgive us our sins, for we also forgive everyone who is indebted to us. And lead us not into temptation."*

Reclining on his bed after his shift at work, he began to feel some peace. With his hands behind his head, he pondered the words, "Thy will be done" and as he did, his eyes closed and he drifted off to sleep.

33

AUGUST 1961
HIGH ALERT LOCK DOWN

Butch was on duty from 4 p.m. to 12 p.m. the Saturday night Hahn Air Force Base went on High Alert. It had been a beautiful summer day. He and Lt. Perkins were leaving football practice to clean up, eat lunch, and get ready for work in the Combat Operations Center.

"You did good today, Panko. Those workouts have really made a difference, haven't they?"

"Yes, sir, I see it in my endurance, strength, and speed. I'm looking forward to the next practice and the beginning of the season in a few weeks. I'll be ready."

"I know you will. The coach has noticed, too. I think you'll get more play time."

"From your lips to God's ears."

Lt. Perkins slapped Butch across the back as they headed to the locker rooms.

While in the mess hall, he ate quickly. As soon as he had gulped down his soda, he ran to his room to get some study time under his belt before leaving for work. An "A" on this tough history test tomorrow would look good on his transcript.

The crisp mountain air put a spring in his step. The cloudless blue sky made it hard to think about studying or working a shift in an underground bunker.

With a productive study session under his belt, Butch walked from his barracks to the Combat Operations Center. It'd have been nice if he'd had the day off. Immediately, he brushed that thought aside and considered that eight hours from now his shift would be over and tomorrow was supposed to be just as gorgeous as it was today. Buoyed by that thought, he nodded at the guard as he showed his badge and passed through a security checkpoint outside the entrance to the center. Butch regained his professional composure upon descending the two flights of stairs to the facility. He showed his badge once more as he passed through another security checkpoint to get to the Com Center.

During his shift, he noticed the theme of the messages coming in was of increasing urgency. He couldn't shake the gut feeling of impending doom. Alarm bells ringing confirmed that feeling. The noise became incrementally louder indicating an incoming high priority message. Butch walked to the machine, grabbed the document, and in the decoding room, deciphered the first of many high priority messages that night. The first one changed the status of the base from Low to High Alert.

The airmen sprang into action. High Alert status mandated the decoding tables now change every hour instead of once or twice a day. An emerging crisis mandated that all the crypto people had to be mentally nimble. Messages coming in could have their encoding changed midstream and whoever was decoding would have to be alert for those changes.

My spine stiffened. I was prepared to guide and protect my man. This dire situation would end badly if either side lost their cool.

As if he heard me, Butch put his hand over his shirt pocket, saying a silent prayer. The alarm bells rang again. In the crypto room, he initiated the decoding process. I knew the message was serious because I could feel the vibration of his trembling hands as he viewed the "Eyes Only" message to the Base Commander, Colonel Andrews.

Butch called the Officer on Duty, Captain Jackson, to tell him about the "Eyes Only" message for Colonel Andrews."

"I'll contact him immediately. Thank you, Airman."

Heavenly Father, guide the decisions made by heads of state making life and death decisions for millions of people.

Attending a party on base at the Officer's Club, Colonel Andrews saw the Air Police enter the room. Instinctively, he knew the Berlin Crisis must be coming to a head.

"Sir, you're needed at the Combat Operations Center for an emerging situation."

The Colonel turned to his wife, leaning in to whisper in her ear, "I have to go." She nodded, knowing the gravity of the situation in Berlin.

The commander hastily left the Officers' Club, escorted by Air Police.

Security was now tighter, both inside and outside the COC. Checkpoint personnel snapped to attention as they saw the Base Commander arrive and proceed down the stairway. He strode purposefully past the second checkpoint headed directly to the communications area. The Colonel approached Butch and Captain Jackson.

"Sir." Butch handed him the Top Secret message.

As he read the words on the paper, Colonel Andrews issued orders. "I want all Squadron Commanders to report to the Combat Operations Center immediately."

The Colonel gazed around the room, taking in the huge Plexiglas board showing positions of aircraft in the air and on the ground within the area served by the 50th Tactical

Fighter Wing. The planes carrying nuclear warheads were noted. He observed the hand-written list of the Victor Alert pilots, their chiefs and armament men. He noted who was on the pad ready for the "Go" sign. The colonel had a lot of respect for these highly-trained people whom he knew personally. Finally, the base prepared defensive actions against Eastern attacks and for retaliatory strikes in the Soviet Bloc countries.

Aircraft and pilots, many of whom were friends with Butch, moved onto the runway from the Victor Alert sector to facilitate a quick launch. The pilots were ready for takeoff at a moment's notice. Remaining in the aircraft until ordered to stand down, they were only allowed out of the cockpit for one minute every hour. Each had orders to strike predetermined targets within the Soviet Bloc countries.

These extraordinary young men worked 48-hour shifts, eating in a separate mess hall nearby and sleeping on the launch pad during the entire shift.

Support aircraft gathered on the tarmac, also preparing for launch.

After briefing with the Colonel, the Squadron Commanders left the Combat Operations Center to carry out preparations for the defense of the base and American interests in Europe. Everyone would be watching and waiting for the Soviets' next move.

Colonel Andrews paused for a moment with Butch and Captain Jackson. The Colonel nodded at Butch, "How old are you, Airman?"

"Nineteen, sir."

The colonel looked carefully at Butch's ID, "Airman Panko, well done. You kept a cool head in a tense situation. I know I can count on you to remain steadfast in this crisis."

"Yes, sir."

"Captain Jackson, this airman is a credit to you and the squadron."

"Yes, sir, thank you, sir," replied Captain Jackson.

The officer hastily turned and left the Com Center to attend to other matters.

As soon as Colonel Andrews departed, the Combat Operations Center was ordered into "Lockdown." Heavy steel doors clanged shut and locked, unable to be opened from the outside. No one could come in without special clearance; no one could leave the underground structure until further notice.

Every man in the COC was a professional quietly doing his job, unimpeded by personal concerns and emotions. Detailed information was streaming into the Center through encoded messages, verbal communications and surveillance reports from the front lines. The 17th Air Force Headquarters was up to speed on every development as it happened. Mission and target information was fluid, changing with each action of the Soviets.

"Lockdown" lasted three days. Three days of having meals brought in by Air Police, three days of no showers and no sleep, three days of no sunshine and three days of wondering who would fire the first shot.

United States Secretary of State Dean Rusk was said to have commented in a meeting, "Berlin is not a vital interest." With that in mind, intense diplomatic negotiations to defuse the situation took place between President Kennedy and Chairman Nikita Krushchev. Strangely, KGB spy Georgi Bolchakov served as a go-between for the two most powerful men on earth. During these talks, the two men agreed to withdraw their tanks in a very simple manner. First, the Soviets moved one of their tanks backward five meters, then an American tank moved backward five meters and so on until all of the massive machines had assumed a non-aggressive posture. This action alone started easing tensions, and finally, a resolution was agreed to by both powers. It was a starting point for new negotiations. President Kennedy stated, "It's not a very nice solution, but a wall is a hell of a lot better than a war."

Hahn Air Force Base canceled the "High Alert" status, "Lockdown" was rescinded, and relief came in the next shift of personnel. Bone tired and drained emotionally, the weary airmen and officers all wanted a good meal, a hot shower, and much-needed sleep.

Butch went back to his room to do just that. With every step, he offered prayers of thanks for the avoidance of armed conflict, for being able to keep a cool head and for doing a good job. The Lord had blessed him.

> *Get some rest, Butch. You did a great job, and I am so proud of you. If only your dad could see you now, he'd be popping the buttons off his shirt with pride.*

George and Gladys were reading newspapers and watching television with rapt attention, hoping for a diplomatic resolution. They prayed day and night for their eldest son. When the standoff was resolved, it was an answer to prayer.

George was comforted by knowing Butch carried his missal; the prayer book had a protective nature, he was convinced of that. He also knew Butch would be safe, no matter what.

34

1962
AIN'T NO MOUNTAIN HIGH ENOUGH

Having done outstanding work for nearly a year, Butch was chosen for rotation to the most important aspect of his career, Victor Alert. He was elated to be handpicked for this position. Each man working in this highly classified area had been chosen for his capabilities under stress, his level of maturity and, of course, additional Top Secret clearances.

Butch and the other airmen in Victor Alert had knowledge of all targets within the Soviet Bloc countries. Most importantly, he was responsible for passing on the correct target information to the fighter pilots provided by 17th Air Force headquarters. Part of his job entailed the launch of aircraft and plotting the weather in both the target and recovery areas in the event of an armed conflict. Rotating to this specialized area every other week was an honor and a privilege.

Butch had an exciting job that he loved and felt fortunate to be stationed at Hahn Air Force Base in the beautiful Eiffel Mountain region of Germany. He and some of his friends had begun traveling around Europe on their days off experiencing some of the finest skiing in the world and enjoying the exceptional regional cuisine. He was playing football and taking college classes, both of which were personally satisfying. None of this would have been remotely possible at home. Butch was going to make the most of every opportunity. Life was good and he was grateful!

Both he and his parents were glad he wasn't in a shooting war; bullets would be a complication, yet Butch was about to be faced with making some crucial decisions. He would need good advice from people he trusted. His metamorphosis had begun.

35

1962

IN HIS FATHER'S FOOTSTEPS

The Berlin Crisis had made Butch grateful for his routine. His mentors were as proud as any parents to see him doing well in class and football.

His focused efforts paid off. In the second year, Butch made the travel team. Having gained thirty pounds of solid muscle through intense physical conditioning, he was indeed bigger, faster and stronger.

The Hahn team played other Air Force bases across Germany and France in a ten-game schedule followed by a playoff game. Each year, at the end of the season, the European Air Force All-Stars played the European Army All-Stars in the Freedom Bowl in Frankfurt, Germany. For the players, it was a prestigious honor to receive an invitation to this event. For the coaches, it was a pleasure to create a dream team from the best players of all the European teams.

Every man strived for a bowl game invitation and Butch was no exception. In previous years, the invited players traveled to Frankfurt to begin practice as teammates for an entire week before the Freedom Bowl.

Playing the Bowl had been Butch's aspiration since his first year on the practice squad. Traveling Europe with the football team for two years across the French and German countryside led to an epiphany: he pondered what he and his dad had in common other than the military missal both of them carried.

On the bus heading back to the base after a game, he turned to his friend Fritz. "You know, I've been thinking a lot about my dad fighting to liberate these same cities and towns we're traveling through. We're geographically following the path of the 289th Cannon Company from twenty years ago. Look around at this Europe today; it's rebuilding and thriving. My dad and other soldiers who fought here made it possible. Fritz, you and I have it made, no one's shooting at us."

Fritz grunted in agreement, his head bobbing, bouncing his chin off his chest with every bump in the road.

"Fritz, my dad was a hero. All those guys were heroes. They sacrificed years away from their homes and families. I don't even remember my dad until I was almost three years old."

Butch now had Fritz's attention.

"Do you realize how much time my dad spent behind German lines gathering intel?"

Fritz shook his head. "No, not really." The question was rhetorical because Fritz had no idea what Butch's father did in the war.

"He was lucky he wasn't killed or captured and always gave credit to this prayer book he carried." Butch patted his breast pocket. Feeling overwhelming admiration and respect for his father, Butch vowed he'd write him a letter as soon as they got back to base.

Fritz wondered if it was safe for him to go back to sleep when Butch stopped talking and became lost in thought.

I was grateful that he'd had this insight. I'd been praying this would happen. Butch finally has formed a unique, mature bond with his father here in Europe.

God is good.

36

1962
THE CUBAN MISSILE CRISIS

T he decade of the Sixties signaled the beginning of the nuclear arms race between the Soviet Union and the United States. The two superpowers each had enough nuclear weaponry to wipe out the entire world and each side had developed an antimissile defense system.

In October 1962, the headlines screamed, "Soviet Missiles and Bases in Cuba—90 Miles Off Florida Coast!"

President Kennedy demanded that the missiles and bases be removed. When they refused his ultimatum, he set up a naval blockade of Cuba. The Soviets attempted to bargain and offered to remove the missiles if the United States would dismantle its military bases in Turkey. The United States refused.

The United States military went on alert. The missiles in Cuba were pointing directly at Florida. Though Hahn Air Force Base was thousands of miles away in Europe, there was no guarantee of safety. No one knew if the crisis in Cuba was a diversion for impending Soviet military action in another part of the world and all American forces had to be ready.

Although on alert, the COC at Hahn was not ordered into "Lockdown." They watched and waited. All personal leaves were canceled. The airmen and officers anticipated diplomatic resolution but prepared for action.

Khrushchev contemplated the consequences of continuing the standoff and, after a week of tense diplomatic negotiations, agreed to remove the missiles in Cuba. The dismantling of the Russian missile bases in Cuba was scheduled, and the threat to the southern coast of the United States gradually lessened.

When the Soviet leader backed off, the alert was canceled, and Hahn Air Force Base and Butch's routine went back to normal.

God is with us, Butch, but normal is just a setting on the washing machine. Stay alert.

37

1963

A LIFE-CHANGING DECISION

Summoned by his Squadron Commander, Butch strode across the base to Major Langdon's office in January 1963. He was just shy of his twentieth birthday and a bit apprehensive about today's meeting. Arriving at the one-story gray cement building, he entered the first suite on the left. Butch announced himself to the First Sergeant who showed him into the major's office.

"Airman First Class George J. Panko reporting as ordered, sir."

"At ease, Airman Panko. I have something important I want to discuss with you." The major pointed to a chair. "Please sit."

"Perhaps you've heard of the cheating scandal at the Air Force Academy in Colorado Springs." Major Langdon picked up a pen on his desk and began to write on a tablet as he spoke.

Butch nodded "Yes sir."

"The scandal resulted in the dismissal of all those involved. Consequently, the Air Force is actively seeking airmen of exemplary character to fill the empty slots at the Academy. I've recommended you as a possible candidate. Airman, in my opinion, you fit the Air Force Academy profile."

Butch was stunned. This opportunity was something out of left field. He had to digest this. The silence in the room was deafening.

"Airman Panko?"

Butch snapped out of his momentary shock. "Sir, I'm honored, but how do I know I'm qualified for the Academy?"

"You'll have an interview with Colonel Andrews. If he approves of your candidacy, you'll go to 17th Air Force headquarters at Wiesbaden for academic testing. When we have the results of those test scores, you can make your final decision. What I need to know, do you want to move forward with the next step? Are you interested?"

"Yes sir, I am. I'd like to see if I qualify."

"Glad to hear that, Airman Panko. My First Sergeant will set you up with an appointment with Colonel Andrews." The major escorted Butch to the door.

The next day, Butch met with the Colonel. He felt the interview went well. The officer seemed like a down-to-earth guy. They talked about many things both in and out of the Air Force.

Colonel Andrews recognized Butch from their meeting during the Berlin crisis and had made a few notes about the Airman at that time. He reviewed Butch's on-base college course grades and promptly recommended academic testing for the Academy.

Butch exited the Colonel's office with his head spinning. In two days, he and five other airmen left the base for Wiesbaden.

A few days after the test, he reported to the Commander's office for results.

After being ushered into the room, Butch nervously waited for the Colonel to arrive, not knowing what to expect.

The Colonel strode into his office and proceeded to the swivel chair behind his desk, sat down and opened a folder to review the papers inside. "Sorry for keeping you waiting, Airman. You haven't disappointed me. You did well on the testing and are now considered a formal candidate. This slot at the Academy requires a timely decision. Unless you have a definitive answer for me right now, we'll meet again tomorrow after you've had time to think. Feel free to seek advice and discuss this important decision with others. Is this acceptable?"

"Yes, sir." Butch rose from the chair, saluted and left the office in a daze.

> I never had a moment's doubt. My charge is an extraordinary young man. I'm so proud of him and his accomplishments. I know this monumental decision weighs heavily on his mind.

All Butch could think about as he ambled to the Combat Operations Center (COC) to work his 4 p.m. to 12 p.m. shift was the opportunity before him. If he accepted, he'd leave Hahn within days for Colorado Springs to be present for spring semester registration. The decision to accept the appointment to the Air Force Academy would be life-changing.

There was no time to write his parents and wait for a reply. Besides, he didn't want to be swayed by their emotions. Phone calls were only for emergency situations and had to be approved by the brass. It was up to him to solicit unbiased opinions.

The two people on base he highly respected were his football teammate and mentor, Lt. Perkins and his Squadron Commander, Major Langdon, who made the initial recommendation. Butch was lost in thought as he walked, "I'm working the same shift as Lieutenant Perkins and can talk to him this evening. I can see the major during office hours tomorrow morning before I go to work."

When Butch arrived at his station in the COC, Lt. Perkins was at his desk. He sipped his habitual mug of coffee and nodded for Butch to pull up a chair. "Coffee, Airman?"

"No, thanks, I've had my allotment of caffeine for today, but I would like your input on huge decision I've got to make."

Perkins' eyes widened over the rim of his mug. He lowered it slowly and said, "Go ahead, tell me what's on your mind."

Butch reiterated the past week's conversations and important opportunity facing him.

Perkins thought a moment. "Well, it means another four-year commitment at the Academy, and an additional six years once you become an officer. Are you up for that?"

"That's what I'm not sure about, Lieutenant."

"I have no doubt in my mind you'd make an excellent officer. You're suited for the military and its structure, Butch. My question for you is, does it fit into the plan you see for yourself?"

"I've never in my wildest dreams thought I'd have a shot at the Academy. The last thing I want to do is pass up a great opportunity.

"You're afraid you'll make the wrong decision?"

"Exactly."

"I can't make the decision for you. You need to talk it out. Put the pros and cons down on paper where you can see them. Sometimes that helps to clarify an issue. For myself, I know you can do it. I know that you would give it your all and be an excellent officer, a credit to the Academy. I also know you'd make a darn good pilot if that's the direction you want to go."

Butch thanked him and went back to his work station.

Lt. Perkins had given him a lot to think about. If his shift was quiet that evening, he'd make that T-chart with the pros and cons.

The next day, Butch got up early and was at the Squadron Commander's office when they unlocked the door. Waiting ten minutes, he sat forward in the chair, resting his elbows on his thighs, hands clasped tightly in front of him. His brow furrowed with the thought of the decision before him. He needed to compose himself. He heard his name called.

Major Langdon looked up at Butch as he entered the room.

"Something I can do for you, Airman Panko?" His eyes twinkled as if he knew exactly what was on Butch's mind.

"Yes, sir. It's about this opportunity to the Academy. I'd like to consider every angle before making a decision. I wanted to check in with you to make sure I'm not missing anything."

"Can't say that I'm surprised, Airman. I'm glad you're giving it so much thought." He got up from behind the desk and walked over to a console where a coffee maker was perking away. "Let's talk about it." Pouring two mugs of steaming caffeine, he offered Butch some warm *fasnachts* on a beautiful ornate plate.

The nervous airman declined.

"Pretty, isn't it?

"Sir?"

"The plate. I bought it for my wife. It's hand-painted antique Dresden china. I had a once-in-a-lifetime opportunity to buy it in a small out-of-the-way shop, and I jumped at it. Turns out, it came in handy today for the doughnuts." He chuckled.

The Major sat down with his coffee and fasnacht in front of him. He tossed Butch a notepad to use as a coaster. Butch caught it with one hand and put it on the edge of the desk before setting down his mug. He noted the colorful Air Force logo facing him. A coincidence?

Major Langdon bit into the confection. He closed his eyes and murmured, "Oh, my, the bakery outdid themselves with this batch. Are you sure you don't want one?"

When Butch caught the tempting aroma of the doughnut, his stomach involuntarily growled. "No, thank you, right now it would be a distraction." He tried to ignore the involuntary gnawing in his gut.

"Okay, back to the business at hand. This, like the antique plate, is a once-in-a-lifetime opportunity for you. Life changing, in fact. "

"Yes, sir. That's putting it mildly and is what makes this so difficult. I know the pros and cons. I-I just have to make the right decision."

"I suppose you know all about the additional service time to which you'd be obligated."

"Absolutely."

"I also know what a hard worker you are. Dedicated, focused and determined. Airman, you'll be a success whatever you choose to do." He got up and came around the desk. Leaning forward, he made sure he had Butch's full attention. He lowered his voice. "Don't be intimidated by the fact that this is the Air Force Academy; it's a means to an end. Think long and hard about what you see yourself doing, make the decision, then go after what you want with fierce determination."

That statement hit home with Butch. He nodded and listened while the Major shared his insights.

"When do you need to let Colonel Andrews know?"

"This afternoon."

"Well then, I better let you go, because you have a decision to make."

"Thanks for your time, sir." Butch left the Major to enjoy another doughnut and a second cup of coffee.

He didn't have to ask a single question, but he had all the information he needed. What he needed now was time for prayer and meditation.

In spite of the educational opportunity, extending his commitment to the Air Force was a huge consideration.

Holding me in his hands, he prayed for guidance. Within five minutes, Butch slipped me back into his shirt pocket and left for lunch in the mess hall. He sighed deeply, but I noticed a spring in his step.

That afternoon before reporting for work, Butch met with Colonel Andrews for his final decision. I listened carefully.

"Have you made your decision, Airman?" The colonel inquired, prepared to make notes on a tablet in front of him.

"Yes, sir, I have. The Air Force is the best thing to happen to me, providing opportunities I wouldn't have had otherwise. This particular opportunity is an incredible honor, but I must respectfully decline the appointment to the Academy. Thank you very much for considering me."

The Colonel nodded and sat back in his chair tugging at his left ear lobe.

The young airman continued, "I've decided to keep working toward a degree while I'm here and after I complete my enlistment." Butch felt surprising relief at hearing himself say these things.

"What a loss for the Air Force Academy. I want to remind you Airman, that you were not only considered, but you qualified by passing all the requirements. That, in and of itself, is quite an accomplishment. I wish you well in school, Airman Panko. I have no doubt you'll be successful."

The two men saluted. The colonel extended his hand. Butch shook it, and left feeling better than when he had come in.

As he came down the steps and turned toward the barracks, he ran headlong into his friend, Fritz.

"Hey, what's happening?" Fritz asked. "You look like you're in another world."

"I am." He inhaled deeply and let it out slowly. "You heard about the chance to go to the Academy?"

"Yeah, I know the last few days have been a whirlwind for you. Figured we'd catch up one of these days. I can tell you've been under a little stress."

"Well, I turned it down. Fritz. I turned down the appointment to the Academy."

"You did? Why pray tell?"

"I felt something was missing and finally figured out what it was. I don't have a burning desire to be a pilot or to attend the Academy. Even though it was a great honor to have been chosen and an even bigger deal to pass the test, it proved something to me. I can do anything I want, including getting a degree in civilian life. I know one thing for sure, I don't want to commit myself to ten more years in the Air Force." An involuntary sigh escaped his body, and he knew his decision was the right one. It was clear as day.

He and Fritz went their separate ways. As Butch walked back to his quarters to rest before going to work, he pondered the last few days. Tracing my outline in his pocket, he thought, "I know I did what was best for me." He bowed his head, "Thank you, dear Lord, for guiding my thoughts and helping me see clearly."

> I also knew this. Philippians 4:6 said it best: *Have no anxiety, but in every prayer and supplication with thanksgiving let your petitions be made known to God.*
>
> What's more, I knew he'd be needed at home.

38
ROMAN HOLIDAY

B utch went to church on base every Sunday. When the Chaplain posted a sign-up sheet for a tour to Rome in early spring of 1963, it was no surprise to him that Butch Panko was one of the first names on the list. The cost was two hundred dollars a person, which included bus and train transportation, meals, and lodging for one week. It was an unbelievable opportunity.

Awed by the ancient city and the classic beauty surrounding them, the group organized their schedule around Rome's schedule. In the early morning, tourists visited a collage of piazzas before having lunch. When Rome was napping, some of the group members napped while others visited the gardens. Evening excursions consisted of what remained on their "must see" list. Whether tossing coins into the Trevi Fountain, visiting the Colosseum or the Pantheon in the Piazza Della Rotunda, the group from Hahn crammed as much sightseeing in as they possibly could.

Sunday morning, they walked to St. Peter's Square at the Vatican to attend Mass and the excitement only grew as the crowd gathering for the Celebration of the Mass continued to swell.

Anxiously awaiting the appearance of the pope, the throng looked up. Appearing at the large window overlooking the square, Pope John XXIII waved and blessed the people. They cheered the beloved man. Butch pinched himself to make sure this was happening.

Butch had only seen pictures of this event, but he was emotionally moved. It was known that the pontiff was sick. The pope had been diagnosed with stomach cancer in September 1962. One could see the toll the disease was taking on the man as he became paler and weaker with each occasional public appearance.

> *Pope John XXIII had offered to mediate talks between President John Kennedy and Nikita Khrushchev during the Cuban Missile Crisis in October 1962. I knew he'd be Time magazine's "Man of the Year" for his deep commitment to peace.*

When Mass in the Square was over, the tour guide ushered them to the perimeter of the area and conferred with the base chaplain.

Turning to his entourage, the chaplain said, "I have some exciting news. We'll be entering the Basilica for an audience with the pope." His face beamed with excitement.

There was a collective gasp.

"I knew this was a possibility, but I didn't want to say anything in case it didn't materialize due to the pontiff's precarious health. I'm beside myself that we have this incredible opportunity."

On the pope's part, when he found out that a group of United States military and their families were attending Mass, he insisted on granting them an audience.

The tour guide ushered them into the breathtakingly beautiful St. Peter's Basilica. He talked a little about the famous church as they walked down a side aisle into a smaller chapel. The group gathered along the kneeling rail which divided the room. The tour guide fell silent, and suddenly, without fanfare, Pope John XXIII was ushered into the chapel with priests on either side of him.

Butch thought he could've heard a pin drop. The group was appropriately reverent, awestruck, and overwhelmed with the experience of being this close to the Pope.

The pontiff smiled. "How is everyone?" he asked in broken English.

"We are blessed to be here, your Holiness," the Chaplain replied as their spokesman.

"Thank you for coming. It is always good to see members of the United States military and their families." He proceeded to walk alongside the kneeling rail handing each person in the group a bronze papal medallion. With insight to his mortality, the pope continued to speak, "That which happens to all men perhaps will happen soon to the pope who speaks to you today." He paused to take a deep breath. "Now, please bow your heads for a special blessing."

> Butch reached into his pocket to retrieve me. While everyone bowed their heads, Butch held me in the air. The papal blessing was bestowed and the pontiff noticed the airman holding up the military missal. Approaching the railing closest to Butch, the holy man beckoned him to approach. Still holding me in the air, Butch took two steps, close enough for the pope to take me from Butch's hand. The pontiff made the sign of the cross over my worn cover and handed me back.

> I was just blessed by the pope! Undoubtedly, I'm the luckiest military missal in all of Europe. Forgive my vanity, Lord, but could the pontiff have sensed that I was a unique prayer book?

The pope turned, waved good-bye, and left the room. Murmurs of delight broke the silence. What a day this had been!

Stunned, Butch stood holding me in his hands for a few moments. He was deeply moved and humbled by the encounter.

"You are one lucky son of a gun," someone said as they clapped him on the back.

Dazed, Butch was the last one to wander out of the Basilica.

> I know that Butch felt blessed in many aspects of his life, but the experience at the Vatican confirmed it. Pope John XXIII died June 3, 1963. Known affectionately as "Good Pope John," his cause for canonization was opened under his successor, Pope Paul VI in November 1965.

There is a time for everything,
*   a season for every activity under heaven.*
A time to be born and a time to die.
A time to plant and a time to harvest.
A time to kill and a time to heal.
A time to tear down and a time to rebuild.
A time to cry and a time to laugh.
A time to grieve and a time to dance.
Ecclesiastes 3:1-4

39
NOVEMBER 1963
THE WORLD IN SHOCK

The United States and the USSR were starting to realize there would be no winner in a nuclear war and the world would be much safer if they started agreeing on some controls regarding their nuclear weaponry and testing. In July 1963, the U.S., Russia, and Great Britain approved a treaty to stop the testing of nuclear weapons in the atmosphere, in outer space, and under water.

The U.S. and Russia set up a hot line between the White House and the Kremlin in August 1963. This direct link would reduce the risk of accidental nuclear war. Two months later, the UN unanimously adopted a resolution forbidding the use of nuclear weapons in outer space. Global relations were improving.

On November 22, 1963, the unimaginable happened. President John F. Kennedy was assassinated in Dallas, Texas.

> *Chills ran up and down my spine. This horrible event would affect the entire world. Solomon's words from Ecclesiastes were running like a ticker tape through my consciousness.*

40

NOVEMBER 1963
THE AFTERMATH

All military bases went on high alert. It wasn't known immediately who the assassin was or on whose behalf the deed was committed. The sudden death of the young president shocked the world.

Hahn Air Force Base was no exception. The 17th Air Force Headquarters had informed the base of the assassination. Those who were on duty in the COC were notified before the base went to High Alert status. Airmen and officers alike were stunned and saddened by President Kennedy's death. As highly-trained members of the finest military in the world, they focused on the task at hand and performed their jobs to keep the base and the country safe.

The Soviets stood down, seemingly as stunned as the rest of the world. They did nothing to take advantage of a grief-stricken nation.

41

NOVEMBER 1963
UNINTENDED CONSEQUENCES

B utch was not on duty when he heard the President had been shot. He was packing to leave the base for a week's practice for the Freedom Bowl in Frankfurt when one of his roommates burst into the room.

"The President's been shot."

Stunned and surprised, Butch stared at him. "What President?"

"Our President. The President of the United States, President Kennedy. He's been killed!"

At the horrifying news, Butch sat down on his bunk, head in his hands.

Lifting his head, he asked, "Are we on High Alert?"

"Yep, all leaves are canceled. You know the drill."

"Yeah, I know the drill. Who did this?"

"They think there was a shooter or shooters in a building targeting the presidential motorcade. It'll be in the news as soon as they nab the people who did it."

I was in his pocket, having heard it all. God in Heaven, what is happening in this world?

Three weeks earlier, Butch had achieved one of his goals when he received the coveted invitation to play in the prestigious Freedom Bowl. Scheduled to leave for Frankfurt on November 23rd, the selected players were supposed to have their first practice for the Bowl Game the same day. This was his last year to play football for the United States Air Force.

Not this year; not this game, not for Butch. In deference to the fallen Commander-in-Chief, the Freedom Bowl was canceled.

He was heartsick at the news of the assassination; he was also extremely disappointed to lose his last chance to play in the Freedom Bowl.

> *This news is hard to bear for you, Butch. You worked so hard to become eligible to play, but it's all put in perspective by the assassination of the Commander-In-Chief. I'm not sure which situation makes you feel worse.*

42
WINTER 1964
THE INNSBRUCK OLYMPICS

S ix months earlier, in June of 1963, Butch and two of his close friends had begun making plans to attend the '64 Winter Olympic Games in Innsbruck, Austria. It was a 16-hour trip from the base by car. Having lost the one chance he had of playing in the Freedom Bowl, Butch threw himself into his classes and looked forward to this once-in-a-lifetime event.

One day in the first week of January, Fritz showed up in Butch's room. "Mike sent me over to see if you want to get together to finalize the plans for our trip to Innsbruck."

"Where does he want to meet?"

"In his room. You ready to go?"

"Yep." Butch grabbed a folder out of his top desk drawer. "Oh, by the way, Fritz, I saw something interesting on TV this week about preparations for the events." He locked his door, and they started down the short flight of stairs. "The lack of snow this year is causing a problem in Seefeld and Innsbruck. The Austrian army has to truck in thousands of blocks of ice for the luge and bobsled tracks and tons of snow to the Alpine skiing slopes."

"Wow, I didn't realize it was that bad. Do you think they'll have to cancel any events?"

"Hey, man, this is the Winter Olympic Games. I think the Army will truck in as much as they need for as long as they need it. No doubt in my mind."

They arrived at Mike's room and knocked on the door.

"Come in. It's unlocked."

"Hey Mike, we've got all our paperwork; where do you want to start?"

He had pulled his desk away from the wall so all three of them could gather around.

"I'll start." Fritz opened his folder to display event passes and ski school information. "Here's a calendar for each of us. The opening ceremony is January 29 and those are separate passes." Fritz started a pile of paperwork for each of them. "The closing ceremony is the evening of February 9th, and it'll go late. We should head back to base early the next morning. Butch, you were able to use the telephone at the COC to call the travel agency for hotel reservations. Is everything confirmed?"

Butch opened his folder. "Yes, indeed, we are confirmed. Hotels are booked within a hundred mile radius, but I think you're gonna like what the agent was able to do for us." He handed Mike and Fritz a colorful pamphlet on a bed and breakfast in Seefeld. "We're in the home of a doctor and his family. We get breakfast before we leave in the morning. It costs each of us seventeen American dollars a day. We can drive to all the events, I have a parking pass for whatever vehicle we drive. We can also use the train in Innsbruck once we've parked the car."

"Cool." Mike pumped his fist in the air.

Fritz referred to his folder once again, pulling out other passes already on lanyards. "When we planned this trip back in June, we chose the downhill events in Innsbruck and cross-country in Seefeld." He handed out those passes. "Butch signed up for a week of instruction at the Toni Seelos Ski School in Seefeld. You can pick either morning or afternoon instruction depending on the event schedule. Oh yeah, they provide the equipment." He handed Butch the ski school information.

"Wow! Thanks, Fritz."

"Mike, we didn't know how we were gonna get there six months ago. Where do we stand?"

"I bought a second hand VW beetle. I've been fixing it up, with the help of the guys in the motor pool and I'm pretty sure it'll get us there and back."

"Okay, so that's taken care of. Any questions about anything?"

"You're sure that old beetle can make it through the Alps? At that altitude? We've got at least a 16-hour trip." Butch walked over to the window to look out at the quad. He waited for Mike to answer when he heard Fritz coughing.

"In the middle of winter?" Fritz sputtered.

"Okay, I understand your hesitation about the vehicle, but I thought, to ease your minds, we'd drive as far as Munich, have dinner, and spend the night. No sense in pushing it. We'd have to get up early to get back on the road to Seefeld. All in daylight, guys."

"Even in daylight, we'd better be prepared with blankets and food to venture into the mountains in any car." Butch mused aloud from the window.

"Okay, you're in charge of those supplies," Fritz announced. "So you're in?"

"I'm in." Butch walked back over to the desk, grabbed a pen and paper to start making a list of supplies to take.

"I'll tell you what, I can't wait to try the food and beer in Austria! This trip is gonna be a blast, and we're up for some cool skiing, man." Fritz rubbed his hands together in excitement.

Butch nodded. "I agree one hundred percent. In three weeks we'll be going to the 1964 Winter Olympic Games!" He pointed upward, and said aloud, "Thank you, Lord."

On the day of departure from the base, they left in the afternoon and drove to Munich as planned. At dusk, a large bright moon began to rise over the horizon illuminating the countryside as if it were daylight. When the trio came out of the restaurant, not a single cloud disturbed the showcase of stars and the brilliant winter moon was now a giant spotlight in the sky.

A discussion ensued. "Mike, I'm game to keep on driving. There's no snow falling, we have an incredible bright sky, and the car has been running great." Fritz gently patted the side of the vehicle.

Butch agreed. "I agree with Fritz. We'd get there earlier and have more time to get our bearings in Seefeld."

Mike scratched his chin. "I'm okay with it if you two are. I've got all the stuff I need to get 'er going again if she quits on me. Let's do it." They jumped in the car, left Munich and headed South to Seefeld.

The optimistic feeling about the car car didn't last long. The VW broke down two hours after leaving Munich.

"Mike, is it something you can fix?"

"Yeah, Butch, I've dealt with this before." He opened the trunk and hauled out some fluid to pour in one of the engine compartments. "We have to wait about fifteen minutes before trying to start her up again. Better pull out the blankets and put on your wool hats. You know how cold it gets up here."

Huddled under blankets, wool caps pulled down over their ears, the men had nothing to do but gaze out the windows.

They marveled at the star-studded sky. Light from the full moon reflected off the snow, creating a brilliance none of them had ever seen at night. Snow-covered mountain spires, devoid of vegetation, towered above them majestically. The valleys below twinkled with tiny lights from houses warmed by wood fires. Chimneys belched fingers of grey smoke reaching into the sky. It was peacefully quiet and still. Not another vehicle was on the road. Although somewhat unsettling given the VW breakdown, the lack of traffic added to the serenity of the night.

Even wrapped in blankets, they all were shivering. They'd be in dire trouble if the car didn't start. But when Mike turned the key in the ignition, the engine sprang to life. He let it run for a minute before turning on the heater. Chilled to the bone, each of them was grateful when the fan started pumping warm air into the passenger compartment. Guided by the bright moon, Mike resumed driving.

Arriving at the B & B in Seefeld just after dawn, the trio met their hostess who had just put on a fresh pot of coffee and was beginning to set out rolls and breakfast cakes. She took time out to show them to their room.

All three of them were pleased with the large room containing three double beds. Attached was a small bathroom with only a commode and a sink. They were given directions to the public baths in town. It definitely would be a new and unusual experience.

Too excited to rest, they unpacked their bags and had breakfast downstairs. Afterward, they took a walking tour of quaint downtown Seefeld. It wasn't hard to find the public baths to which they were directed by the owner of the B & B and the men were relieved to find it also offered private showers. Later that afternoon, all three of them napped in preparation for the opening ceremony in Innsbruck that evening.

The Vienna Philharmonic kicked off the opening ceremony with a concert conducted by Karl Bohm performing Beethoven's 7th and Mozart's 40th symphonies. Meanwhile, the guys from Hahn Air Force Base took note of all the famous celebrities and athletes mingling among the Olympic goers.

Butch was walking about when the crowd parted like the Red Sea. A growing murmur alerted him that something was happening when a vision in white fur appeared before him. He stopped in his tracks to see Elizabeth Taylor. There was no mistaking that gorgeous face with those violet eyes and dark double lashes. He sucked in his breath and couldn't have moved if he wanted to. The fur clad star brushed by him followed by a man he'd seen before, in the movies. "Man, this is unreal! Elizabeth Taylor and Richard Burton just touched my sleeve! The guys are going to lose their gourds when I tell them what just happened." The three had gotten separated in the massive crowd.

When they met up at the car to drive back to Seefeld, Butch could hardly talk.

"You're not gonna believe this, but Elizabeth Taylor bumped into me in the crowd."

"What?" They said in unison.

"You heard me. And right behind her was Richard Burton."

"Wait a minute!" Fritz held up his hand. "Isn't Liz married to Eddie Fisher?"

"She sure is." Mike gushed. "I read those magazines. Liz and Eddie are getting divorced. She and Burton were both in *Cleopatra*, you know, the movie. All the gossip columns said they had a 'thing going on,' but that was a couple of years ago. They've been seen all over Hollywood together. I bet it all started when they did that movie."

Butch and Fritz stood there with hands on their hips seeing a side of Mike they never knew.

"Well, that's good to know." Butch opened the car door. "Are we leaving, or not?"

They drove back to the B & B. It had been a long day.

The '64 Olympic Games saw the debut of athletes from Mongolia, India and North Korea. In the bobsled competition, athletes raced on artificial ice for the first time proving to be much less dangerous. Eight hundred ninety-two men and 199 women participated in 34 events. During training, two athletes died which cast a pall over the games. The U.S. figure skating team had to start from scratch after the loss of the entire team and their family members in a plane crash three years earlier.

In addition to attending the downhill and cross country events, Butch, Fritz, and Mike skied on nearby slopes outside Seefeld unrivaled in challenges and beauty. They fell into bed each night exhausted and arose early each morning to start all over again. They seldom saw their host or hostess except if the trays of sweets were being refilled at breakfast.

The morning after the closing of the Winter Games, the Airmen loaded the VW and headed out northbound for Hahn Air Force Base. The lady of the house had left tins of cookies, pastries, and candy on the buffet to take on their journey. This time, the trip was uneventful, and the VW had no seizures.

When they returned, Butch had mail waiting for him. One was a letter from home explaining that his mother was sick and needed surgery as soon as Butch was discharged in early July. The letter was rather non-specific as far as explaining what exactly was wrong. He was convinced that his parents wanted to spare him undue anxiety. However, it achieved just the opposite. Butch's imagination ran wild, imagining the worse possible scenario. He wrote back asking questions, hoping for specific answers.

Nancy Panko

I knew what was in store for Butch in the coming months. In a panic, he turned my pages searching for a prayer to touch his heart and calm his mind. He came across the "Prayer for Relatives of Service Men."

He read the passage: *"Grant, O Lord, to those homes from which have come our country's defenders, the peace which You alone can give. Make those at home strong to meet their trials, to overcome the pain of loss, to meet bravely whatever You have in store for them. May these trials be as well and bravely borne as Your Own Immaculate Mother bore her loss at the foot of the Cross. Amen."*

Butch sat on the edge of his bunk for a few minutes then rolled back, turned on his side and fell into a deep sleep. His furrowed brow relaxed.

43

1964
AN EARLY DISCHARGE

It took two weeks for him to receive an answer to his letter. His parents gave a brief overview of his mother's condition, multiple strictures of the esophagus, which had deteriorated to the point where she could only consume small amounts of room temperature liquids. Surgical intervention was needed as soon as possible. With all her heart, Gladys wanted to wait until Butch was discharged in July to have it done. It was an admirable plan on her part but proved to be foolish to put off the care she desperately needed.

One day in late May 1964, the Red Cross delivered disturbing news to Butch. His mother's condition was such that they had to move up the date for surgery. Butch knew she had put it off too long. Reluctant to postpone the necessary treatment any longer, his father had taken the bull by the horns. He and Gladys' doctor contacted the local Red Cross in Scranton who, in turn, contacted their European agencies. Butch was coming home early, and Gladys was going to be admitted the day after he arrived in Scranton.

The squadron commander, Major Langdon, interceded with Colonel Andrews to arrange an immediate honorable discharge for Butch, several weeks ahead of schedule.

Sad to see him go, coworkers and friends gathered to send him off. It was hard to say good-bye to those who had mentored him and with whom he'd shared so many moving experiences. He had come to Germany a boy, not yet fully grown. He was returning home a man, physically, mentally and certainly spiritually.

Within two days, Butch left Hahn Air Force Base for the last time. Emotionally, it was best for him this way.

Fritz offered to drive Butch to Rhein Main Air Force Base in Frankfurt to catch the military transport home. The trip took them about ninety minutes from the base at Hahn. They began in silence as Butch reminisced about his three years in Germany.

"I'm really sorry to hear about your mom, Butch. Hope everything works out."

"Thanks, Fritz. I'll be sure to drop you a note to let you know how she is after surgery."

"I'll be praying for her." Fritz changed the subject. "Hey, do you remember when we were first learning our way around base and couldn't find the mess?"

"Oh boy, do I." Butch laughed.

Verbal flashbacks covered the adventures they had while in Europe to amazing plays in football games throughout the last two years. They exchanged ideas of what they were going to do when they got discharged, although Butch was in that spot now with his plans temporarily on hold.

"I really can't devote much time to job hunting until I know where Mom is going to be in her recovery. I have to help Dad with my brothers …" He couldn't even finish his sentence.

"It's okay, Butch. It'll be okay."

After arriving at the airfield, they had some time to kill before the flight left. As usual, food factored predominantly in their minds, so they continued the conversation in a small coffee shop. Butch ordered his last authentic Bavarian crème pastry and Fritz dove into a cherry strudel. They promised to get together back in Pennsylvania over coffee and a slice of Pennsylvania Dutch shoofly pie. After eating, the two friends shared a laugh about Mike's car breaking down in the middle of the night while crossing the Alps. They parted with a bear hug and a handshake.

Butch walked to his gate and saw the flight was on time. Within minutes they called for boarding. "How odd," he thought to himself as he trudged up the steps to the plane. "I'm the only one boarding." Inside the aircraft, he counted the seats.

"... Eleven, twelve, thirteen. Well, I'm the only one here," he mused until he saw the cargo.

His fellow passenger was a large jet engine and it took up a good bit of space in the fuselage strapped securely to rails bolted to the floor of the plane.

Butch chose one of the thirteen seats, and made himself as comfortable as possible in the sparsely-cushioned seat. Even if he did feel like having a conversation, the jet engine was not going to be a good conversationalist.

One of the pilots stopped by to chat. "Airman, we're going to make a quick stop in Paris to pick up other cargo. The operative word is 'quick.' France has strict guidelines on military aircraft taking off after 6 p.m., and I really don't want to butt heads with the air traffic controllers. We can't get grounded overnight 'cause we're on a tight schedule." He hustled off to the cockpit to begin pre-flight checks.

A bit puzzled, Butch lifted his cap, scratched his head and looked around. As far as he could tell, besides the remaining dozen seats, there wasn't a whole lot of room for additional cargo.

The flight was supposed to be a relatively short one, hardly long enough for a good nap, but they ran into some pretty strong headwinds which made for a later than desired touchdown in Paris.

When they landed in Paris, one of the pilots told Butch they'd be taking off as soon as loading was complete.

The plane taxied to a remote hangar and steps were rolled up to the open door. Ten seconds later, an even dozen Army Special Ops troops boarded in full combat gear. They saw the expression of surprise on the airman's face as they took the twelve remaining seats. The steps were removed, the door closed and the plane taxied to the runway. It was 6:15 p.m. The pilot asked an air traffic controller for permission to take off.

The Frenchman sputtered and cursed in French, saying in English, "You do not have permission."

The American pilot responded, "Give me a runway, I'm taking off."

The control tower said, "It's after 6 p.m. It is against our rules."

"I don't care about your dang rules; I'm on a tight military schedule. Cut me some slack. I need coordinates and a runway, now! I have special forces on board who need to be in the States in the morning."

The testy air traffic controller and the insistent American pilot verbally sparred a few more times.

Finally relenting, the air traffic controller cursed again and shouted, "Stubborn Americans!" Reluctantly, he proceeded to give out coordinates and a runway. He secretly enjoyed fighting with American pilots and knew their persistence was going to result in a takeoff with or without permission.

The pilot hollered over his shoulder. "They sure do have short memories, don't they? If it weren't for Americans, these guys would be speaking German. Next stop, Shannon, Ireland, for refueling. Then it's non-stop to McGuire Air Force Base."

The men nodded to Butch and settled into their seats.

Butch leaned forward. "Where are you guys headed?"

The man next to him replied. "Vietnam, Southeast Asia."

"Obviously, you're getting another ride once we get to our next stop at McGuire," Butch stated as a matter of fact.

One of the other men joined in. "You got it. We'll be taking military transports all the way to California and on to our final destination. Our internal clocks will be all messed up, traveling more than half way around the world."

The squad leader eyed the ribbons on Butch's uniform. "Airman, when you think about re-uppin' would you consider the Army? Right now, they call us 'advisors,' but we're gettin' shot at and we're shootin' back. I call that fightin'. More and more of us are being sent to 'Nam' every day. I've heard that jungle ain't pretty in any sense of the word."

Butch laughed and shook his head. "Any re-enlisting would be right back in the Air Force. I had three hot meals a day and decent quarters to lay my head at night. My dad was in the Army and from what I know, it's not for me. I'm not even considering re-enlisting at this point."

The banter continued for a short while until sleep overtook them, one by one.

The long flight gave him time to reflect. Besides a nagging worry about his mother, Butch contemplated how his family would react to seeing him again and noticing how much he had changed. He was worlds away from that newly-hatched high school graduate who needed his parents' signature to enlist. Now self-reliant and self-sufficient, he knew he'd be out on his own as soon as possible.

When the flight landed on Memorial Day at McGuire, the soldiers heading to southeast Asia went their separate way, and Butch looked for his family. His father, George and middle brother Ron were there to meet him. Thirteen-year-old Joey had stayed home with his mother and his grandparents who were caring for her. It felt good to be in the States, but going back to Scranton was going to be strange for him. They had a lot to talk about on the way home. Butch wanted to know so many things about his sick mother, but his father didn't have answers. They were all anxious.

I could only remind him of the words of Psalm 20:1, *In times of trouble, may the Lord respond to your cry. May the God of Israel keep you safe from all harm.*

Butch prayed for his mother.

44

MAY 1964
HOME SWEET HOME

G ladys was being admitted to the hospital the next day. On the car ride home, his dad told Butch what he could about his mother and her surgery with his limited understanding of medical jargon. His brother Ron peppered him with questions during the entire ride. As soon as he walked into the house, Butch fell into his mother's waiting arms. Both wept unashamedly as George and Ron escaped the emotional scene and moved past them into the living room. Having experienced intercontinental travel, Butch was exhausted. His parents understood when he went to bed and slept for fifteen hours.

Upon awakening, he stretched his legs and arms, sore from the long flight. He lay in bed a little longer, thinking about his mother's impending surgery. He couldn't bear the possibility of losing her. The doctor had reassured the family that having tried all other treatment modalities, surgery was the only viable treatment for her present condition. Butch showered and dressed quickly so he could accompany his father in taking his mother to the hospital for her admission. His larger bag remained on the bedroom floor, full of the trappings of his last three years in Germany. The chore of unpacking would give him something to do in the coming week. There were more important things on his mind right now.

Finding me on his nightstand, Butch held me in his hands and prayed for his mother. Instead of returning me to the cedar chest, he placed me in his pants pocket. He knew he would need my comforting words as a constant source of strength and guidance in the coming days and weeks. He planned to continue carrying me.

The lengthy and complicated esophageal surgery was a success and Gladys began a long recovery. The household continued to run in an efficient manner because George could cook and housecleaning wasn't beneath him. He delegated specific chores to each son commensurate with their abilities.

Several days after his mother's surgery, Butch walked into his bedroom after his daily visit to the hospital. Nearly tripping over the unpacked bag which stuck out from the foot of his bed, he muttered, "This darn thing is a hazard, it's about time I take care of it." He hefted it up on the bed. Opening the suitcase, he began methodically sorting his clothes when he came across a bulky sweatshirt uncharacteristically rolled up. And he remembered, I did this to keep it safe during that long trip. As he unrolled the shirt, his mind went back to Germany and a football banquet five months ago, well after the season had ended.

"I know you were all disappointed that the Freedom Bowl was canceled due to the untimely death of our Commander-in-Chief. We coaches were, too. We thought we had the talent and the will to beat the Army all-stars and bring home the trophy for the Air Force. Another time, another year. However, tonight's banquet is a celebration. You guys did one heck of a job not only this season but in the past two years in team building and strength training, both on offense and defense. We applaud you for those achievements."

Butch remembered every word as if it was yesterday. He remembered the meal, the atmosphere of camaraderie and the pride of being part of a winning team. His reverie continued.

"Now that your bellies are full, we coaches want to recognize the superlatives this season." One by one the outstanding players were called up to the podium, lauded for their performance on the football field and presented with a trophy. The coach turned to his audience once again and said, "There's one award left, and I'd like to say a few words about this player. This guy went from being on the practice team the first year to making the travel team for the next two years. It's an honor to coach someone with so much determination and heart for the game. He's one of the hardest working players we've ever seen. Without further ado, Airman Panko, come get your award for being the Most Improved Player for the 1963 season."

Butch's eyes misted over when he recalled the overwhelming feeling of surprise as he moved toward the front of the room as if in slow motion. The coaches were smiling and applauding, for him. The head coach handed Butch his trophy and shook his hand; the other coaches followed suit. He looked out over the room and saw his applauding teammates standing, for him. Butch swallowed the lump in his throat, but he couldn't wipe the goofy grin off his face as he made his way back to his seat. Teammates reached out to clap him on the back and congratulate him.

Butch shook his head, the sound of applause stopped, and he snapped back to the present. He held the trophy in both hands reading the inscription. He'd never be able to adequately describe that feeling to his family, especially when the sideboard in the dining room downstairs held Ron's football trophies and Joey's baseball trophies. Butch had only one, and it was going to stay in his room. Someday, maybe someone would ask about it. Someday, maybe he'd tell them about his football playing years.

Final separation from the United States Air Force came in July 1964. Butch returned to McGuire Air Force Base to complete the paperwork, making it official. His active duty obligation was completed.

On the weekends, Butch enjoyed taking Joey fishing as he had before he went in the Air Force. It gave them a chance to talk about school and anything else on the teen's mind. Ron had become a high school football star, and Butch enjoyed watching the team practice as the season approached. He looked forward to the spirited Friday night games under the stadium lights. It brought some nostalgic feelings about having missed the Freedom Bowl. Butch regretted that lost opportunity. More than that, he wished his dad could have seen him play football. He couldn't help but wonder if his dad would be as proud of him as he was of his younger brother, Ron.

The news broadcasters reported daily on the conflict in Vietnam. Exceedingly grateful he didn't have to serve in Southeast Asia, he let his mind wander to the men on that military transport which brought him home. He thought aloud, "God be with them."

With his mother on the road to recovery, Butch felt free to pursue a career. He concentrated on developing a strategy for finding a job and continuing his education.

> One day, instead of putting me in his pocket as he'd gotten used to doing each day, Butch picked me up from the top of his dresser and walked to his parents' bedroom. He knelt in front of the cedar chest, lifted the top and took out quilts and blankets to make a safe spot for me. Pausing a moment to contemplate not only the part I played in his life, but his father's as well, Butch silently offered a prayer of thanks and placed me in the bottom of the cedar chest.
>
> I was resigned to being put away. I'd done my job for another military man. I knew his heart and his faith. I had served another well. I could rest easy, for a while.

45

1965

A FAMILY OF HIS OWN

B utch began the interview process and found a job. He moved ninety miles south of Scranton to Allentown to pursue a career in business and finance. He continued working toward his degree availing himself of every educational opportunity offered through his employer.

It was there he met his future wife, Nancy. They married in 1965 and had two children. Their first-born, a daughter, Margie and then a son, Tim, added tremendous joy and fulfillment to the couple's lives and life was good.

> Now twenty-three years old, I rested in the cedar chest at his parent's home, awaiting the day I might be called upon to support and guide another person in this family.

> The day will come, I feel it in my spine.

46
1970's
LIFE GOES ON

B utch avidly followed the news about developments in Vietnam. For years, Americans acted in the capacity of military advisors like those combat troops who accompanied him on the flight from Paris to McGuire Air Force Base. He remembered their comments about Vietnam being a nasty conflict. He felt strongly that the US needed to "fish or cut bait." He was disturbed when President Lyndon B. Johnson committed combat troops to Southeast Asia in 1965 as the politicians micro-managed the war. Having been in the military, he knew politicians didn't know how to win wars.

Night after night, the evening news showed protestors in the street. In towns and cities across the country, families were split and alienated over the legitimacy of the undeclared war.

Ten years later, after declaring a cease-fire in 1975, the United States counted over 58,000 American troops dead and more than 300,000 wounded. The physical and social wounds of the country healed over time, but the nation would not easily tolerate another Vietnam.

Now a father, Butch deeply felt the sadness of so many young lives lost in an undeclared war. He hoped that it would never happen to one of his own.

In 1974, Butch, Nancy, and their young family moved to north central Pennsylvania, settling into a new home in Lock Haven, the home of the Piper Cub airplane. Everyone at Woolrich, Inc, the family-oriented company for which Butch worked, knew him as George.

The young family settled in becoming active in their small community while Butch established a name for himself in the thriving outerwear company.

The United States enjoyed peacetime for some years in spite of periodic isolated skirmishes in different parts of the world. Americans experienced economic prosperity and the abolishment of the draft.

> *I slumbered in the cedar chest among the quilts and blankets. Yearning to guide another military person, I felt up to the challenge in spite of my age. I knew of the unrest in the world and the growth of evil influences. I felt the day was coming and I wanted to be involved. The timing, however, was not up to me.*

> *All things in God's time.*

47
1980's & '90's
A New Breed of Enemy

"Mr. Gorbachev, tear down this wall!"

Butch had come home from work and was watching the 6 o'clock news. His ears caught President Reagan's line during his speech. It was June 12, 1987, and the U.S. leader was in West Berlin. "Nance, come here. You gotta listen to this."

A busy working wife and mother, Nancy was dusting a shelf unit in the adjacent room while dinner was cooking. She ran the soft cloth over her husband's football trophy and placed it carefully in the center of the shelf. Hearing her husband call, she ran into the TV room. "What's happening?"

He told her what the President had said in his speech. "I was stationed in Germany when that wall went up. I wonder how Gorbachev is going to deal with it."

The wall had divided West and East Berlin since 1961. That speech wasn't the only time Reagan addressed the Berlin Wall. Time and time again he asked the Soviet leaders, "Why is it there?"

"I just read in the paper yesterday that fifty thousand people demonstrated against Reagan's presence in Berlin. The government even sealed off large areas of Berlin hoping to suppress the protests. Something's going to happen here." He looked inquisitively at his wife. "What's for supper and how soon are we gonna eat? I'm kinda hungry."

She leaned down and brushed his cheek with her lips, "Your favorite meatloaf and mashed potatoes are just about done, Mr. Most Improved Player. Aren't you lucky I had off today and had the time to cook? How about getting washed up and coming to the kitchen in about five minutes."

He grinned and thought, "I'm such a lucky guy."

Several weeks of civil unrest in Berlin followed in July and August. On November 9, 1989, the East German government lifted the ban on travel between East and West Berlin. Crowds gathered at the wall and started chipping away at the structure taking chunks of it as souvenirs.

Butch saw it all on the news. "I can't believe I lived to see the wall come down." He stood watching film crews talk to people pounding away at the infamous structure. "I have goose bumps, Nance. Wow, does this bring back a lot of memories."

"I can understand. I have chills too, and I don't have the connection like you do. This wall coming down is history in the making, and it's an awesome step forward for the freedom of people in Germany. "Oh, by the way, we're going to the neighbors for dinner tonight. Frank got a deer, so Mary Beth is doing a venison roast with red skin potatoes."

"Oh boy, can't beat that with a stick. They know we love venison. What are we taking?"

"I made a green salad and just took a pound cake out of the oven. Why don't you pick out a bottle of wine and put it in the carrier? We have to be there at five o'clock."

Butch pondered his wine choice.

The German government brought in heavy equipment to tear down what remained of the infamous wall. By 1992, in its absence, the country was once again unified. Praise The Lord!

Also in the late 1980's, Butch began reading about a network of radical Islamic fighters known as al-Qaida under the leadership of a Saudi Arabian, Osama bin Laden. Born into a wealthy family, bin Laden used his wealth to recruit and train young Muslim Arabs to fight against the Soviet troops who invaded Afghanistan. At that time, these fighters were supported by the United States. They succeeded in ousting the Soviets from Afghanistan in 1989.

Butch thought at the time, "Good for them." He had no idea of the hell which would be inflicted on the United States at the direction of this man. Smug in that monumental success, bin Laden returned to Saudi Arabia.

In August 1990, every print and TV news outlet was covering the invasion of the tiny nation of Kuwait by Iraqi dictator Saddam Hussein who was also threatening Saudi Arabia in a dispute over oil, money, and land.

Nancy tossed and turned nightly, dreaming about the unrest in the world. "Are we going to get involved in this conflict?" Nancy asked her husband who could only shrug his shoulders.

Economic sanctions were imposed by the UN Security Council after the world body ordered Iraq to leave Kuwait. The world waited hoping sanctions would work to stop Hussein.

Meanwhile, the United States approached its political allies in the Middle East. They sought friendly territory for air bases from which to launch air strikes. King Fahd of Saudi Arabia responded by allowing additional U.S. forces to use their territory for air bases. President George H.W. Bush vowed to protect them from an Iraqi attack and sent armament and troops to the Saudis to discourage Iraq.

Osama bin Laden was becoming rebelliously outspoken. Angry that King Fahd allowed U.S. forces on Saudi soil, bin Laden believed Islamic law required the Saudis to support their fellow Muslims, the Iraqis. Placed under house arrest for criticizing the king, bin Laden escaped Saudi Arabia to the Sudan. There he continued to build up the radical terrorist al-Qaida network with plans to turn it against its new enemy, the United States.

Inspired by the show of force against Iraq, a large nation threatening a much smaller Kuwait, the classic good against evil scenario, many young men and women enlisted in the all-volunteer military. Patriotism in the United States surged, and yellow ribbons were displayed everywhere.

Both Panko men, former military veterans, understood this feeling. They, too, were thankful that Tim was still in high school and there was not another likely young man in the family to feel the pull to serve.

> I knew what was ahead and also knew their hearts would ache in a way never anticipated. Meanwhile, I lay dormant in the cedar chest as I aged gracefully. Although worn and tattered on the exterior, my insides were rich with timeless wisdom.

48
December 1990
Be All That You Can Be

Terry Owen Williams, nicknamed T.O., was no exception in feeling a surge of patriotism. He'd graduated with a Bachelor's degree in Criminal Justice from Penn State University, Allentown Campus, and was contemplating a career with the Pennsylvania State Police.

He remembered attending a job fair on campus where all branches of the military were present. T.O. had gathered information from each table. He had a deep respect for the military because many of his family members had served.

T.O. watched the television screen intently when President George H.W. Bush stood up against Saddam Hussein when he threatened Kuwait in December 1990.

Pamphlets were now spread out on the table before him, and one by one, they were tossed into a waste can until there was only one left. It said across the top, "Be All You Can Be." The slogan appealed to T.O. and had deep meaning for him at this stage of his life. He had the urge to enlist. He wasn't interested in becoming an officer; what appealed to him was the infantry. He knew all about hardships. He knew about being in the trenches of a tough life and, to him, the infantry was the embodiment of pushing through difficulties.

The yellow ribbons and TV coverage of the impending showdown spoke to him. He felt an overwhelming patriotic duty to be part of something bigger than himself. At twenty-two years of age, he was ready for adventure and up for any challenge. Having overcome many obstacles throughout his life, T.O. was bursting with confidence.

Visiting the Army recruiters was enlightening. He learned they would pay off his student loan debt, a huge incentive.

Holding his breath when it came time for his physical, T.O. hoped his complicated medical history wouldn't hold him back. It didn't. The Army physicians were not able to find deficits of any kind and were delighted to clear him. He sailed through the testing and enlisted in the Delayed Entry Program in December 1990. He didn't have to leave for basic training until April 1991. Meanwhile, the United States went to war in the Middle East inflicting "Shock and Awe" on Saddam Hussein's army.

Riveted to the TV screen, Butch and Nancy watched as the United States struck targets in Baghdad and Kuwait on January 17, 1991. All the regular TV programming had been interrupted with the breaking news.

The show of force was substantial and unrelenting, and by February 27, 1991, President George H.W. Bush declared a cease-fire. Coalition forces had achieved their clear objective by liberating Kuwait from Iraqi forces. Although tempted by the prospect of invasion, the President didn't want to risk a protracted war by going after Saddam Hussein.

> *I continued to rest in the cedar chest, among the blankets and quilts, knowing my time was near to be a guiding force once again. The Lord's will be done.*

49
1991

U nabashed news junkies, Butch and Nancy were becoming quite concerned with what was happening in the Middle East. Nancy fretted about her children who lived far from home in opposite directions. Twenty-four-year-old Margie worked in Pittsburgh, three hours away. Eighteen-year-old Tim was attending his first year of classes at East Stroudsburg University in the far eastern part of the state.

Nancy's fears were not unfounded. Perhaps she had an inkling of things to come.

The couple also dealt with concerns for Butch's parents. George now lived alone. His beloved Gladys had suffered a major stroke and was in a skilled nursing center. George had to be driven to dialysis treatments three times a week, and the role of overseer fell to Butch's youngest brother, Joey who lived in Scranton and worked on the railroad as a conductor. Butch and Nancy made the two and a half hour trip to visit his parents as often as their work schedules would allow.

With the help of the mass media, bin Laden's radical Islam was growing. Terrorists sought to destroy both secular and democratic-leaning societies.

Odd as it may seem, all of these world events were going to come into play for this family. My intuition told me I was going to be actively involved.

The atmosphere in Somalia on the Eastern coast of Africa in 1991 was downright hostile. Wracked by war among rival clans who interrupted the flow of goods and supplies, the country experienced a severe famine followed by the deaths of millions of people.

In the United States, organizations began collecting food to send to a starving nation.

Peacekeeping troops and humanitarian aid workers were confronted with a confusing array of clans and private armies squabbling over the distribution of food and supplies. It soon became apparent even the security guards hired to protect the convoys of food were competing over this cash crop. They began hijacking the U.N. supply trucks. The bandits sold the food on the black market for more than what it was worth.

When warring clans got in on the action, they used the proceeds to buy weapons and drugs. Food was a precious commodity, and it wasn't getting to the starving people who needed it.

The U.N. and private volunteer organizations resorted to hiring help from local tribal technical assistants, dubbed "technicals." Driving around in open bed trucks or land cruisers armed with machine guns or mounted heavy weapons, they were often high on a drug called "Khat" and contributed to Somalia's well-deserved reputation as a dangerous, lawless country.

> *I called upon The Almighty to stem the tide of this callous brutality. We could use a little bit of your "Shock and Awe," Lord.*

50
1992
A FATEFUL MEETING

After three months of basic and subsequent Advanced Infantry Training, T.O. showed tremendous talent in handling weapons. His superiors noted steady hands and accuracy in his shooting skills perfectly suited for a sniper. He remembered a time when it would not have been remotely possible.

T.O. advanced to Sniper School at Fort Benning. At the time of enlistment, he signed as part of a Cohort unit attached to the 10th Mountain Division. He wouldn't know which brigade or battalion to which he was assigned until the end of basic training. The Scout Platoon Leader and First Sergeant from Fort Drum, New York, traveled to Fort Benning to interview prospective candidates. Six men out of three hundred were hand-picked for the 2nd Battalion/14th Infantry Regiment. Decisions were based on scores throughout basic training and how each man handled himself during the interviews. It was an honor to be chosen. When T.O. learned he was one of the six, he was stoked.

In August, T.O. went home on 30-day leave. The Army had sculpted both his body and mind through basic training and sniper school. His mother, Anne, noticed the difference in him immediately. She was extremely proud of the man he had become. She and his younger sister Emma were thrilled to have him home for those thirty days. When he left to return to base, his mother wept at his departure. She only wished he could share his successes with his father who had left the family when T.O. was nine and Emma three. It broke Anne's heart.

In September 1991, T.O. arrived at Fort Drum in Watertown, New York. It didn't take him long to get acclimated to the base. He got into the routine of training, PT, road marches, field exercises, patrols, and shooting range time. The goal was to get all the new guys trained up to 2nd Battalion/14th Infantry Regiment (2/14) standards, so the brigade was combat ready.

When not training, the men had weekends off. During the summer months, many soldiers enjoyed going to Alexandria Bay, a picturesque tourist town on the American shore of the St. Lawrence River in upstate New York. Known by the locals and the soldiers from Fort Drum as A-Bay, it was about thirty miles from base and offered a variety of restaurants, bars, and clubs along the waterfront. Vacationers, summer residents, and soldiers frequently ended up together at any one of a number of hot spots in town enjoying the music, food, and drinks.

One night in late June 1992, Margie Panko met T.O. Williams at a noisy night club in Alexandria Bay. She spotted him from across the room. He stood head and shoulders above the others at the bar and was drop dead gorgeous.

Grabbing her cousin, Denise, by the arm she got up from the table saying, "Come on, we're going to the ladies room."

"But I don't have to go," Denise protested.

"Just be my wingman," Margie whispered with a sly grin.

"Ohhh, I get it." Denise popped up out of her chair and followed her cousin across the room. As they sashayed by the bar, Margie reached out and tapped the shoulder of the dreamy guy deep in conversation with another man. She kept moving toward the ladies' room. Did he feel the tap? She wasn't sure.

When they exited the restroom door, T.O. was leaning against the wall with his arms crossed. He had practiced the perceived "model" pose in his barracks room in front of the mirror.

Using a similar tactic stolen from a fellow soldier he'd observed weeks ago at the same club, T.O. nonchalantly flexed his biceps and said, "You tapped?" A slow smile spread across his face, and his eyes twinkled with mischief.

"Uh, I guess, really, I just, well, um, I don't know what you're talking about," Margie stammered, losing her courage.

"I'm pretty sure one of you ladies tapped me on the shoulder." Reaching up to rub the back of his neck, while remembering to flex again, he hoped he wasn't mistaken. Squinting his eyes, he tried to play it cool. Man, he hated being inexperienced at the flirting game.

"Seriously, we didn't."

"I think you did."

"Why do you think it was one of us?" Margie furrowed her brow. Denise took a cue from her cousin and furrowed her brow as well.

He was beginning to doubt himself, and his face turned red with embarrassment. An old familiar insecurity crept into his subconscious to mock him: "She'd never even give you a second look if she knew 'the real you.'"

He was brought back to reality when both girls started to giggle as their facade crumbled.

"It was you! You just gave yourselves away." His well-muscled arms dropped and he clapped his hands. "Bravo, good performance!" He banished his demon of insecurity. He wasn't the same person now.

Margie held both hands up as if in surrender. "Yeah, it was me, I'm guilty. I'm sorry. I'm not usually so forward; it's totally out of character for me."

Denise coughed violently. "I'm sorry, I have something caught in my throat, maybe a hairball. I need to see how the rest of the group is doing."

Margie thought it was sweet how much her cousin wanted to give her a chance to talk to this fine man alone. She gave her a signal letting her know she didn't need to run off just yet.

T.O. turned his attention to Margie and held out his hand. "Terry Williams, my friends call me T.O. I think we need to discuss this deplorable action." Attempting to maintain a scowl, he burst out laughing, unable to get his face to cooperate with the intimidating line.

Margie shook his hand, jumping slightly from the tingling sensation racing up her arm. "This, this, uh, is, is my cousin, Denise."

"Nice to meet you, Denise." Terry never took his eyes off Margie.

Taking Margie by the elbow, he steered her toward the bar. "Would you like a drink?"

Denise stood by herself as the couple walked away. She shrugged her shoulders muttering, "And the cheese stands alone." The wingman who had morphed into a third wheel turned to walk back to the table, but called over her shoulder, "We'll be watching." She couldn't wait to get back to her cousins, Angie, Julie, and Tim waiting patiently at the table for her report on the hook-up taking place.

T.O. and Margie began talking over drinks and hit it off immediately. It didn't take long for them to find out they both were from Pennsylvania.

"Are you here on vacation?" He was suddenly aware of his heartbeat. He thought he'd drown in her big, brown eyes.

She made him a little nervous, and he couldn't quite put his finger on what was happening.

"Yes, a special vacation." She felt herself blush. The tempo of the music picked up.

"Aren't all vacations special?"

She picked up her wine cooler and took a sip at the same time nodding her head in agreement. He was one of the most handsome men she'd ever seen. His olive complexion was highlighted by compelling green eyes, his rugged face framed by close cut dark hair. This man seemed unaware of his own appearance. He had leaned closer in order to converse over the loud music. She inadvertently held her breath.

He spoke into her ear. "Let me guess, you're staying at The Riveredge or the Edgewood." His mind was working overtime. "I know the area," he thought, "and those are the two most popular hotels, gotta be one of them."

"No, we're staying at Briar Bay."

"Never heard of it, is it in town?"

Over the increasingly loud dance music, Margie laughed, "It's our family summer home about ten miles north on Route 12."

"What's so special about this vacation?" He shifted on his barstool, and his knee was now touching hers. She flinched from his touch, feeling another electric shock.

"My grandparents are celebrating their fiftieth wedding anniversary this week. They wanted the whole family here to celebrate with them, all twenty of us. So yes, this vacation is special."

"Oh, now I understand. Are you and Denise here by yourselves?"

She laughed. "Hardly, I'm here with my brother and three of our cousins, including Denise. We're more like siblings than cousins. If one goes to A-bay, we all go to A-Bay."

She gestured to a table under a multi-colored neon sign of a dancer moving on the wall in sync to the pumping music. Her brother and their cousins were smiling and watching. They all waved, knowing full well they were making Margie and the handsome guy at the bar a little uncomfortable with the scrutiny.

"It's totally obvious I'm gonna have to get your brother's approval, not to mention those three ladies with him, if I want to spend more time with you." As he leaned even closer to Margie to see everyone on the opposite side of the room, he whispered in her ear, "You smell good." T.O. smiled and waved at her family at the table across the dance floor. He sat back not realizing the effect he had on her.

Margie had chills racing up her spine. She tossed her hair over her shoulder and gave a throaty laugh. "As far as approval goes, you'll have to get it from everyone at that table. And, thank you, my scent is Eau de St. Lawrence. I've been in the river all afternoon."

"Well, it's one I could get used to." He loved what he saw. Long, thick hair, beautiful smile, a musical laugh, a great set... "Hold up, buddy," he thought. "Get a grip."

"I like to see a close-knit family. It's something I want for myself someday."

"It's special; I can't imagine not having my cousins. Each one is more like a sibling. Do you have any brothers or sisters?"

"A younger sister, Emma. We're really close, even though she's a few years younger than me. She's still in high school."

Margie liked his response to her family. She had already guessed that T.O. was a military man by his haircut, "high and tight." She tilted her head. "What brings you to A-Bay?"

He smiled, showing beautiful white, even teeth, immediately making him more attractive. "I'm stationed at Fort Drum with the 10th Mountain Division."

"Oh, you're in the Army. What do you do?"

"I'm a sniper scout."

"Are you making it a career?"

"I'm not planning on it."

"What will you do when you get out?"

"There's not much job opportunity for snipers in civilian life, other than SWAT." He began, chuckling. "I have a criminal justice degree, and all the men on my mother's side of the family are in law enforcement, so it's almost predetermined that I join that brotherhood."

She was fascinated. "A sniper/police officer," she mused, "I'm sure he'd look good in any uniform." She smiled at the visual.

Her daydream was interrupted when he reached for her hand.

"Would you like to dance?" A slow song had started to play. He led her out onto the dance floor and held her close while they talked, laughed and swayed to the music.

She was attracted to this dark, handsome man. Shivering with pleasure, she put her arm around his neck as they danced slowly in a circle. Margie snuggled close to his chest and smiled. After a few indulgent seconds, she pulled back and lifted her chin to study his face. His voice interrupted her thoughts.

"You have a great personality," he blurted. "Oh, brother," he thought, "that sounded so lame." He smiled sincerely and tried to recover, "What I, I, mean is, I'm having a great time tonight. This trip to A-Bay, well, I've enjoyed meeting you and, uh, really, you do have a great personality."

"I bet you say that to all the girls, T.O.," she lightly teased. Being gullible was one of her greatest faults, and alarm bells were going off. She thought, "Pull yourself together, girl."

"Oh, boy," he mused, "if she only knew how little experience I've had with girls." He took a deep breath to relax and enjoy the moment.

Like her mother, Margie possessed a sixth sense that said T.O. felt something as well. She had to ascertain whether it was a true interest in getting to know her.

"It wouldn't have anything to do with a girl who has access to a family summer home on the St. Lawrence River, would it?" She needed to find out if they had more in common.

"Only in the sense that if you didn't have a family home here, you and I might not have met here tonight." The song changed, and the couple walked back to their seats at the bar.

"Do you like to fish?" she asked

"Are you kidding me? I love to fish. Are you telling me that you do?"

"Yep, my dad took me fishing for the first time when I was three. He taught me to bait a hook and I'm not afraid to take the fish off the hook." She stood a little taller having said that.

"I may have met my match," he said, grabbing his beer from the bar and taking a swig.

T.O. slipped into a momentary reverie of his boyhood. His troublesome symptoms had diminished significantly when he was fishing. It was one of the few times the demons inside of him quieted and he felt any peace.

That night, they had fun clubbing in A-Bay. T.O. enjoyed meeting Margie's brother and her three cousins. All of them shared a pizza at the end of the night. T.O. and Margie exchanged phone numbers and made plans to get together the following day.

The couple had made a love connection. They saw each other every day that week until it was time for Margie to return to Pittsburgh, where she lived and worked. Between Fort Drum and Pittsburgh, nightly long-distance phone calls allowed T.O. and Margie to get to know each other. Regardless of what T.O. shared about himself, Margie couldn't escape the feeling that he was holding something back.

51

August 1992
A Family Vacation plus Two

Late in August, Butch and Nancy returned to the summer home to visit her parents for a ten-day vacation. They were hoping to arrange a meeting with the man Margie talked about so much. After all, Fort Drum was only 45 minutes away. They planned to invite him for dinner and fishing sometime during the week-and-a-half they were going to be there.

On the second evening Nancy's mother, Mary, announced that there was going to be company for dinner. New neighbors had bought a house down the road and had accepted an invitation earlier that week. Nancy set the table for six, after struggling to put two contrary leaves in the small round table. At 6 p.m. they all heard a knock on the door.

Nancy's dad, Art, got up to answer the door, while Nancy and Butch wondered about meeting the new neighbors. But instead of two strangers, Margie and a tall handsome young man greeted them.

"What in the world? This has to be T.O.!" they chimed together.

Pandemonium broke out as everyone laughed and talked at the same time.

Margie hugged her parents. "Were you surprised?"

"Totally. We had no idea that you were coming. We really did think we were meeting the new neighbors."

Nancy turned to her mother. "Are we meeting new neighbors?"

"No, that was just an excuse for you to put two leaves in the table and set it for six people." Mary giggled at the deception and winked at her granddaughter. "We sure put one over on you."

"I'll say." Butch turned to his daughter. "Do you have vacation or are you just here for the weekend?"

"We both have a week of vacation, another surprise."

"Great, we look forward to having you both here with us." Nancy excused herself to help her mother put the finishing touches on dinner. Joyful laughter was heard coming from the other room as the women dished up the evening meal.

The ruse concocted by the young couple and Margie's grandparents had been executed beautifully. Art and Mary were delighted to be in on the surprise.

For the entire week, Butch and Nancy made an effort to know their daughter's new love interest. They could tell she cared deeply for the young man. Spending many hours on the boat fishing, talking over meals and relaxing on the river bank gave them a chance to size him up as a prospect for their daughter. They found themselves liking T.O. quite a lot. On the surface, he appeared sincere and respectful. It would seem his mother had single-handedly done a fine job in raising him. However, he was interested in their only daughter, which meant they needed to know him better.

When it was time to go home, everyone was reluctant to leave the riverside paradise. Margie and T.O. had driven in together, and she'd drop him off at the base in Watertown on her way back to Pittsburgh.

Margie teased him, "I'll slow down when we get to the base exit, and you can tuck and roll. How 'bout that?"

Everyone laughed at the visual.

T.O. thanked everyone for their hospitality. "I appreciate including me in your family vacation." He shook hands with Butch and hugged Nancy.

Art grasped T.O. by the shoulder. "You come back anytime you can get away from the base. It's only 45 minutes away. All you have to do is call to make a reservation for fishing and dinner."

T.O. smiled. He and Margie's grandfather had hit it off. They would never know how much it meant to him to be accepted. It felt good.

52

1992

T.O.'s Confession

One day T.O. called Margie from the base. "Do you have any plans for this weekend?"

"Only to clean my apartment and do my wash. Why?"

"I'd like to drive to Pittsburgh to spend the weekend. I need to talk to you about something important."

"I thought you were on field maneuvers this weekend. What happened?"

"They were canceled."

"Okay, back up a minute. What do you mean 'talk about something important?' Are you okay? Is there something wrong?"

"No, nothing's wrong, but before we take this relationship any further, there are things you need to know about me and my family that can't be adequately explained on the phone."

She was getting worried and wondered what could be so important. "Okay, I always look forward to seeing you. Can you at least give me a hint what this is about?"

"Here's your hint: I have to tell you about my childhood."

"Okay."

"It could affect any relationship I have."

"It sounds serious. I'm certainly curious, but I'll just have to wait until you get here. Be careful driving. I'll have pizza and beer here for late supper."

"Later, babe."

T.O. arrived on her doorstep in Pittsburgh Friday night just after eleven.

After having a few slices of pizza at the kitchen table, they settled themselves on the sofa. T.O. took a long draw on his beer. Margie turned toward him waiting patiently, hands folded in her lap.

T.O. felt as if he were about to jump into a deep, dark lake. He looked at the sweet expectant face next to him and began in a rush of words, "When I was five years old, my parents noticed me acting funny. They took me to our pediatrician who eventually referred me to a neurologist. By the time I was six, I was diagnosed as having a movement disorder and had been referred to a psychiatrist and a psychologist. I had a mess of tests and, long story short; every specialist agreed that I had Tourette Syndrome, obsessive-compulsive disorder (OCD), attention deficit disorder (ADD) and oppositional defiance disorder (ODD).

"Wow!" She was floored by the information. She grabbed a pillow and wrapped her arms around it on her lap. She saw T.O. through different eyes, as a troubled little boy and wanted to hold him in her arms.

"Margie, it was a mess of weird, changing behaviors which were confusing for me as a little boy, and a mounting challenge for my parents. It was extremely stressful for their marriage. Emma was a newborn and, there I was, a kid with all these weird issues."

Margie was wide-eyed, listening intently. She wanted to reach out to stroke his arm or hold his hand, but he had gotten up and started to pace. She adjusted the pillow instead.

"At first, the symptoms showed up as rapid eye blinking and sniffing. I had to sniff everything, and I couldn't control it. I was aware that I was different from other kids and I was so embarrassed. Just when I got used to those tics, others surfaced. I never knew what was coming. My parents and I felt helpless and scared."

Listening intently, Margie pulled one leg up underneath her. She bit her lower lip. Her eyes filled with tears.

T.O.'s words were spilling out as if a dam had burst. "It got so bad I couldn't function at school or home. We had multiple specialists involved and endless appointments, but finally found a doctor and a medication regimen that worked better than anything had before." He stood, raised his arms above his head taking in a deep breath, blowing it out slowly as he lowered his arms.

"Margie, I need a quick break." He called over his shoulder, "Let's put some music on."

She got up, striking a yoga pose to stretch her legs, walked to the stereo set and found a favorite smooth jazz station. She kept the volume low. The dulcet tones soothed her jangled nerves. She hoped it would help T.O.

"I like that." T.O. walked out of the bathroom bobbing his head in time with the silky music. He got another beer from the refrigerator and stepped toward a nearby chair. "Okay, where was I?"

Margie asked, "There's more?"

"Oh, babe, I've just begun. Fasten your seat belt; there's a lot more." He perched on the edge of the chair. "My mom was and is a saint! She became an expert on Tourette syndrome and kept a detailed journal on my changing symptoms. She met with teachers and counselors at each school I attended, educating them on my condition."

T.O. took a deep breath, swallowed hard and continued. "I was bullied, taunted, threatened, and even beat up on the bus and in school, every day. Mom was always fighting my battles."

Margie had tears in her eyes thinking of him as a little boy enduring this cruel treatment.

"My dad ..." T.O. looked up at the ceiling to stem the tears from flowing at the mere mention of his father. "He pulled away. I guess he couldn't stand the turmoil, the stress. He began smoking pot in the garage and staying out late. When Mom called him on it, all he could do was accuse her of not giving him time with his friends." T.O. made air quotes with his fingers. "It was such a copout. Mom begged him to go to marriage counseling. He refused."

Margie reached out to him.

He held up his hand. "I just need a minute." Music softly played in the background. With the back of his hand, he wiped at a tear trickling down his cheek.

"I'd sit on the stairs and listen to their arguments, over me. I thought if they didn't have me, this wouldn't be happening. Finally, one night he didn't come home at all. A few days later, he announced he wanted a divorce and was moving out." This time he couldn't wipe the tears away fast enough. They streamed down his cheeks. Margie got up and brought him a box of tissues. He blew his nose. Squeezing the bridge of his nose with two fingers, he held them there until he could talk again.

She put a gentle hand on his shoulder and spoke softly, "T.O., you didn't make your dad leave. There was a weakness in your father you had nothing to do with. He was escaping the responsibility of being a husband and father."

He got up from the chair and came closer to her sitting at the opposite end of the couch. "That may be true, but I felt the burden especially when I saw my father leave. I actually tried to stop him. I stood in the doorway with my hands on both sides of the jamb, but he just pushed me out of his way. I was screaming and crying, trying to make him stop and think about what he was doing to our family, but his face was a stone mask. My symptoms and behaviors got worse after that. I know now it was stress. Even a little kid can internalize a lot of stress, and it comes out in unhealthy ways."

"I got a whole new perspective on not having a father around when just a few years ago Emma and I were talking about Dad's leaving. She told me she doesn't remember Dad ever living at home with us. I was shocked. She didn't know what it was like to have an intact family. I was incredibly sad for her, but then I thought, if she doesn't know what it was like, then she doesn't miss it like I do."

Margie squeezed the pillow tighter as T.O. continued with his heart-wrenching story. She reached for a tissue and dabbed at her own eyes.

"My psychologist, Doctor Bryant, helped me through the next ten years. He made me feel safe, and I could tell him anything. I actually began to feel like I had some worth."

T.O. stood and began to pace again. "When I was ten, I wanted to kill myself."

Margie put her hands to her mouth, "Oh, my gosh!"

"Yep, I threatened to jump out of my bedroom window and was perched on the sill with the window open, both legs dangling outside. It was two stories up. I still have nightmares where I'm on the window's edge and see the fear on Mom's face. I remember telling her that I couldn't live with the tics and the bullying and I'd rather be dead. Mom yanked me off the window sill by the back of my pants; I landed hard on my butt. She dragged me into her bedroom so she could get to the extension phone to call my father. When he answered the phone, she begged him to talk to me. He wouldn't; told her to 'just handle it.' Can you believe it? He couldn't be bothered and basically told her, 'he's all yours.'" He stopped pacing briefly and shuddered at the memory.

"Mom was desperate. She called Doctor Bryant. He was super kind and calming, talking me down from my hysteria. He and I made a deal that I wouldn't ever do anything to hurt myself without talking to him first. Mom held me in her arms that night until I fell asleep. We went to see Doctor Bryant the next day."

Margie looked at the clock. It was 3 a.m. "T.O., it's late. This conversation has been exhausting, and you must be tired from driving."

He held up his hand, "I hafta finish, Margie. There's a reason for all this, and I'm almost done saying what I have to say." He sat down again and sighed deeply.

"When I hit puberty, everything changed. The symptoms were worse, no longer responding to the dose of meds I was on. The docs said my changing body chemistry, you know, those raging hormones turned everything upside down."

"Meanwhile, Mom found a behavioral therapist who was conducting a clinical trial on Tourette's patients. Mom signed me up for the three-month trial. Once a week, she drove me a hundred miles round trip to see this therapist. Mom worked a full-time job. I don't know how she did it." He got up and walked to the window. Pulling the curtains aside, he stared out at the pitch black sky.

"Well?"

"Well, what?" He was beyond tired.

"Did the therapy work?"

"Oh. Yeah, it did." He turned and walked over to his corner seat on the sofa. He sat but leaned forward with his elbows on his knees, his hands were clasped together. "I learned ways to control my tics and disguise them when they occurred.

It was amazing. He taught me deep breathing exercises and relaxation techniques and, miraculously, it worked."

"So they're gone?"

"Not entirely, but for once in my life, I felt as if I had some control. The docs reminded me that I could also be in the process of outgrowing the disorders."

"You can outgrow them?" She pulled her hair up to put it in a ponytail but changed her mind when she realized that she didn't have the familiar band around her wrist. Instead, she dropped her hair, letting it cascade over her shoulders again.

He watched her intently. He loved her long hair, and it temporarily distracted him. After a second or two, he focused.

"Kind of like outgrowing asthma, I was told. When Mom heard the doctors say that some kids outgrow the tics and twitches, she became a prayer warrior."

Margie had to smile at that. It was endearing to see T.O. appreciate his mom for all her efforts. She liked this man even more now.

He yawned. He was exhausted, but he had almost reached the surface of the water he'd dived into, three hours ago. "By the time I was twenty, all of my meds had been tapered successfully. But, I still needed my attention deficit med for me to focus in college. One day the doc asked us how we felt about discontinuing the rest of the meds on a trial basis. I could tell Mom was hesitant, but I was excited. I wanted to go for it."

"What happened?" Margie asked leaning forward.

"We followed the doctor's recommendation for tapering the meds. I began to develop a social life in college. My tics were nothing more than an eye blink or a shoulder shrug. Mom tells everyone she saw me blossom. I finished college, passed the Army physical and enlisted. Then I met you."

"Is that all you needed to tell me?"

"Not exactly." He hesitated and reached across the space between them to grasp both her hands. "I wanted you to know all this because I am falling in love with you; a grown-up, happily-ever-after love. I need you to know who I am and what I've been through."

She looked at him adoringly and whispered, "I'm falling in love with you, too."

He raised her warm hands to his lips and kissed them, one at a time. "It's something you need to think about. Anyone who loves me and becomes my wife needs to know the chances of our children inheriting these disorders and has to be prepared to deal with them." He was quite serious. "I really want you to consider everything I've told you." He pulled her close and kissed her tenderly. "I'll understand if you don't want any part of, of, this potential drama."

She cupped his face in her hands. "I promise I'll consider everything. Right now, we need some sleep, whaddya say?"

T.O. yawned again and nodded in agreement.

"I'm gonna brush my teeth and get ready for bed. I'll be right back." She rose and walked down the short hallway toward the bathroom.

"I'm just gonna rest my eyes." T.O. was spent. He put his head back on the sofa and closed his eyes.

When Margie came out of the bathroom, he was sound asleep. Margie carefully unlaced his shoes and gently slid them off his feet. She lifted his long legs, turned them and placed them on the couch. Covering him with a light blanket, she gingerly pushed a pillow under his head and kissed him on the cheek. He rolled onto his side, softly snoring.

She smiled and went into her room. She had a lot to digest.

On Sunday afternoon, T.O. returned to base. Their relationship had changed. It had grown richer, deeper and more meaningful to both of them and it looked like they had a future.

53
NOVEMBER 1992
A BIG SURPRISE

T.O. and Margie continued their long-distance courtship for five months.

The week after Thanksgiving, Butch and Nancy got a phone call.

"Hi, Mom and Dad! I have something important and exciting to tell you."

Each parent was on an extension. "Did you get a promotion? A raise?" They were anxious to hear the news.

"No, it's not about my job." She paused. "T.O. asked me to marry him."

"What? You haven't known each other very long." Her mother scowled into the phone.

Her father chimed in, "Since the end of June."

"I said yes."

"Why?" her father croaked, taken aback.

Both parents were surprised and dismayed, to say the least. Margie and T.O. had only spent a total of a few weeks together since meeting five months earlier. Alarm bells were going off.

"Are you sure about this?" Butch was starting to feel a little miffed because T.O. hadn't asked him for his daughter's hand in marriage. "He could have picked up the phone to talk to me," he muttered under his breath.

"Dad, don't grumble, it's going to be a long engagement. We aren't going to get married for two years. In fact, the date we're tossing around is August of 1994, after T.O. gets out of the Army. You asked why I said yes; it's simple because I love him!"

Her parents were coming to the realization that to resist their daughter's wishes was futile. The last thing they wanted to do was alienate her.

There was a thoughtful pause before her mother spoke. "We wish you all the best, honey. You're twenty-five years old, and we have to trust your judgement. The news just took us by surprise and, well, it seems like you just met." Nancy did her best not to convey her dismay.

"I'm happy, Mom. It's going to be fine." She was patient with her parents, knowing that they would feel some hesitation. "I've never felt this way about anyone. I want to have the same kind of marriage that you and Dad have."

The two people on the other end of the telephone line were silent.

She certainly knew how to seal the deal.

54
DECEMBER 1992
SAD TIMES

On December 16, 1992, Butch was in New York City on business when he got a message from his New York office to call Nancy at home.

He found an empty cubicle and an available phone line. When his wife answered, he could tell something was wrong. "Honey, I'm so sorry to say your dad has died." Although it was expected, the news caught Butch off guard.

"When?" Suddenly, his legs felt weak, and his heart was heavy.

"Joey just called from the hospital."

Ailing with kidney failure, his father had been on dialysis for the last three years.

Butch sighed and choked down the lump in his throat. In spite of years of anticipatory grieving, his father's deterioration and passing left him feeling sad and empty.

"Was Joey with him when he died?"

"Yes."

"I'm glad he wasn't alone." Butch sounded subdued. Having a minute to lay out a plan in his head, he instructed his wife, "I'm going to wrap up my business here and drive directly to Scranton to help Joey any way I can. I want to stop at St.

Patrick's Cathedral and say a prayer for Dad. It's not going to take long, and I have to pass the church on my way to the parking garage. I'll call Joey and tell him I'm coming. Have you told Margie and Tim yet?"

"They're the next two calls on my list."

"Give them both my love. I'm worried about Tim because he's in the middle of finals and Margie has to drive in all the way from Pittsburgh."

"It's okay, Butch. You concentrate on what you have to do. I'll deal with the kids. I'll remind Margie to drive safely, and I want you to do the same."

"Nance?"

"I'm here."

"I think Tim should stay and finish exams unless he doesn't have one on the day of the funeral. He can't afford to lose any ground, especially during finals. He can't have another bad semester."

"I understand. I'll talk to him, and we'll figure it out, okay?"

"Okay. I'll call you when I get to Scranton. Love you."

"Love you, too."

Butch quickly concluded his business in the city. He was glad he'd taken the ten minutes to stop at St. Patrick's because it gave him some inner peace and strength to sustain him for what was to come.

He drove directly to Scranton to meet Joey at the nursing home and together they broke the news to their mother.

Gladys was happy to see her two boys but became alarmed at the expression on their faces. When she heard the news, she lowered her chin to her chest and slowly began to moan. "No, no, no!" Lifting her head, she began to rock back and forth in her wheelchair howling like a wounded animal. Her once strong, handsome soldier, her protector, was gone. Her sons, the oldest and the youngest, stood at her side openly weeping with her.

Nancy called her children.

Margie could hear the emotion in her mother's voice. "Mom, something's wrong for you to call me at work in the middle of the day."

"Yes, sweetie, Grandpa Panko died this morning." She heard the intake of breath on the other end of the line and then soft sobbing. "He passed away in his sleep and wasn't in pain."

In an instant, Margie pulled herself together. "Mom, I can leave work now. I was going to Watertown for the weekend and already have my suitcases in the car. I'll drive to Lock Haven and pick you up, and we can drive to Scranton together."

"Sounds like we're on the same page. Dad sends his love and wants you to travel safely."

"I will, I promise."

Nancy made the second call after taking a deep breath and wiping the tears from her eyes. Tim was in the middle of finals at East Stroudsburg University. This was going to be hard for him to hear. She was relieved when her son answered the phone.

"Hi, honey, I'm calling with some sad news about Grandpa Panko.

Tim felt a foreboding. "Oh no! What is it, Mom?"

"He passed away this morning. Uncle Joey was with him."

"I'm sorry, Mom." His voice was shaky with emotion. "I, I don't know what else to say. How's Dad taking it?"

"Dad is focused on finishing business in New York and getting to Scranton. He's grieving in his own way, but glad

Grandpa isn't suffering anymore. Dad and I are concerned about you missing exams. What's your schedule for the next couple of days?"

"I had one final today, two tomorrow and two the day after. My study group is intense, Mom. I'd like to be with the family for Grandpa's funeral, but it means I'd have to get a deferral for exams and take them the beginning of next semester. I don't know how I'd do then. I've worked really hard to be more prepared this time. I know I have to do better than last semester or Dad won't pay for any more school."

"Well, Tim, I think Dad and I can make it a little easier for you. We talked about this scenario just a little while ago and we both feel you should stay there and finish exams. Grandpa would want the same. He was so proud of you and what you're doing in school."

"Okay, Mom, thanks. I love you and give my love to Margie, Dad and the rest of the family. I'll see them soon."

"I will. Love you too, sweetheart."

She hung up the phone and started making a mental list of all she had to pack. Margie would be there in less than three hours. Pulling the suitcase out of the closet, she started grabbing clothes to pack. December 16th was a sad day. It was going to be one somber holiday season.

Oh Nancy, you and Butch have no idea how emotional the holidays are going to be.

55
DECEMBER 19, 1992
AN UNUSUAL REUNION
AND A FUNERAL

Having met with his brother Joey and the funeral director, Butch was satisfied with the simple arrangements they had made for their father. The boys knew their mother would agree. Wanting to relax, if possible, before the viewing that night, Butch drove the short distance to the house, still his father's house, in which he lived as a child. He felt the huge knots in his neck and shoulders start to release. He was home.

Unlocking the back door, he stepped into the kitchen. Sadness permeated the house. It was starkly quiet. There were no delightful aromas of his dad's freshly baked bread or homemade *pierogies* waiting to be tasted and savored. He felt his parents' absence more than ever.

Gladys remained a resident in a nearby skilled nursing facility. Before his most recent hospitalization, George had remarkably managed to visit his beloved wife on the days he didn't have kidney dialysis.

The house was chilly, prompting Butch to adjust the thermostat up. He made a mental note to remember to turn it down again when they left the house the next day. As Butch continued to wander through his boyhood home, he gazed at pictures displayed on the sideboard and the walls.

A usually stoic guy, he was surprised to feel tears well up and trickle down his cheeks.

Butch took his bag upstairs to the master bedroom, his parents' room, and set it down on the worn rug. He looked around the familiar room, remembering how his mother used to paint it a new color every year before she had her stroke.

He recalled their voices, "Glady, we never have to worry about this house falling down, it has three 'hunderd' coats of paint to hold it together."

He remembered that his mother would always giggle and answer, "Hush, George, I want this new color for spring (or summer or fall)."

The thought of their banter made Butch smile. He heard car doors closing and went downstairs to see if Nancy and Margie had arrived. Wiping the tears from his face, he poked his head out of the storm door to see who was there. He saw his girls running to him across the porch. Then the three of them stood silently, sharing a tearful embrace.

A shooting star streaked across the navy blue sky.

When the family entered the kitchen, the same feeling of sadness enveloped the girls as it had Butch.

"It's not the same without Grandpa and Grandma here." Margie's chin quivered, and tears rolled down her cheeks. She sniffled into a tissue.

Butch helped carry their bags upstairs.

Once again in the master bedroom, Butch noticed the old cedar chest. It had been moved from the foot of the bed to underneath the window. He made a mental note to look inside for anything important. He wondered if the prayer book he and his dad had carried was still kept there. They were on a tight schedule that evening, and he looked over his shoulder at the chest as if to say, "I'll be back later."

"Let's go, ladies, we've got to eat something and get to the funeral home." Obediently, they followed him down the stairs and into the kitchen.

He was so close to me and yet didn't open the top of the chest. I know he'll come back for me. Butch was aware of the bond his father and I had. I hope Butch felt that same bond as well. I've been waiting for a long time to be set free again.

Butch, Nancy, and Margie sat down at the kitchen table. They gave thanks for the food in front of them. Conversation resumed as they opened the tightly-wrapped sandwiches that the girls picked up at a hoagie shop. With the first bite, each of them realized how hungry they were and talking ceased. When the sandwiches were gone, they cleaned up and left the house to meet Joey and Ron and their families at the funeral home.

Everyone arrived promptly at 7 p.m. The funeral director was doing the family a huge favor in expediting the services to accommodate work schedules and travel for those coming from out-of-town. Gladys arrived in the nursing facility's handicapped equipped van. Her boys helped maneuver her wheelchair out of the vehicle and up the ramp into the funeral home. She broke into tears seeing her still handsome husband lying in his casket. With her good arm, she stroked his hand.

George had suffered through three heart attacks and three years of dialysis. The once strong, agile soldier had grown frail and sick. He had known his time was coming.

In the greeting area, the family recalled many funny stories, and shared tender memories of a loving father, grandfather and war hero. It was certainly cathartic to be together sharing hugs and tears. Gladys sat in her wheelchair parked next to the coffin; she would not leave her husband's side.

The nursing home van arrived to return Gladys to the facility, the driver promising to have her back in the morning for funeral services. The rest of the family retired to their respective homes or hotels to get a good night's rest.

The 9 a.m. Mass was held at the neighborhood church to which George and Gladys had belonged for decades and where George was a Eucharistic minister and altar server.

Before the service, Butch went upstairs to his parents' bedroom to get his coat and tie. A brilliant ray of sunshine bounced off the top of the cedar chest, reminding him to look inside for the prayer book. He crossed the room, knelt down and carefully lifted the lid. His mother kept everything in the cedar chest. He found handmade quilts, bedding, and family pictures.

Butch was worried that it wouldn't be there. He was the last one to carry the prayer book, and he'd put it back in the cedar chest after his mother's surgery in 1964. Lifting the quilts aside, he spotted the familiar military missal, the one his father always referred to as his soldier's Bible. Reaching down to pick up the tiny book, he found stuck to it a crumpled, worn citation for a Bronze Star issued to his father for heroism in action during the Battle of the Bulge. The rest of medals, awards and citations were missing. Where were they?

> Oh my, after all this time I see the light of day. I'm not sure what's happening, but there certainly is change in the air. It's better than the aroma of moth balls. Butch is picking me up. He's got plans for me, I can feel it down my old spine. This is a reunion with Butch for which I've been waiting. At fifty years of age, I look a little rough around the edges, but my pages hold the timeless Word of God.

Butch sat back on his heels. "I remember seeing those medals years ago. Where would Mom or Dad have put them?" He bent over the cedar chest once more to see if they were in a corner when he remembered something. "Mom used to hide some things in shoe boxes in her closet. Could she have put them on that top shelf to keep them out of the hands of little boys?" After unsuccessfully sweeping the cedar chest one more time, he got up and walked over to his mother's closet. Reaching up on the shelf to take down the few shoe boxes stacked neatly to one side, he lifted the lid on each box, one by one until he hit pay dirt in the last box. "I was right! Here they are, all Dad's medals and souvenirs from France, Belgium, and Germany." He tucked the special box under his arm, walked out of the closet to his suitcase, opening it to make room for the box of medals. He felt immense relief having found them.

Butch went downstairs with the fragile missal gently cradled in his hand. In the kitchen, he searched for a plastic zip bag. Carefully placing the fifty-year-old prayer book in the bag, he sealed it and put it inside his jacket pocket. In another plastic bag, he put the smoothed-out bronze star citation, tucking it in another pocket. Finally, he remembered to turn down the thermostat and take out the garbage. Leaving the house by the back door, Butch locked the door and paused a moment to take a last look.

Memories flooded his mind as he peered through the pastel ruffled cafe curtains he'd helped his mother hang years ago. He swallowed hard, blinked back the tears and picked up the suitcases on the porch. The eldest son left his boyhood home and, with bags in hand, walked slowly to his girls waiting for him in the driveway.

Butch and Nancy hugged their daughter tenderly before she got seated in her car and drove out of the driveway for Watertown, New York. T.O. was being deployed to Mogadishu, Somalia, in the Horn of Africa and Margie knew where she had to be.

They stood waving as the car drove over the crest of the hill. Margie had struggled with the decision not to attend her grandfather's funeral. Her parents insisted she drive in daylight when weather wasn't a factor. She had a four-hour trip ahead and they worried about her safety. They reminded her Grandpa Panko, a former infantry scout, would have understood the circumstances.

Butch and Nancy got in their car and left for the church and the funeral services. The presence of the familiar missal in his pocket was a comfort. It was something only he and his father had shared and certainly brought them together spiritually, today more than ever.

The ache of sadness in Butch's heart was acute. He needed the comfort of his father's prayer book in his pocket today for more than one reason. December 19, 1992, was a day Butch would never forget. He attended his father's funeral and left his childhood home for the last time.

Butch, I understand why you got me out of the cedar chest. You needed comfort, support and spiritual guidance. Heavenly Father, bless this man who's bidding farewell to his father.

Blessed are those who mourn, for they shall be comforted.

56

DECEMBER 19, 1992
AN EMOTIONAL ROLLER COASTER

T wo weeks earlier—
Margie called her mother from Pittsburgh.

"How are you, honey? How's work? What's new with T.O.?"

"I'm okay; work's okay. Everything's fine. Well, not everything. T.O.'s being deployed to Somalia, in East Africa."

Nancy could hear the change in her daughter's voice. "Oh, my gosh. How soon?

"They're supposed to leave December 21st. He's part of a Quick Reaction Force, QRF, for short. You've seen the news of the starving people on the news. The blue helmets, the UN forces, are being regularly attacked by bandits and militants who steal the food."

"That doesn't sound good."

"You're right Mom; it could be dangerous. The President named it Operation Restore Hope. Supposedly, it'll be a mission to protect the distribution of food stores to the people who need it. But T.O. tells me that it's deteriorated to firefights and all-out assaults on the UN forces. It could be a dangerous mission."

"I hope the forces are prepared for that."

"Yeah, Mom. Me too."

"Gosh, Margie, are you going to get to see him before he leaves?"

"Well, that's kind of why I called. You know we've made all these plans for a big wedding and reception when T.O. gets discharged from the Army in August 1994?"

"Yes, I do. I have the wedding notebook started, and each page is …"

"Mom, stop a minute. I'm trying to tell you something. When T.O. got his deployment orders, we started talking about getting married before he leaves."

"You're kidding. Margie, there's no time. We can't put it together. There's no time to get everything we need."

"Mom, stop! We talked to a priest on base about marrying us at the chapel, but he wouldn't do it on such short notice."

Nancy thought to herself, "Oh, thank God."

Margie continued, "There are a lot of risks to a deployment where the people are shooting at you. A fiancé doesn't have survivor benefits and, well, we've decided to get married by a Justice of the Peace in Watertown."

"What? Oh my gosh!" Nancy wanted to scream, No!

"Mom, I want you and Dad to be there. T.O.'s calling his mom, too."

"Of course, of course, we'll come. You're our only daughter; we could never miss something so important. But what about all the plans we started for the church wedding and big celebration afterward?"

"Somehow, I knew you'd ask me that. We want to have our marriage blessed in the church and throw a big party afterward. I promise we'll get to carry out every single thing in that wedding notebook you've been working on. We'll have more than one thing to celebrate; we'll also be toasting T.O.'s homecoming and Army discharge."

"So when is this, this elopement with parents going to take place?"

"Next weekend."

Nancy echoed, "Next weekend?"

"Yep, December 12th. I know it's soon. But, they are supposed to deploy on the 21st. Don't worry; it will all come together. Have faith, Mom."

As fate would have it, Mother Nature delivered a surprise. White fluffy snow began falling in Pittsburgh on Thursday, December 10th and by Friday, December 11th, the city was blessed with three feet of the stuff. Impassable roads in all areas of Pennsylvania and New York prevented any of the family from traveling.

Undeterred, Margie and T.O. announced the family elopement was the following weekend, December 19th.

> Little did she know that her grandfather would take a turn for the worse in early December and pass away on December 16th. I sensed her grief even though the family had all watched him suffer for more than three years. She was "Grandpa's girl," the first born grandchild. Night after night, I heard George pray for her. He'd done this from the time she was born.

When Margie found out her grandfather's funeral service was on December 19th, she cried. "Mom, what'll I do? I just can't call off our wedding. T.O. and I need to be married before he leaves. I sound so selfish, don't I? I'm sorry, I'm just so conflicted. Would Dad be upset if I missed the funeral?"

Nancy needed to be honest. "Calm down, honey. I believe that your grandfather would not want you to change your plans. You know how much he loved you. He's gone now. You spent time with him while he was alive when he knew you were there. You may get some criticism from your uncles, but these circumstances are unique, and your father and I will handle your uncles."

With her guilt put aside, Margie gathered with everyone to attend her grandfather's viewing and have dinner with the entire family afterward. Her aunts, uncles, and cousins all wished her well on her wedding journey.

The drive to Watertown the next morning was difficult. Margie shed some tears at first, but the closer she got to her destination, she smiled in joyful anticipation of being with the love of her life.

> I was awaiting a new assignment and contemplated 1 Corinthians 13:7, *Love bears all things, believes all things, hopes all things, endures all things.*

December 19, 1992, the day of her grandfather's funeral was also the day of Margie's marriage to Terry Owen Williams.

57
December 19, 1992
You Lift Me Up

For Butch and Nancy, the four-hour drive to Watertown after the funeral was a quiet one. They were both emotionally drained. Each was lost in their thoughts about the events of the past week and worried about their daughter's emotional fragility. After all, T.O. was deploying to a dangerous, war-torn country.

Nancy broke the silence. "I feel the weight of the world on my shoulders right now." She paused, "Even though Dad's been failing for years, I feel a kind of heart-wrenching sadness. It's the end of an era. What's more, I feel the same for Margie and T.O. with this deployment hanging over our heads. It's overwhelming."

Butch could only say, "I know." He felt it too. He had a hard time finding words to express his thoughts, but his wife never did. She could always put things in perspective and translate them into words. He envied that ability.

Nancy continued to sort out her feelings verbally. "I know I've got to put the doom and gloom aside if I'm going to support Margie right now. I can only pray the Lord gives me grace and strength to do it."

Butch responded succinctly, "Me too, Nance."

She began to hum the familiar hymn, "On Eagle's Wings."

Nancy Panko

It was therapeutic.

T.O. was going to be a part of operation Restore Hope; an admirable mission, but growing increasingly dangerous. He was slated to deploy in two days. I was in Butch's pocket, hearing this conversation. I felt intense emotions swirl around the interior of the vehicle. I wanted so much to be able to console this couple and tell them these feelings would pass and they would feel a sense of peace someday. I wanted to feel useful once again.

58

December 20, 1992
Passing on a Family Treasure

Arriving at the motel in Watertown, Butch and Nancy had an hour to unwind before getting ready for the ceremony. They unpacked, hanging their clothes for the wedding in the closet. Stretching out on the bed, they both fell asleep. The last two weeks had taken a physical toll on both of them.

> Later, while dressing for the ceremony, Butch reached for the plastic bag containing the missal. He hesitated, gazing at me through the plastic, then carefully placed me on the top of the dresser. I was aware that my usefulness was not yet over. Although I was fifty years old, tattered and worn, there was still a plan for me. Obviously, Butch had something in mind. Do I have a new charge or don't I? What gives, Butch?

A knock on the door startled him.

"I've got it." Nancy stepped out of the bathroom and opened the door to a radiant bride-to-be. Margie beamed.

"Hi sweetie, come in. We're almost ready." There was a catch in her voice when she realized her only daughter was going to be married within the hour. "You look absolutely stunning." They embraced, and a tear escaped from Nancy's eye. She brushed it away, not wanting the emotional dam to burst.

Margie wore an off-white wool pleated skirt and a matching silk blouse. Simple jewelry adorned her ears and neck. Her long hair was pulled back and fastened with a rhinestone clip at her neck. She radiated joy.

"I'm excited, but a little nervous. Do I look like a bride?"

Butch looked at his daughter and, with a huge lump in his throat nodded his head. "Yes, you have that bridal thing going on." He waved his hands in the air as if that would help him find adequate words, finally giving up and saying, "And you look beautiful."

"Margie, we want only the best for you and T.O.: a long and happy life together. Today is just the beginning of that time, and I know neither of you is thinking much beyond this deployment. However, just as the Bible says, 'This, too, shall pass.' You'll get through this with the help of the Good Lord. Trust Him."

With that, he helped each of his girls into their coats, and the three of them left the hotel for the short ride to the Justice of the Peace.

The civil ceremony took place in the home of a judge near Fort Drum. In a lovely room, warmed by the glow of fire emanating from a large fieldstone fireplace, the couple nervously waited while the judge donned his black robe. Margie had taken her mother aside to ask if she'd be the Matron of Honor. Nancy tearfully accepted and stood in front of the fireplace as directed by the judge. T.O.'s mother, his little sister, Emma and some of T.O.'s army friends stood around the perimeter of the room.

Mysteriously, Butch and Margie disappeared while T.O. stood next to the judge with his best man, Bart. The judge began to hum the wedding march, and all heads turned to follow the judge's smiling gaze. Butch and his lovely daughter entered the room from the kitchen doorway, arm in arm.

Margie wanted the honored tradition of being "given away" by her father woven into the hastily-put-together wedding ceremony.

The event was over in less than fifteen minutes. After signing the required paperwork, the judge and the young couple posed for pictures in front of the fireplace, followed by more poses with family and friends. Lasting memories were captured on video.

The newlyweds and their parents adjourned to a restaurant overlooking the St. Lawrence River, now frozen over in its winter splendor. No one talked about deployment. The group drank champagne and ate wedding cake, hopeful conversation filling the air with the couple's plans.

In the morning as he dressed for the day, Butch reached for me again. I knew something special was in the wind. I'm ready for any mission, Butch.

The families met for breakfast at a nearby restaurant. Everyone feigned normalcy, even though they knew an emotional parting was imminent. T.O.'s mother showed the strain; her eyes were red-rimmed and shimmered with tears. Sixteen-year-old Emma nervously fidgeted and frequently wiped her face with a tissue.

Butch and Nancy were quiet, anticipating having to support their daughter. The last few weeks had left them emotionally drained and, once again, their hearts were breaking as they expected a heart-wrenching parting. Even Butch, usually stoic and calm, had a lump in his throat.

After breakfast, they adjourned to the parking lot to say final goodbyes. It was a bright, sunny winter day that belied the swirling emotions. Margie was already sobbing and it was decided that Nancy should drive Margie's car for safety's sake. T.O., his mother, and Emma bid each other an emotional goodbye. Tissues were being passed from one person to another. Butch and Nancy waited their turn to address their new son-in-law. Butch retrieved the missal from his pocket.

It was then I was certain I was being passed to another soldier. The tradition would be carried on as I, the military missal, was carried within the uniform of the newest family member. Yes! The word of the Lord between my covers would guide, protect and support him.

Butch chose his words carefully while weaving his way through an emotional minefield. "T.O., my father carried this military missal during World War II. He called it his soldier's Bible. He was convinced the prayers and scriptures in this book guided his every decision and every step." Butch found it difficult talking about this special book and its history less than five days after his father had died. He lowered his voice and continued, "Dad told me this was in his combat jacket pocket from basic training until he came home in 1945. He gave it to me when I enlisted in the Air Force, and because he carried the missal, I did too. I believe this prayer book is unique; my dad did too. I feel the word of God bestowed a kind of holy armor on us, protecting us from harm. I know it sounds strange, but both Dad and I experienced it."

He handed me to his new son-in-law. T.O. had tears in his eyes as he realized what a special moment this was. His father wasn't there to offer words of encouragement or to give him a military missal, but his new father-in-law accepted the honor willingly. I felt a charge of love and respect surge through me at the moment both men had their hand on me.

"My dad was a fellow army scout. I know he'll be watching over you." Butch cleared his throat. The next statement carried an emotional impact: "I want you to bring this missal back to me."

The two men embraced and tried, unsuccessfully, to hold back the tears.

"I'm honored to be the next one to carry this prayer book. Thank you for trusting me with it." T.O. carefully folded the plastic bag and placed the missal in his pocket.

> The prayers within my pages gave each former soldier a sense of the power of the Lord. Please, T.O., let me do this for you as well. You're the third link in this family chain. I'll guide you when you're frightened and give you hope of returning home. It's not about you taking care of me; it's about my role as a conduit for the power of the Lord to take care of you.

Nancy tearfully embraced T.O. "Welcome to the family. You know what that means?"

"No, what does that mean?"

"You'll have lots more family praying for your safe return." She hugged her new son-in-law tightly. Tears squeezed their way out of tightly closed eyes and spilled down her cheeks. "God bless and keep you." She released her grip and stepped back to make way for her daughter.

Butch and Nancy started walking toward the car to give the newlyweds some privacy as they said good-bye. He was scheduled to deploy the next day, December 21, 1992.

The couple embraced until T.O. pulled away. "It's time to go, sweetheart. I love you."

Margie sobbed softly and placed her hand over his heart. "I will love you forever."

These same words had echoed across the decades from another tearful parting in 1944.

Arm in arm, T.O. walked his wife to the passenger side of Margie's car. He opened the door for his bride. She lowered herself into the seat, swung her legs around and fastened her seatbelt. She reached for his hand and kissed it, then held it against her cheek. T.O. leaned down for one last lingering kiss. He gently closed the car door as Margie rolled down the window.

"I love you."

"I love you, too," she sobbed.

He stepped back and waved.

Nancy started the car and negotiated the vehicle out of the parking lot onto the highway, Margie pressed her hand against the window until she could no longer see T.O. With the radio playing in the background, the women drove. Neither spoke. Margie wept softly off and on for the next five hours.

That night she spoke to her new husband on the phone until he had to relinquish the phone. Exhausted, she cried herself to sleep.

59
DECEMBER 24, 1992
STAND DOWN

The newlyweds spoke on the phone several times the next day. T.O.'s unit had not yet deployed. He insisted he had no idea what was happening. For the next two days, they wondered when the proverbial ax was going to fall.

Margie complained, "This is torture! It's the day before Christmas Eve, you're still in the States, yet you can't come home, and I'm not allowed to visit you. I wish they'd let you know what's happening."

Christmas Eve morning, T.O. called while Margie was out doing some last minute shopping. Nancy answered the phone.

"Hi and Merry Christmas. Our unit has been ordered to stand down."

"What does that mean, 'stand down?'"

"It means we aren't leaving. Deployment has been delayed and they're giving us two weeks leave."

"Two weeks leave? When?"

"Starting now."

"How soon can you leave base? Are you packed to come home, I mean here, for civilian life?" She was so excited for her daughter, she was beside herself. She could barely finish a sentence.

"I don't want to interrupt your holiday plans," he stammered.

"Are you kidding me? Buddy, you just married into the family. Your wife is here, and you're gonna be part of this family's whole crazy holiday celebration."

Holy mackerel, he sure is a green newlywed. He hadn't gotten the family thing down yet.

She shook her head in disbelief and laughed. "Yes, you can come here; you and Margie are married. Our home is your home."

"I want to surprise her. I'm just about ready to leave. I can be there in about five hours. Can you keep the secret?"

"You bet I can! I love surprising my family and I promise I won't slip up."

"Oh, by the way, what's for dinner?" He laughed, knowing his mother-in-law would get a kick out of him asking. Even though they hadn't known each other that long, T.O.'s asking "what's for dinner?" was a running joke between the two of them.

"Roast 'beast,' smarty pants. Be careful driving; we'll be watching for you."

For the next five hours, Nancy and Butch were bursting at the seams, keeping the secret. They kept a watchful eye on traffic on the road, waiting for a blue truck to appear. When T.O. pulled into the driveway, Nancy quietly opened the door to let him in.

Margie was in the bathroom applying makeup for Christmas Eve church services. Nancy pointed down the hall to the bathroom door. T.O. approached the door and knocked.

Thinking that it was one of her parents, Margie said, "Come in."

When she didn't open the door, he knocked again.

Margie hollered out, "Come in."

To get her to open the door, he knocked again. His strategy worked. The door flew open.

Nancy heard a loud gasp and watched her daughter become airborne as she flew into her husband's arms.

"Did you go AWOL?"

He laughed. "No. Our unit was ordered to 'stand-down.' We're not being deployed to Somalia right now."

She started crying and buried her face in his chest. "Thank you, God." Happy tears coursed down her face, streaking the freshly-applied makeup.

"The best part is, I'm home for Christmas," He paused and looked her in the eyes. "And, I have two weeks' leave."

She squealed in delight. Despite the tears, there was no happier couple that day. Evening Mass was a celebration of praise and gratitude.

Christmas of 1992 was transformed from sadness to great happiness and much thanksgiving. The newlyweds spent the holidays with both their families, treasuring the memories of their first Christmas together. The gifts under the tree were secondary to the gift of this couple having more time together. God is good!

> T.O. carried me in his pocket, and I was witness to this lovely reunion. I recalled the words of Psalm 98:4, *Sing joyfully to the Lord, all you lands; break into song; sing praise.*
>
> I knew that hard times were coming and these cherished holiday memories would help sustain both of them.

60

January 1993
Competitions and Awards

At the end of his two-week leave, it wasn't easy for T.O. to return to Fort Drum. But knowing it was only a matter of time before he'd be deployed to Somalia, he forced himself to get back into the daily training routine. His shooting range practice paid off as he was chosen to participate in two separate 18th Airborne Corps sniper competitions at Fort Bragg, North Carolina.

> It was hard for me to believe that this young man had once been diagnosed with Tourette syndrome and all the accompanying disorders with the shooting skill he was demonstrating.

During the contest, the two-man teams competed in several events including, among other things, a sniper stalk, urban shooting and orienteering exercises, firing under stressful conditions and other tests of marksmanship and sniper skills. Each man created a ghillie suit from moss, leaves, twigs and other camouflage materials worn during one phase. To stay invisible in a ghillie, one has to look like a clump of grass or moss. During the event, a sniper must get from point A to point B, get off a shot undetected, and hit the target. To make things more challenging, other soldiers walk the fields, trying to find the sniper. It takes practice, skill, and patience.

In the first match, T.O.'s team placed second; in the subsequent one, his team took first place. First place came with an automatic invitation to attend an All Army sniper competition. In that prestigious competition, their team took second place.

The Command Sergeant Major of the 10th Mountain Division went to North Carolina for the awards ceremony. Noticing the absence of airborne wings on T.O.'s uniform, the senior ranking NCO approached him afterward. "Specialist Williams, report to my office when you return to Fort Drum, and I'll personally see you schedule an airborne school date."

T.O. responded crisply, "Yes, Sergeant Major." The prospect of airborne school and wearing those wings was exciting. Besides, as a bonus, this school might delay his deployment to Somalia. That would save his new wife a lot of anxiety.

Boy did that thought sound familiar to me, echoing back from 1944.

As he sought out division headquarters once he was back on base, T.O. was excited about another adventure—airborne school. Entering the office, T.O. asked for the sergeant major.

An aide quietly took him aside, "The sergeant major unexpectedly dropped dead of a heart attack while on a PT run this morning. I'm sorry."

T.O. left division headquarters shocked and disappointed. He thought, "Wow, he was a fit soldier. Nothing like bringing the subject of life and death to the forefront of your mind." The 10th Mountain Division had lost a good man, but T.O. felt even worse for the man's family. What a shock.

T.O. had missed his connection to the much coveted airborne school but had been jarred into thinking about his mortality. Putting those feelings aside, he went back to his routine of training and preparing for deployment.

I knew the outcome before he did. I'm sorry, T.O., but your experience in Somalia will keep the thought of your mortality in the forefront of your mind. And it will repeatedly test your faith.

61

Early Summer 1993
A Deteriorating
Humanitarian Effort

N ancy and Butch were looking at a map of Africa.

"Here's Mogadishu, Somalia, on the eastern coast. No wonder this area is called the Horn of Africa; it looks just like a rhino horn, don't you think? How many people have ever heard of this place?" Nancy asked her husband.

"I guess not many. You and I are fairly astute, and we'd never heard of it. Now that it's making the nightly news and we're hearing about all the starving children, we'll get a steady diet of the conditions there." Butch walked away and opened the refrigerator door to hunt and gather. He was hungry.

"Look, it's bordered by Ethiopia and Kenya. All we ever hear or read from this part of the world is about famine, disease, war, and brutal clan feuds which seem to happen in epic proportions." Nancy was still staring at the map.

Butch was building a masterpiece of a sandwich. He started with two thick slices of homemade bread. Nancy had attempted making it with George's recipe and was anxious to get her husband's feedback. She wondered, "Did I get it right this time?" She was warily watching for her husband's reaction to his first bite. But right now he was concentrating on building it.

"It'll never change, Nance. That part of the world is always at the mercy of really inhumane warlords or cruel dictators." He picked up his creation to take a bite.

"When you put it that way, I wish with all my heart T.O. didn't have to go." She looked down at the map at a country halfway around the world.

"Look Nance; he's gonna be part of a big UN Operation. Troops from many countries are working together to get food to the starving people of Somalia. How stupid do those warlords have to be to challenge all those nations? Why don't you come over here and get something to eat. This BLTC is really good." He took another big bite and rolled his eyes in ecstatic satisfaction.

"What's the 'C'?"

He chewed a while, swallowed and answered, "Cheese."

"How's the bread?" she asked tentatively.

"It's getting better, hon. You did a good job, but it's still not quite Dad's."

"I'm determined to get it right, you know. Someday, it's gonna happen, and you'll know it for sure!"

"I'll know when it's right by that amazing aroma, Nance. You'll know it too; there's something familiar about the distinct aroma of Dad's homemade bread."

> How stupid do those warlords have to be? I knew the question was rhetorical because the open conflict had already killed thousands of innocent citizens, particularly in the city of Mogadishu.
>
> From the time T.O. was originally scheduled to deploy to Somalia in December 1992 to his actual deployment date in July 1993, the political landscape had drastically changed. Somalian warlord Mohamed Farrah Aidid was a wanted man. The military had tried unsuccessfully to capture him. It made for a hostile environment and was the

setting for events that would change lives forever. God bless all those people who happened to be in that dreadful place at the same time for what can only be described as a tinderbox.

When Butch picked up the evening paper, he uttered, "Oh, dear God!" It was loud enough for Nancy to hear while she was cleaning up the kitchen and thinking about her next attempt at baking bread.

"What?"

"Oh, it's just an article relating an incident in Somalia."

"Read it to me."

"Mohamed Farrah Aidid has savagely disrespected the UN organization. Oh, boy, this is not good."

"Why, what did he do?"

"Okay, here it is, and I quote: 'At the end of June, his Somalia National Alliance forces ambushed and killed twenty-four Pakistani soldiers, beheading many of them. Forty-four were wounded.'"

Nancy stopped what she was doing. "Lord, have mercy!" She held her hands to her mouth. "It's getting worse."

News reports the next day said the UN Security Council approved a resolution adopting a more aggressive military stance asking member states for more troops and equipment.

Subsequently, Nancy and Butch listened as TV reporters talked of increased missions in the capital city of Mogadishu destroying Aidid's weapons storage facilities, vehicle compounds, and a propaganda radio station. A warrant for Aidid's arrest with a $25,000 reward attached hardened the political lines.

Later, a Fox News anchor broadcast the following: "On July 12th, a mission involving the American Quick Reaction

Force (QRF) conducting helicopter raids, attacked a major Aidid compound. After the attack, a hostile crowd near the compound killed four western journalists who had been covering the action. The Somalis proudly displayed the bodies for the whole world to see."

The couple was sickened to think that their new son-in-law would be in the midst of this.

T.O. Williams deployed to Mogadishu ten days later.

My work is cut out for me. T.O., I implore you to let me be a conduit for divine help. Ask the Holy Spirit to guide you with every step you take.

62
LATE JULY 1993
WELCOME TO SOMALIA

As the commercial aircraft which carried the men of the 2-14 infantry approached Somalia, the pilot made an announcement, "Gentlemen, we are being diverted to Athens. The airport at Mogadishu is taking heavy mortar fire which would make an attempted landing dicey."

T.O. turned to his best man and seat mate, Bart, and said, "That's our welcoming committee. Do you think they're trying to tell us something?"

Their layover in Greece lasted approximately 10 hours until all was clear. When the Mogadishu airfield was deemed safe for incoming traffic, the plane took to the air attempting the approach once more. The men were instructed to "lock and load" their weapons before they deplaned.

Upon landing, the pilot spoke over the PA system. "Welcome to Somalia. We will expedite disembarking, so we're not a target any longer than we have to be."

T.O. knew the area would be "hot" from the time the aircraft door opened and not only from the air temperature which was always over 90 degrees.

"Hot and stinky, like the inside of a barn," Bart made a face.

The soldiers were loaded into the back of trucks, and taken to the University compound where they were billeted according to companies.

Passing an open air market, the troops watched shoppers examining wares displayed on rickety tables in uneven rows. A limited supply of meat, fruits, and vegetables, encrusted with black flies, lay in the scorching sun,.

T.O. questioned aloud to no one in particular, "And they eat that food?"

He got more than one affirmative murmur from the guys in the vehicle with him.

The Somali shoppers watched the truck convoy with hostile curiosity.

As they pulled into the driveway of their destination, T.O. elbowed Bart. "Look, I don't know about you, but I'm glad I see armed security guards at the gates of the university compound."

"Barbed wire fencing on top of a stone wall surrounding these buildings. Whaddya think T.O., to keep us in or keep the bad guys out?"

"I'm taking it as a definite ominous sign."

"Yeah," Bart replied, "for sure."

Inside the gates, weapons had to be unloaded of ammunition. T.O. remarked snidely, "This regulation is just stupid. We're targets, and the attacks on UN workers and soldiers are on the increase. What in the world are we supposed to do if they get inside the gates, shoot spitball at them?"

The men occupied empty classrooms, about 35 to a room with no air conditioning, no fans and no privacy. The bathroom facilities consisted of latrines, which were nothing more than outhouses with screened tops to allow for air circulation. If it was meant to dissipate the stench, it wasn't effective. Hit square in the face with the putrid odor of Mogadishu; a mixture of raw sewage, burning rubber and garbage, it was in their nostrils until the day they left Mogadishu. Even though there was a constant breeze from the ocean, flies were everywhere.

T.O. and Bart got settled in and stowed their gear. Within the hour, the university compound experienced mortar fire.

The first sergeant stuck his head in the room and shouted. "Flak vests on, helmets at the ready for anyone not on patrol."

Perimeter security was provided by soldiers from Tunisia. They often left the bullet-ridden bodies of Somali intruders hanging on the barbed wire fence as grim reminders to future offenders.

I remembered the Soviets doing the same thing during the Berlin crisis thirty years ago. The cruelty of man on man is infinite. God help us!

On August 8th, the day after T.O. arrived in Somalia, Aidid's forces detonated a mine under a U.S. military police vehicle in Mogadishu, killing four U.S. MPs. Two of them were from T.O.'s QRF team. The explosion was of such magnitude that pieces of the Humvee in which the MPs were riding were found on a rooftop. As a result of this attack, a new military road was built around the city to enable UN forces unimpeded access to the airfield from the university compound. It was constantly patrolled.

Start praying now, T.O., this attack has al Qaeda written all over it. We're not going to get through this without the help of the Lord.

As the situation worsened, UN Secretary-General Boutros Boutros-Ghali asked the new U.S. President Clinton to assist in capturing Aidid. In retrospect, it was reported many Somalis felt Clinton was duped into providing the muscle for the UN Secretary-General. It was later ascertained there was a bitter clan rivalry between Boutros-Ghali and General Mohamed Farrah Aidid.

Hmm.

63

AUGUST 1993
THEN AND NOW

T.O. was not just an infantryman; he was a specialist, a trained scout-sniper recruited to join the Rangers and Delta Force special operations forces in Somalia for a specific mission. When they weren't on patrol, they trained together.

Task Force Ranger and the special ops of Delta Force weren't in Mogadishu to feed the hungry. They had other missions. From late August to early October, they raided locations where either Aidid or his lieutenants were believed to be meeting; they were a no-nonsense group of soldiers.

Unfortunately, the military brass had a more sensitive mission in mind, and it didn't include T.O. The Rangers and Delta Force were the primary soldiers selected to carry out this secret mission.

Dejected at missing a chance to carry out a mission with the "D" boys and Rangers, T.O. now had more time to train with his QRF Company and take his turn patrolling the streets of Mogadishu from the sky. When he had down time, he'd lie in his bunk and think about being home with his wife.

Reflecting on Grandpa Panko's service in World War II, T.O. realized that his occupation as a scout/sniper and Grandpa Panko's experience as a scout/forward observer was only similar in name. Fifty years ago, Grandpa was often behind enemy lines equipped only with a map, compass, binoculars, a radio and a .45 handgun. His enemy wore a distinctive uniform.

T.O., on the other hand, had a little more technology on which to depend. T.O.'s map and compass was a GPS system; his binoculars were night vision glasses, his radio was a small headset, his weapon, a .50 caliber sniper rifle. His enemy didn't wear a distinctive uniform and could be a man, woman or even a child. Despite the current technology, T.O. had the highest respect for Grandpa Panko, a member of the Greatest Generation, accomplishing what he did with such primitive equipment.

> T.O. kept me in a leg pocket of his BDU (Battle Dress Uniform) pants, safely inside a plastic bag. I knew he remembered my legacy and wanted to keep me safe. He didn't understand my job description, which was to guide him and keep him from harm. He'll have a learning curve, the same one that both men before him experienced.

64
SEPTEMBER 1993
INTO THE FIRE

T.O. usually saw Mogadishu at night through the open door of a helicopter. He sat on a wooden bench, resting the barrel of his .50-caliber sniper rifle on a 550 parachute cord stretched across the doorway. Behind him, facing the opposite door of the MH-60 Black Hawk helicopter, a second sniper sat on a matching bench, his weapon also facing out. The men wore night vision goggles to scan the city streets for Somali militia up to no good. If they saw any, the snipers would, in Bart's words, "offer a little .50 caliber discouragement."

From the air, Mogadishu was a maze of narrow streets, buildings ravaged by gunfire, garbage piled high in the streets and abandoned vehicles left to rust. During skirmishes, the militia created roadblocks by stacking old tires in the streets and setting them on fire. The thick black smoke summoned fighters into the fray. It was a wonder anyone, even the enemy, could find their way around in this city.

Seeing the smoke, civilian onlookers also poured into the streets. Old men, gold-toothed women in their long caftans and children were often used as shields by the militia during battle.

Herded in front of fighters, the women and their long colorful robes hid the weapons that came up from underneath those caftans. This act preyed upon the cultural sensitivity of UN troops until they learned it was shoot or be shot, kill or be killed.

On the night of September 25th, a Black Hawk helicopter was shot down. When T.O. heard the news, he was sick. It was the same chopper in which he had patrolled the two previous nights, covering for someone who was ill. On September 25th, it was supposed to be T.O.'s night to patrol, but he had off, having worked the previous two nights in a row. Someone else was sitting in his spot on the bench, the bench which was blown to smithereens. Three crew members were killed. T.O. thought, "That could've been me."

He reached down to his pant leg pocket and outlined my form with his fingers.

"Thank you, Lord."

He was starting to understand the Lord's protection. The learning curve begins, his growth in trusting the Lord has begun.

T.O.'s unit, Charlie Company, was the Quick Reaction Force (QRF) sent into the city to secure the crash site. Squatting in the dirt to assess the situation of victims trapped in the helicopter, T.O. realized that none of the men had survived. There was precious little time for analysis at the crash site. As civilians amassed in the street, behind them the militia gathered. The QRF was fired upon from all directions with small and larger weapons, including RPGs. With the help of withering fire from helicopters overhead, T.O.'s group of soldiers managed to make it to the rooftop of a nearby building where they provided cover fire for others extracting the bodies of the men from the helicopter.

Above the din of battle, T.O. heard someone yell, "T.O.'s been hit!" He hadn't felt anything, didn't have any pain, and couldn't stop firing to find out if he'd been wounded.

He shouted, "I'm okay! I'm okay!"

His squad leader knew it was common for those who'd been shot to be impervious to the initial pain. When he saw the back of T.O.'s pants soaked in blood, he crawled across the flat roof to check on him.

"Williams, drop yer pants."

"I'm kinda busy," Terry barked while still firing.

The squad leader yelled, "This is an order, Williams, drop your pants. I need to look at your backside!"

"Okay, Sarge." T.O. put his weapon down. Others covered for him as he crouched and dropped his drawers for the first sergeant to look at his butt and upper legs.

The helicopters circling above witnessed a bare backside being scrutinized on the rooftop while other soldiers continued to fire on the enemy. The chopper radios crackled with chuckles and comments about the "full moon over Mogadishu."

Satisfied that T.O. wasn't injured, the squad leader shouted above the din. "Okay, soldier, pull up yer pants and get back to work."

The humor of the scene didn't escape the men. It was tempered by the amount of militia fire they were taking, and the realization the blood probably belonged to one of the helicopter crew killed in the crash.

With the bodies of the crew from the downed helicopter evacuated, the soldiers realized they had to exit the rooftop and fight their way back out of the alley the way they came in. Exiting the stairway, the men fanned out into the dusty, narrow street. Survival strategy and training required leapfrogging forward while laying down cover fire for each other.

T.O. could see bullets kicking up sand all around his feet as he ran to the nearest cover. It seemed to be happening in slow motion, and he kept thinking, "Why aren't they hitting me?" He crouched behind a hard structure to lay down cover fire for the next man when he felt a concussion in his shoulder and chest. He could see that blood wasn't oozing or spurting through his uniform. He could breathe and was moving all his limbs; he'd take stock of his body later. T.O. kept firing until all the men made it to safety.

Sergeant Reese was the first member of Charlie Company hit that night.

Someone screamed, "RPG!"

A flash, followed by an explosion where Sergeant Reese had squatted for cover, stunned everyone. The RPG hit and detonated Reese's AT-4 Rocket Launcher lying on the ground next to him. The blast tore Reese's left hand and right leg off. It peppered his groin with shrapnel. Both of his eardrums were ruptured, and he was blinded by the explosion. His men, who had witnessed the incident, had to quickly get Reese out of the line of fire while continuing to fight the militia.

T.O. thought Sergeant Reese was dead, but seconds later, heard Reese screaming. He was alive! Keeping him alive depended on how quickly they could get him evacuated. The only thing T.O. could do was to lay down more cover fire to protect the sergeant and the men who were aiding him. Retreating to a rally point, his men loaded Reese onto a Pakistani vehicle headed back to the compound.

> *God help us! I'm overwhelmed by the compassion the soldiers have for each other. Knowing the way Somalis treat their captives, the American soldiers don't want to leave any man behind. Memories of World War II and the Battle of the Bulge flooded my consciousness. No matter how long I've been in this business, I've not gotten used to the brutality of battle.*

It wasn't until after they were back at the University compound that T.O. was able to assess his own body for a wound. His shoulder and chest were bruised and discolored from the concussion, but his skin wasn't even broken. He realized how close he'd come to being wounded when he saw the hand guard on his weapon. The jolt he'd felt in his shoulder and chest was the recoil of his gun as his hand guard was being shattered by a Somali militia bullet. "That was a little too close for comfort," he muttered.

T.O. ruminated about every aspect of the firefights that day. The scenes played over and over in his head. It seemed as if he had been in an impenetrable bubble. He remembered seeing bullets bouncing in the sand all around him. He immediately thought of what his father-in-law told him about the Military Missal.

He had a moment of clarity. "I'm being protected by the Holy Armor of God!" He fell to his knees beside his bunk and with his head in his hands gave thanks. He reached down to the pocket in the leg of his BDU's and extracted the prayer book. Paging through the missal, he read the same passages as two men before him had decades ago.

Praise God. The boy got it!

T.O. slept fitfully that night. He was not alone. In spite of being exhausted, every soldier wondered why they were in Somalia. This was no ordinary conflict; it wasn't even a declared war. The enemy didn't wear a uniform and sometimes wasn't even a man. What was the mission?

Saint Michael, the Archangel, defend us in battle; be our protection against the malice and snares of the devil. We humbly beseech God to command him, and do thou, O prince of the heavenly host, by the Divine power thrust into hell Satan and the other evil spirits who roam through the world seeking the ruin of souls. Amen

65

SEPTEMBER 1993
A SIGN

T.O. felt a degree of freedom from the stench and filth of the war-torn city below when overlooking Mogadishu from the open door of the helicopter. In spite of the danger inherent in being on helicopter patrol, he liked this part of his job. What he didn't like was being a target.

The sudden screams of, "RPG, bank left, bank left" punctuated by the explosion of a grenade was always terrifying but became routine. Feeling the blast of heat from the exploding RPG was nerve wracking. It was always a relief when the chopper stayed in the air and made it back to base. T.O. had the good fortune to fly with superior pilots with razor sharp skills. Flying above Mogadishu was like playing a real life video game. It only took one hit to lose. Each succeeding night patrol involved at least one attempt by the militia to realize a "kill" with their RPGs. The Somalis deemed it sport and a badge of honor to shoot down an American helicopter.

When his feet were back on the ground, T.O. needed time to decompress. With thirty-five men to a room, there was little privacy except in the latrines. While there he prayed fervently, "Lord, thank you for keeping me safe. Please let me make it out of this alive. Allow me to get back home to my wife. I don't want to die in the dust and filth of this third world country. Lord, please send me a sign that things will be all right."

He looked up to the blue sky visible through the mesh screen. He blinked his eyes several times as a white dove softly landed on the mesh and began to preen his feathers. The only birds he'd seen in Somalia before this were sea gulls and buzzards, certainly not doves. Quietly, a second white dove fluttered to the screen joining the one already there.

A sign? I'll give you a sign. How about two white doves?

Without a doubt, T.O. knew this was his answer.

"Thank you, Father." T.O. bowed his head and prayed in gratitude.

I sing the words of Isaiah 40:31, They that hope in the Lord will renew their strength, they will soar as with eagles' wings; they will run and not grow weary, walk and not grow faint.

T.O. will need his strength in the coming days.

66
October 3-4, 1993
Blackhawk Down

Eight days later, October 3, 1993, the Somalis ramped up their attacks resulting in a ferocious two-day battle. Militia members armed with RPGs shot down two Blackhawks and crippled three others that fortunately made it back to base. Unrelenting attacks trapped American soldiers in the city overnight. Eighteen Army Rangers were killed, dozens were severely wounded, and helicopter pilot Mike Durant was taken prisoner by the Somalis. Bodies of dead Americans were desecrated and dragged through the streets of Mogadishu as Somali civilians cheered.

It had begun as a mission to capture wanted militia leader Mohamed Farrah Aidid and his advisors. On the afternoon of October 3rd, a group of Rangers and Delta Force operators descended from hovering helicopters on thick ropes. They surrounded a building where top leaders of the militia gathered. The intended mission was a success as the leaders were cuffed and taken into custody until unexpected resistance rained down upon the Americans.

Somali militia, summoned by tire fires, poured into the area, subjecting the Americans to heavy fire. The original mission was supposed to last an hour but didn't end until the next day.

The assault team found themselves in quite a pickle. Some men, thinking they'd be back at the airport compound within the hour, neglected to take drinking water or night vision goggles with them, a crucial error.

Enemy fire was getting heavier. Officers watching on screens in the command center were unnerved to view what was happening in real time. Afterward, a general observed, "It was as if their men had poked a hornet's nest." Cameras on aircraft circling overhead captured crowds of Somalis building barricades and igniting mounds of tires to summon help. Helpless, the Joint Operating Command could only watch.

A Black Hawk helicopter piloted by Chief Warrant Officer Michael Durant was shot down. He and his three crew members were severely injured in the crash. Durant was trapped in the wreckage. Two Delta Force soldiers went to their aid, managing to hold off the attacking Somalis until they ran out of ammo. Militia stormed the site of the wreckage, killing the Delta Force operators as well as the surviving crew. Angry Somalis pulled the bodies of the dead men out of the Black Hawk and dragged them and the bodies of the Delta Force men through the streets of Mogadishu, putting them on display.

Mike Durant, still trapped in the wreckage, could only listen to what was happening. He heard the firing cease when the D-boys, who had come to save him, ran out of ammo. He knew they'd been killed when they no longer answered him. When the attacking Somalis saw the pilot was still alive, one man realized Durant's value as a hostage and stopped the rest of the angry mob from killing him. The intervening Somali planned to ask a sizable ransom for his return. Pulling the screaming pilot out of the wreckage, they carried him off. Durant had suffered a broken back, a compound fracture of his femur, bullet and shrapnel wounds to his shoulder and thigh. He was now a hostage.

Back at the base, the QRF, T.O.'s unit, heard by word of mouth a mission was going down and they needed to be ready for action. The order came in the Army's trademark phrase: "Get it on."

T.O. retched loudly, trying to cover it with a fake cough.

His friend Bart looked at him sideways. "Get it together, man, you gonna puke or what?"

"Nah, I'm just coughing." He reached down to his BDU pants pocket to outline the military missal with his fingertips. "Help us, Lord," he prayed silently. His queasy stomach settled.

"Hey, I'm nervous too, T.O. Nuthin' to be ashamed of. We got a job to do, so let's get our shit together, okay?"

"Okay. Done."

The unit loaded into trucks and left the university compound for the airfield and headed into Mogadishu. Before it had gotten a half mile, the company was ambushed at a roadblock. Two of T.O.'s buddies were wounded. The trucks, unable to push through the barrier, returned to base to take care of the wounded and formulate a new strategy.

> I don't like what is happening any more than you do, T.O., I urge you to remember the words of Psalm 23:4 *Even though I walk in the dark valley I fear no evil; for you are at my side with your rod and your staff that give me courage.*
>
> Pray, T.O., the battle is just beginning.

67
OCTOBER 3-4, 1993
THE RESCUE CONVOY

The American commanders had a problem. Back in August, they'd requested additional mechanized and armored infantry teams with a platoon of tanks, but Secretary of Defense Aspin had not approved the request. As a direct result, men were trapped in the city, and the Somali militia had just proved that trucks alone were not going to get through. The Americans had neither tanks nor armored personnel carriers (APCs), and it would have been foolish to risk more Blackhawks.

It took hours to put a rescue convoy together. Using tanks borrowed from the Malaysians, the Americans blasted their way into the heart of Mogadishu. Small arms fire and rocket-propelled grenades came at them undeterred. As one soldier aptly put it, "It was the Mogadishu Bullet Car Wash!"

Six hours later, after fierce fighting block by block, T.O. and his fellow soldiers climbed out of their vehicles and ran into a maze of shacks surrounding Durant's helicopter crash site. They were joined by a Delta Force operator who had also made his way to the scene as a lone wolf.

They found many spent shells, pieces of torn clothing, blood pools leading into trails of blood, however, they found no sign of survivors. Searching the area while shouting the names of the downed crew was an exercise in futility. The only responses they heard were the echoes of their voices bouncing off the walls of the buildings in the narrow streets. Before leaving the scene they destroyed Durant's helicopter with incendiary grenades because it carried sensitive electronic equipment.

T.O. and his comrades leapfrogged their way back to the main street, one group providing covering fire as the other ran. When they arrived at the designated rally point, the men were devastated to find the APCs, which brought them into the city, had been destroyed by RPGs, and the Malaysian drivers had been killed. With no idea how many hours it would take to marshal extraction vehicles, the men were left to fend for themselves. It was now a fight to stay alive.

The sheer amount of enemy fire was enough to evoke dread because eventually, someone was going to get hit by a lucky shot. As the men continued to leapfrog their way to hard cover, a scream was heard: "I'm hit!"

T.O.'s friend and best man, Bart, was sprawled in the dusty street, writhing in pain. A pile of burning tires twenty feet away spewed out thick black smoke, making it hard to see or even breathe.

T.O. called out, "Bart, play dead, lay still." He could see Bart was bleeding from a chest wound and his right arm was hanging at his side.

Without another thought T.O. called out to his fellow soldiers, "Cover me!"

He sprinted to Bart's side. The remaining men lay down protective fire. Bart was conscious but fading. The dark red stain on his uniform was spreading; he'd taken a bullet from a high angle which entered above his flak vest. T.O. prayed that it hadn't hit any vital organs. Crouched over his friend, he hefted Bart's weapon onto his chest and hollered above the din, "Hang on to your weapon with your left hand, I'm getting you outta here."

Grabbing him by the vest, T.O. started to drag him to safety. Enemy fire increased. T.O. raised his weapon and took aim at the flashes he saw from the window of a building. He was pretty sure it was the same shooter who hit Bart. He fired and dragged his friend, fired again and dragged Bart. Everything seemed to be moving in slow motion. T.O. took aim at a new area of fire when suddenly he saw bullets bouncing off an invisible barrier in front of him.

Holy Mother of God, what is happening?

The bullets were ricocheting as, time after time, they hit something unseen. He knew he wasn't imagining it because he could see the ammo landing in the street.

"Thank you, Lord, I'll take any help you can give me right now," he was now able to move faster and with a few more steps, pulled Bart around the corner of a cement wall. He turned to ask Bart if he had seen the bullets bouncing away from them, but his friend had lost consciousness.

T.O. loosened Bart's flak jacket enough to see an entry wound. He pulled some field dressings out of his pockets to apply pressure and stem the bleeding. Bart's eyes fluttered open.

"Wha–what happened?" he stammered.

"You took one to the upper chest, buddy. How's your breathing?"

"Okay, I think. There's a lot of smoke. Makes it hard to breathe."

"You're right; they're burning those stupid tires for the weenie roast later."

Bart managed a smile at T.O.'s attempted humor.

T.O. noted that the wound wasn't bubbling with air before he dressed it, pretty much ruling out a hit to the lung. That was a relief.

"I think you're gonna be okay, friend. We just hafta find cover until help comes." T.O.'s mind was racing. "It would be nice if a medic was included with the help, Lord. Bart's lost a lot of blood."

Our God is a mighty God. Even I was impressed with the invisible barrier against those enemy bullets. God is good.

Across the street were pock-marked concrete walled buildings, damaged but still standing. Desperately seeking a safe shelter, the ragtag group of soldiers headed in that direction.

Their progress was interrupted by an RPG which hit about ten yards from T.O., blowing him off his feet.

"T.O., T.O.! You okay?" someone shouted.

Unhurt, but dazed, T.O. nodded his head slowly responding, "I'm okay."

His fellow soldiers, some assisting Bart, some guiding a dizzy T.O., took refuge in a nearby alley. Because of the increasing intensity of weapon fire, the soldiers knew staying in the city was no longer an option. The band of men altered their strategy, forming a plan to keep moving block by block toward yet another designated rally point hoping extraction vehicles would be there. They met militia resistance every step of the way. T.O. concluded that some Somali shooters were surprisingly accurate. Apparently, they'd had training. Fortunately, the average civilian was not such a good shot, but it was known among the troops that Al-Qaida had been proliferating in the country. Regardless of ability, the sheer numbers of shooters on both sides of the street posed a great danger.

All night long the sound of incoming and outgoing gunfire was deafening. The men couldn't hear themselves think, much less use the radio. Instead, they used hand signals as they continually moved from one position to another, taking cover among the flimsy shacks, just trying to stay alive. Somewhere along the way, the exhausted group miraculously encountered a medic who attended to Bart. After some rest and IV fluids, Bart was able to get to his feet and with the help of others, move out on foot.

> *Praise God for a medic! This battle has been truly a trial by fire. Every man concentrated on survival and leaving no one behind. God bless these brave men.*

68
OCTOBER 4, 1993
THE EXTRACTION

Nine hours later, under heavy fire, Malaysian APCs arrived to provide transport out of town. Feeling vulnerable, men jammed into what seemed like a large tin can on wheels. Out of necessity, the bodies of the dead were piled around the walls of the interior as well as on top of the APCs. The ride out of Mogadishu was the same as going in: a shooting gallery. They were sitting ducks for RPG attacks. Each of them prayed to get out alive. The typically short ride took forever to grind through the streets of Mogadishu.

> *Heavenly Father, may the souls of these brave departed soldiers rest in peace. They fought alongside their brothers while alive and are now shielding them in death. Please Lord, have mercy on the remaining soldiers and guide them safely out of the city.*

T.O. and Bart were crammed into a vehicle reeking of urine, sweat, and blood. There were dozens of wounded men, one of whom was the sergeant he'd had dinner with the night before. *Or was it two nights ago?* He couldn't even remember what day it was. Suffering a chest wound, one worse than Bart's, the sergeant begged for water. T.O. attempted to reassure him they'd be back at the compound and medical attention soon. The sergeant later died. Both sad and angry, T.O. felt a cold rage growing in his gut.

The convoy made its way to a soccer stadium where the Pakistani force was bivouacked. It was then that the mission's full carnage became apparent. The wounded, dozens and dozens of them, were spread over the field. Doctors and nurses moved quickly among them, triaging the men and their injuries. A sandbagged area away from the rest of the wounded sheltered a dying soldier with an undetonated RPG embedded in his body. Medivac helicopters came and went as casualties were loaded up and taken to the base hospital. On October 3rd over one hundred men went into Mogadishu. Eighteen were killed, one taken hostage, and dozens were badly wounded.

Several men were physically unharmed, but they suffered nonetheless. T.O. was one of them. Mentally, he was having difficulty processing all that had happened. *How? Why?* Viewing the appalling scene on the soccer field, he was already experiencing survivor's guilt. He found it difficult to feel grateful that he was alive.

In the midst of all the carnage, Pakistani orderlies politely offered water and camel meat to the Americans. As if they were butlers in an elegant mansion, they served the food and drink from silver trays with little white towels draped over their arms. None of this seemed real.

It was too much for T.O. The guy who'd joined the Army looking for a little adventure and to prove something to himself broke down and sobbed uncontrollably.

Hail Mary, full of grace, the Lord is with thee. Blessed art thou amongst women, and blessed is the fruit of thy womb, Jesus. Holy Mary, Mother of God, pray for us sinners now and at the time of our death. Amen.

69

OCTOBER 1993
A VOICE FROM HOME

Unlike in other wars, soldiers were able to call home from time to time. They didn't have to wait for the mail or a telegram to catch up with family. The satellite phone connection could be staticky, you had to remember to say "over" when you were done speaking, and the call could be terminated without warning, but you got to hear your loved one's voice.

Having seen and heard about the horrific battle of Mogadishu on every television channel, and knowing that her husband was involved somehow, Margie was an emotional wreck. She didn't know if he was alive, wounded or dead and didn't have the vaguest notion how to find out. She called another army wife whose husband was in the same company. Amy hadn't heard anything either. Late in the evening of October 4th, the phone rang. Margie raced to pick it up, tripping over the ottoman and grabbing the device on her way to the floor.

"Oomph! Hello? Hello?"

"Margie?" Wracked with emotion, the voice asked again, "Margie?"

"T.O., is that you?"

"Yeah, I'm here. I'm okay."

"Honey, I've been so worried about you. Thank God, you're alright." She was so emotional she forgot the satellite protocol of saying "over" when she was finished speaking. The phone crackled, and she remembered quickly saying, "Over."

Once was all it took to remind them both to get into that rhythm.

"I wasn't hit, but I'm not okay. I'm so freakin' mad about what happened." It was if a dam had burst. "It could have been prevented if we'd had the right equipment. This military operation cost a lot of lives. I lost friends; I had friends wounded."

She let him talk.

"Our government wouldn't give us heavy mechanized and armored vehicles. That would have saved lives. We had nothing. We had to depend on the Pakistanis and the Malaysians." His voice tapered off.

Margie could hear the break in his voice. "I'm so sorry, babe. Is there anything I can do?" She felt utterly helpless.

He rambled on. "Retrieving us guys who were trapped in the city with our equipment and men would have been better than what happened. It was a fiasco. The Rangers, Delta Force and the 10th Mountain Division lost some great soldiers."

Margie heard soft sobbing on the other end of the line and their time was up. The line went dead. Tears coursed down her cheeks. She knew he was in shock and she was worried sick about him A few days later, Margie got another phone call from T.O.'s commanding officers. "Mrs. Williams I've sent your husband, T.O., to Kenya for a few days of R & R."

"Kenya? Excuse me for asking, Lieutenant Bill, how is this going to help?" She shook her head in disbelief. She was concerned and frustrated that she couldn't talk to T.O., himself.

"It gets him out of Somalia and being shot at. He's not alone, several guys went." He cut the conversation short. "I'll have him call you when he gets back." The Lieutenant severed the connection to start another call, to another loved one. Some calls were easier than others.

Three days later, T.O. called his wife. "I'm fine physically, but babe, I'm messed up in the head after what went down in Mogadishu." He couldn't or wouldn't elaborate.

"You sound a little stronger."

"I am. Some strange things happened here."

"What do you mean, strange things?"

"Well, at this point I can only say that I had an angel on my shoulder every time I was in a fight. I'll tell you more when I get home. Right now, I'm not sure you'd believe me."

"I miss you so much. Any news on when they'll send you back to the States?"

Before he could answer, the connection was lost. Margie was distraught, wondering in what condition her husband would be when he got home. She hollered into the dead phone, "I love you."

He wasn't the only one messed up; all the soldiers were affected. They were enraged and fearful and had no outlet for those feelings.

> *It will take time for your soul to be healed. All things happen in God's time.*

70

OCTOBER 1993
HOSTAGE NEGOTIATIONS

The *Philadelphia Inquirer* reported that the ransom demand for helicopter pilot, Michael Durant, was paid by a Somali named Abdullahi Hassan, the propaganda minister for Mohamed Farrah Aidid. For ten days Hassan cared for Durant, washing and feeding him, changing his bandages and through it all, attempting to befriend him.

United States Ambassador to Somalia, Robert Oakley, arrived in Mogadishu on October 8th. Aidid was still in hiding. After several days of negotiating a meeting time and place, Oakley met with Aidid's clan. He convinced them that it was in their best interests to release the pilot as soon as possible. On October 14, 1993, Mike Durant was turned over to Red Cross officials. Doctors examined him, cared for his wounds and administered medication. Durant was flown to the Ranger base the next morning and carried onto a transport plane to Germany, where his wife awaited him. He was going to need more than one extensive surgery and rehabilitation for his injuries, but his wife would be at his side.

In an attempt to maintain a low profile in the press, administration officials decided against attending some of the public memorial services held in the States for the men killed on October 3rd and 4th. Pressure was put on the executive office to recognize the sacrifices of the men who served in Somalia. Finally, Secretary of Defense Les Aspin was pressed into service and agreed to attend a ceremony at Fort Bragg, North Carolina, but television, newspaper or print reporters were not allowed access. The administration wanted the debacle in Somalia to fade away, but it didn't.

One day, the White House received a call from a furious physician at Walter Reed Hospital. He complained that wounded soldiers from the conflict in Somalia had been there for three weeks and not one administration official had been to visit. The next day, President Clinton went to Walter Reed hospital. He visited the wounded, heard their stories of the firefights and the conditions under which they were injured. He seemed to be touched by their bravery. He was especially moved by young Sergeant Reese, who had lost his hearing, his sight, a hand, his leg, and had other severe wounds to his body.

The day after Clinton's visit, on October 25th, Secretary of Defense Les Aspin also visited Walter Reed and the soldiers recuperating there. He had been receiving severe criticism for turning down requests for armored vehicles to protect U.S. troops. Many were calling for his resignation. The trip to Walter Reed was an attempt to repair his image.

One soldier visited by Aspin was Sergeant Reese from the 10th Mountain Division. Reese was one month into his recovery; his hearing had returned, and most of his vision had been restored through surgery. The soldier was waiting for his hand and leg wounds to heal so he could be fitted for prostheses. He was looking forward to getting his new limbs, and with physical therapy, learning to walk again.

Reese had to shield his damaged eyes from the ceiling light as Secretary Aspen stood awkwardly at his bedside. Very succinctly the young sergeant said, "We could've used that armor, sir."

Well said, Sergeant Reese.

71
DECEMBER 13, 1993
PACK YOUR BAGS

On December 13, 1993, T.O. received news that his unit was leaving Somalia in less than a week. Replacements arrived. The traumatized troops packed their gear and were loaded into the back of five-ton convoy trucks. With armed escorts and air support from helicopter gunships, they were driven to the airport.

Before leaving the base, T.O. had a chance to call Margie. When the phone rang in Pennsylvania, Margie answered, "Hello."

"Baby, we're coming home. I'll take a couple of days. I can't wait to see you and hold you in my arms."

"Oh, T.O., me too. Will they notify dependents of the exact arrival?"

"Yeah, the phone chain will be activated. Please pass it on to my mom."

"You know I will. We'll all be there waiting for you. We love you so much."

"I love you too. See you soon." The connection was severed.

I heard her thoughts loud and clear. "He sounded tired and unusually subdued." I felt her urgent prayer. "Please Lord, let the man coming home to me be the same man I met and married a year ago."

Flying from Somalia to Egypt, they stopped in Shannon, Ireland, for refueling before heading to the States. Arriving at Griffith Air Force Base in Rome, New York, T.O. and the rest of infantry regiment were exhausted. The sleep-deprived men were bused from Rome to Watertown where a warm welcome awaited them. Family, friends, and dignitaries greeted the returning heroes as they marched in formation into the assembly hall on December 19, 1993. All the major news networks covered the event.

> It was T.O. and Margie's first wedding anniversary that day. How fitting they should be reunited. I pray for some form of normalcy to return to their lives as God's grace envelops both these young people. God bless them on their special day.

Every soldier looked pale, thin and tired. They had been through hell. Wounded comrades, including T.O.'s friend Bart, who had shipped out after October 4th, were also in the hall to greet the returning warriors. His chest and shoulder wounds had healed enough for him to be present and he looked healthy in spite of an immobilized right arm. Sergeant Reese had been fitted with arm and leg prostheses and, with the assistance of a cane, walked in to greet his company. All of the wounded owed their lives to others who pulled them out of the line of fire.

> Praise God Almighty. We were back. T.O. and I had bonded over six months of life and death experiences. He took good care of me. He also now knows I took good care of him. We both came home unscathed. Praise God for the words from Ephesians 5:20, *Giving thanks always for all things in the name of our Lord Jesus Christ to God the Father.*

President Clinton and his advisors decided to end the American involvement in Somalia immediately. There would be no retribution, no payback, no resignations. Within months, the U.S. troops were gone.

72

DECEMBER 19, 1993
HAPPY ANNIVERSARY

When the 2nd Battalion/14th Infantry Regiment was dismissed from formation, pure bedlam ensued, and families streamed out of the bleachers to each find their soldier. The place was mobbed with TV cameras and reporters from every major network and newspaper, but the families were oblivious. With each family group in the auditorium, there was a story to be told. The reporters were in journalistic heaven.

T.O. and Margie found each other in the crowd. Camera flashes illuminated the romantic embrace as their parents and T.O.'s teenaged sister, Emma stood in the background waiting to hold and touch her brother for the first time. Oblivious to those around them, they looked into each other's eyes. Margie saw circles under her husband's eyes; deep lines creased his face. "He's aged so much in five months," she thought.

"I can't believe I'm holding you in my arms." Margie squeezed him tighter.

"You have no idea how surreal this is for me, either. Twenty-four hours ago, I was still in that stinking country behind stone walls and a barbed wire fence. I think it's going to take some getting used to."

"How 'bout we just take it a minute at a time? Enjoy and savor every second. Right now, there's a line of people behind me, waiting to get their hands on you." Margie gazed over her shoulder at T.O.'s mother, who was dabbing her eyes with a wad of tissues.

She stepped aside and watched as her mother-in-law tenderly embraced her son. Emma joined in the circle of love, burying her face in her brother's chest, her shoulders shaking with each sob.

Margie stood next to her parents, watching the touching reunion. She let tears fall freely. Her father gently rubbed her back. T.O. turned to them as Butch extended his hand and Nancy zoomed in for a hug.

"We thought this day would never come," Nancy sobbed, "We're so grateful you're home safe."

"Nobody's more grateful than I am." T.O. stifled a yawn.

When the soldiers were dismissed, most left the hall with a family who had planned parties, dinners, and celebrations of every kind. T.O. craved a burger but needed to cleanup and change into civilian clothes. This would be his first step in recovering from the nightmare in which he'd been living.

The six of them went back to the hotel so T.O. could take a luxurious shower in a bathroom with modern facilities. Anne and Emma waited in the lobby with Butch and Nancy, relaxing in front of a warm fireplace, recalling every detail of the emotional reunion. Sitting in comfortable upholstered chairs, they found it refreshingly stress-free to chat about where to go for dinner.

Celebrating his homecoming and the young couple's first wedding anniversary was the order of the day. T.O.'s favorite burger place in Watertown was crowded with military families, but the group found a table in the corner, which suited him. Comfortable only if he could have his back to the wall, T.O. kept his watchful eyes continuously scanning the room.

The family had just placed their orders when a member of the wait staff dropped a tray of dirty dishes. The noise was sudden and loud. The entire restaurant became silent and around the room faces of returning soldiers turned white as they gripped the edges of the table. The alert hostess announced, "It's okay, just a dumped tray of dishes. Just wanted to keep you on your toes. It's all good."

There was a spattering of laughter, and then the tempo and tenor of the conversation in the room gradually resumed.

Margie wrapped herself around her husband who was still trembling. "It's okay, honey, we'll eat and leave."

"No, no, I'm fine, just give me a minute." He sipped his soda and took a deep breath. "At least bullets aren't flying." He chuckled, and everyone at the table joined him.

The family simply couldn't get enough of T.O. Everyone was thankful that he was back safe. T.O. was grateful to be home, but he knew the adjustment was going to take some time. It was established early on that he was jittery in a crowd and needed to stay on the perimeter of the room and loud noises had him wanting to dive for cover. The nightmares had not yet begun.

When they had finished eating, T.O. wanted to return to the hotel.

The two-car caravan made the short drive to the hotel. Upon entering the lobby, they found the fireplace continued to give off warmth and comfort on the cold December evening. The families began to bid each other good night.

"You'll have to excuse us," T.O. said. "I'm exhausted, and I need to hit the hay."

"We understand. In fact, it's been an emotionally draining day for us too. I'm ready to hit the sack." After Anne and

Emma had hugged T.O. and Margie, they turned left to walk down the first-floor hallway to their room.

Butch and Nancy waved to everyone. "See you in the morning for breakfast."

T.O. and Margie walked to the elevator hand in hand.

Although exhilaration and joy were the order of the day, it had also been emotionally, physically, and mentally exhausting.

T.O.'s thoughts of a soft mattress and snuggling with his wife consumed him. He knew that he desperately wanted to make love to his wife. He had yearned for her for months and hoped he could stay awake for the event.

The couple's parents, on the other hand, looked forward to lying in bed watching TV, eventually falling asleep before the flickering screen.

Even I need a good rest, Lord.

73

December 20, 1993
Remembering the Gifts of the Missal

In the morning, everyone met for brunch in the adjacent restaurant. At T.O.'s request, the hostess seated the families in a private alcove.

Today was the day T.O. was going to be able to go home on extended leave. He and Margie looked forward to living under the same roof as husband and wife. She had taken a week of vacation from her job to make her husband's acclimation a little easier. She was hoping that time, in addition to her holiday time off, would allow them to get into a calming daily routine.

After finishing a sumptuous brunch, T.O. stood, struggling to keep his emotions in check. All eyes were on him. Reaching into his pocket, he retrieved two decorative replicas of his Combat Infantry Badge. T.O. showed them the badge explaining, "This medal is one given to soldiers who have experienced combat and is most coveted for an infantryman." T.O. cleared his throat. "I want to present these replicas to our mothers who were the grounding forces for both our families." He reached out to his wife, grasping her hand to pull her to his side.

"Without the support of our mothers, neither Margie nor I would have survived this ordeal." He presented a badge to his mother and Margie's mother. Each woman tearfully embraced him.

T.O. remained standing as he reached into another pocket and retrieved the military missal, still in the plastic sandwich bag. With a steady voice, but with tears in his eyes, he began, "It's been an absolute honor to carry this missal. It gave me guidance and hope. I remembered what I was told Grandpa Panko endured during World War II. I was sure he felt many of the same emotions I felt. I am sure his life was on the line more times than what I experienced. His survival gave me hope." T.O. tried unsuccessfully to swallow the lump in his throat.

Looking directly at Butch he said, "Giving this missal to me was an act of trust. I'm convinced, as you and Grandpa Panko were, that it kept me safe."

T.O. fumbled with the plastic sandwich bag to remove the missal. He opened the little book. "I want to read you something from a "Prayer for Soldiers." He carefully turned the fragile pages. Slowly and deliberately he spoke these words: "Preserve them from the wounds and dangers of battle and bring them safely home." He lowered the prayer book. "Without a doubt in my mind, the words in this prayer shielded and protected me in battle."

Hearing the passage, each person murmured a soft, "Amen."

Continuing, he earnestly insisted, "No one will ever be able to tell me that the Lord didn't guide my feet. I know He saved my life on more than one occasion."

Butch approached his son-in-law, putting his hand on T.O.'s shoulder in a show of solidarity and comfort. With tears in his eyes, T.O. said, "Thank you."

Carefully placing the missal back in the bag, he handed it to Butch. They embraced. There wasn't a dry eye around the table.

I knew I was going home. Having been one of the common threads that bound three generations of men together, I was honored to have been their spiritual guide. I was humbled to have been the conduit for the Lord's work and to have witnessed His Mighty Hand. Prayer is a powerful weapon against evil.

That day, Margie, T.O. and their families each left Watertown to travel to their respective homes to prepare for Christmas. It was going to be another memorable holiday with cause for great celebration. They would all be together again in a few days, but the past two days had indeed been special.

74

DECEMBER 1993
A PLACE OF HONOR

When Butch arrived home from Watertown, he placed me on top of his dresser. He needed to look at me every morning when he started his day and every evening before he went to bed. Butch was filled with gratitude for the safe return of his daughter's husband, but more than that, he pondered the the incredible odyssey of the missal. It was a mystery to him that he, his father, and T.O. returned home unscathed when many others carrying similar missals did not.

He wondered aloud. "How does this happen, Lord?"

Sitting on the edge of the bed, Butch quietly meditated. In that stillness, he heard, "Faith, gratitude, and the power of the Holy Spirit!"

He looked around; no one else was there, yet he had heard the words. Butch knew the origin of the response. Looking up, he affirmed, "Yes, Lord."

One week later, Butch placed me inside a glass topped shadow box with other mementos of George's service to his country. A silver star, a bronze star with an oak leaf cluster, his Combat Infantryman's Badge, and other adornments of the Army dress uniform were displayed. Butch added his dad's rosary and souvenirs from Germany,

Belgium, and France. No more dark cedar chest for me. At last, I could rest in a room with a view.

Butch finished arranging the shadow box. Carefully he lowered the glass cover, locked it, and placed the key in his pocket. He turned to leave the room and had only taken a few steps when he distinctly heard a sigh of contentment. Butch stopped to listen; he knew he was the only one there. He paused, and an understanding smile spread across his face as he reached down to pick up his evening newspaper. He tucked it under his arm and, with a spring in his step, walked down the hallway following a distinctly familiar aroma of freshly baked bread.

ABOUT THE AUTHOR

Nancy Panko's novel, *Guiding Missal*, began as a result of an effort to re-create her father-in-law's military history as a gift for her husband on the 50th anniversary of the Battle of the Bulge. As she held the pocket-sized prayer book in her hand, she thought: "If only this book could talk." It was then that the idea for this book was conceived. Nancy is a retired pediatric nurse  and a frequent contributor to Chicken Soup for the Soul and Guidepost magazines. She and her husband moved to North Carolina in 2009 after living and working in Clinton County, Pennsylvania for thirty-four years. They have two children and four grandchildren. They love being in, on or near the water with their family.

The RMS Franconia which took George from NYC to the UK

The SS Léopoldville which took George
from Southampton, England to LeHavre, France

Sweet Gladys

George in uniform

George, Gladys and the three boys

Butch in front
of his squadron
sign at Sheppard
AFB in Texas

Butch in his
uniform in the
living room at
home before
leaving for
Germany

Butch in civilian
clothes in Germany

Butch, Nancy, Margie and Baby Tim

Terry and Laura Emmick,
first military man in the
composite third soldier

Sam Owens, second
military man in the
composite third soldier

George and Gladys
in later years

William Reinbold
and wife, Judy.
William is the third
military man in the
composite third
soldier

Panko Family Heritage Recipes

George's Favorite Yeast Bread

1 medium potato, peeled cubed, cooked + mashed
1 1/2 cup water to cook potato, save 3/4 cup of the water
1 Tbsp milk + 1 Tbsp butter to put in mashed potato
4 Tbsp butter, softened
5 cups flour, plus some for dusting
2/3 cup sugar
1 pkg. active dry yeast
1 1/2 tsp salt
1 tsp grated lemon peel
1/2 tsp nutmeg
3 eggs lightly beaten

In a bowl, combine 3 cups flour, sugar, yeast, salt, lemon peel + nutmeg. Melt remaining butter, cool. Add the cooked potato water + melted butter to the mix; beat until moistened. Add eggs + potato mix (1/2 cup) beat until smooth. Stir in enough flour to form a firm dough. Turn onto floured board, knead about 6-8 minutes until smooth + elastic. Place in a greased bowl, turning once to grease top. Cover, put in a warm place, let rise about 1 hour, until double. Punch dough down, turn onto floured board, shape into 2 loaves. Put in loaf pans, cover, let rise in a warm place about 1 hour. Bake at 325 degrees for about 40 minutes or till golden brown.

Halupki

1 large head of cabbage
1 bag sauerkraut
1 large can tomato sauce
    or diced tomatoes
2 lbs. lean ground beef or turkey
1 egg
1/2 medium onion diced
2 cups cooked rice
Salt + pepper

Wash + core cabbage, let dry, freeze overnight. Take out in a.m. and let thaw, leaves will be limp enough to roll.
Mix meat, eggs, onion rice, salt and pepper. Fashion into a ball, place in leaf + roll, tucking ends in. Place sauerkraut in bottom of casserole dish, place cabbage rolls on top. Add tomato sauce or diced tomatoes and a cup of water. Cook at 350 degrees for 2 1/2 hrs

George's Homemade Pierogies

2 cups flour + enough for dusting board
2 eggs
1/2 tsp salt
butter + onions
warm water

Mix flour, eggs + salt. Add enough water to make a medium soft dough. Knead until blisters appear. Divide into two portions. Roll out one at a time, cut into 3 inch squares. Place a tablespoon of potato mix on each square, fold to make a triangle and pinch edges to seal. Drop into boiling water until they float to the surface. Carefully remove with a slotted spoon and put into a large skillet with melted butter and sautéed onions. Crisp edges of pierogies in the skillet.

Potato filling:
Mashed potatoes, salt, cheese

Kolache

Ingredients:
1/4 cup warm water
2 (1/4 oz) dry yeast pks
1 tsp sugar
6 cups flour, plus some for dusting
3 tablespoons sugar
1 tsp salt
1 cup melted + cooled butter
3 eggs slightly beaten
1 cup sour cream

Filling

Walnut
1 lb. walnuts, ground
1 1/4 cups sugar
1 (12 oz) can evaporated milk
1 cup breadcrumbs plain
1 tsp vanilla
1/3 cup raisins

Poppyseed
1 cup poppyseeds
1/2 cup milk
1/4 cup honey
1/3 cup raisins
1/3 cup chopped nuts (opt)
Dash cinnamon

Directions:
Dissolve yeast and sugar in warm water. Wait until active before adding to dry ingred.
Mix together flour, sugar + salt.
Stir in eggs, melted butter, sour cream + dissolved yeast. Mix well, let dough rest for 10 min., dump out on floured board. Cover with a mixing bowl. Let rise then divide into 4 equal parts. Roll out one 14 x 12 rectangle at a time. Spread with filling to 1 inch from edges. Roll up from 12" side. Seal edge, tuck ends under. Put seam side down on parchment paper on cookie sheet. Cover with cloth. Let rise for 1 hour or until double. Bake 2 rolls to a cookie sheet at 325 degrees for 30-35 min. Transfer to cooling rack. These can be frozen.

CPSIA information can be obtained
at www.ICGtesting.com
Printed in the USA
FSOW01n2218090517
33939FS